The Whispered
Tales of Graves Grove

An Anthology

Edited by
J.S. Bailey &
Kelsey Keating

bhc press™

Livonia, Michigan

About the Type

This book was set in Adobe Garamond This font is a digital interpretation of the roman types of Claude Garamond and the italic types of Robert Granjon. Since its release in 1989, Adobe Garamond has become a typographic staple throughout the world of desktop typography and design.

Graves Grove Concept Created by
J.S. Bailey, LaDonna Cole, and D.M. Kilgore

THE WHISPERED TALES OF GRAVES GROVE

Copyright © 2017 BHC Press

All rights reserved. Except as permitted under the U.S. Copyright Act of 1976, no part of this publication may be reproduced, distributed, or transmitted in any form or by any means, or stored in a database or retrieval system, without prior written permission of the publisher.

This book is a work of fiction. The characters, incidents, and dialogue are drawn from the author's imagination and are not to be construed as real. Any resemblance to actual events or persons, living or dead, is entirely coincidental.

Published by BHC Press

Library of Congress Control Number:
2017933754

ISBN: 978-1-946006-69-1

Hardcover edition ISBN:
978-1-947727-07-6

Visit the publisher at:
www.bhcpress.com

Also available in hardcover and ebook

OTHER BHC PRESS ANTHOLOGIES

In Creeps the Night

A Winter's Romance

On the Edge of Tomorrow

Tales by the Tree

THE TALES

INTRODUCTION

J.S. BAILEY

The Whispered Tales of Graves Grove is a book that was nearly two years in the making. I can remember sitting down with my fellow authors LaDonna Cole and D.M. Kilgore via Skype and brainstorming an epic new short story anthology that was bound to entice authors the world over. We had created two other anthologies before—*Through the Portal* and *Call of the Warrior*—but we wanted to do something different this time.

I don't remember whose idea it was to develop an anthology in which all stories take place in the same town. I do remember suggesting that the stories should take place in a creepy, remote village in the wilds of British Columbia, as at one point in time I had started writing a (failed) short story that took place in such a location.

Amidst various bouts of giggling, LaDonna, D.M., and I formulated the details of this town, which we came to name Graves Grove. We populated it with characters that other authors could use in their stories, such as Mamie Rue Le Doux (LaDonna's creation), Copper the town mutt (D.M.'s creation), and Maggie Pinker (my creation). We created an entire town backstory, typed it out, and opened *The Whispered Tales of Graves Grove* up for submissions.

It took over a year to receive enough submissions to turn *The Whispered Tales of Graves Grove* into a book, and it became a massive challenge to hammer and shape all of the stories into a cohesive whole. We will forever thank every author who participated in this anthology—they helped bring our vision to life!

And now, Dear Reader, do sit back and enter the village of Graves Grove…if you dare.

~ J.S. Bailey, August 2017

The Whispered Tales of Graves Grove

IN THE BEGINNING

J.S. BAILEY

Samuel Madsen Graves had been riding for so long that he'd started to wonder if life had existed at all before he'd won his chestnut mare in a game of poker in a seaside tavern that smelled of tobacco and fish and headed west. He'd lost track of the days, knowing only that he'd left while the snows of winter still blanketed the land and that now it was midway through spring. He had the feeling it might be the end of April, perhaps the twenty-ninth.

If anyone was following him, he didn't know. He'd heard no signs of pursuit.

His entourage rode behind him in silence save for the creaking of wagon wheels and the occasional whicker from one of the horses. It had been slow going the past week or so, what with the land growing more and more treacherous by the mile and mossy trees growing close on all sides; and most of the group was still feeling glum that their best cook had succumbed to dysentery the week prior, so no one really had anything to say.

Samuel wished they'd talk. The voices in his head were much too loud when the rest of the world was silent.

"Do you think we're in Canada by now?"

Samuel turned his head to see Benjamin Jones, one of his more loyal followers, draw up beside him on his black mare. Though Benjamin was only twenty—ten years Samuel's junior—he looked ready to die of exhaustion.

"I imagine so," Samuel said, grateful for the conversation.

"The air is cooler here."

"So I've noticed. I rather enjoy it. Don't you?"

Benjamin's blue eyes reflected unease, and he brushed absently at his tangle of beard. "But our crops—they might not do well here. Winter will come early this far north."

"We will make do." Samuel stared straight ahead at the seemingly endless evergreen forest. He was not the sort of man to fret about things as trivial as food. If his followers should starve, Samuel would find a way to survive no matter the cost.

He always had.

Samuel could feel in the marrow of his bones that they were almost upon the place he'd dreamed of now for years: a utopia of sorts where few outsiders could interfere with his ways. Not even his band of followers knew the full truth. They, like him, were casting off the old in the hope of starting a new life. Some of them were petty criminals, others simply desired a change of scenery from the mundane places they'd always known.

None knew Samuel's ultimate goal. They would think him mad if they did.

The horse crested a small rise, and then the land dipped sharply. Up ahead the trees thinned, and Samuel smiled. *At last.*

He halted the horse and turned. One wagon had stopped at the top of the rise, and its driver, a scrawny fellow named William who'd joined their entourage halfway through Kentucky, stared dubiously at the drop-off.

"Leave the wagons!" Samuel called out, enjoying the way his voice carried. "We will proceed on foot."

He dismounted and strode forward, knowing that the rest would follow. They were like sheep, even Benjamin, and Samuel prided himself in being their shepherd.

Benjamin caught up to Samuel's long strides, panting like he'd never used his legs before. "Sir? Is this it?"

Samuel didn't answer, so determined was he to lay eyes upon his new domain. He'd been waiting for so long, traveling through village and through prairie, through rivers and mountain passes and forests galore, always searching but knowing that his true destination lay far beyond the next ridge or bend in the trail.

At last the trees ended, and Samuel drew to a stop. They stood in a valley between craggy, bald peaks jutting into the sky on all sides. Evergreens growing on the slopes gave the lower elevations a bit of color.

Everything was so *green.*

I'll bet we could build mines in these mountains, Samuel thought as a lone black bird flew in circles in the pale blue sky. Trading with other villages that would surely spring up in the next few years would be great for growth, and an increase in population was exactly what Samuel needed for his plan to succeed.

An increase in population, and time.

"This is a far cry from Chesapeake, isn't it?" Benjamin asked, folding his arms.

"Oh, most definitely." Samuel had told everyone he'd lived in Chesapeake Bay prior to the start of his journey. He'd told them many things, some of which may have been true.

Samuel brushed a fleck of dirt off his crisp yellow shirt and faced his group of followers, the most haggard bunch of men, women, and children he'd ever had the fortune of knowing.

"My friends," Samuel said, though they were not, "we have arrived."

There came a few weary cheers and a "Thank God" from a nun they'd picked up in Kansas. Samuel suppressed a smile.

"Walter, Henry, and Matheson, you start cutting down trees," Samuel said. "Margaret and Lucille, get a nice dinner going for everyone. The rest of you start unloading the wagons."

"What about me, sir?" Benjamin asked.

Samuel clapped him on the shoulder. "You and I are going to look for water."

The trees began again off to the west, and Samuel trudged across the meadow toward them, avoiding puddles from a recent rain so as not to get his boots dirty. His instincts proved correct: within minutes he could hear the telltale trickle of water, and then he and Benjamin found themselves standing before a modestly-sized river cutting through the wood.

"Not bad," Benjamin said with a nod. "Should I fetch some pots?"

"Not yet," Samuel said. "There's something I must do first."

The tree line ended sixty or seventy feet from the water's edge. Most if not all of them would have to come down to provide fuel and shelter for his people.

Samuel closed his eyes and imagined what the settlement might look like in ten years, or even twenty. It would have to be a proper town by then, with rows of clapboard houses, a general store, a blacksmith, probably even a church or two. The town would likely look so normal that no one would bat an eye.

That was the plan, at least.

Samuel removed a pouch from around his waist and untied it, withdrawing a rusty trowel and a wad of paper.

Benjamin eyed both with suspicion. "What's that?"

Samuel unwrapped the paper and beheld the single tiny sycamore seed that had been entombed within. "The future."

He dug a small hole in the damp earth, then stared at the spot for a moment while the sound of an axe repeatedly striking a tree trunk carried through the forest. The sycamore seed remained clenched in his fist.

"This should be a good spot. May I borrow your knife?" Samuel asked.

Benjamin's eyebrows knit together. "Sir?"

"Your knife, please."

Shrugging, Benjamin dug around in his pocke small pocketknife, which he passed to Samuel. Samu gritting his teeth, dragged the blade across his trembling hand right next to where the seed lay against his skin.

"Thank you, Talakoth," he murmured.

"What's that?" Benjamin asked.

"Nothing that need concern you." Samuel owed much to Talakoth. Now all he had to do was uphold the promise he had made to the being, and pray that the being would uphold its promise to him.

He re-clenched the fist containing the seed and let blood drip into the depression he'd made with the trowel. Once he deemed that enough had seeped into the soil, Samuel pocketed the bloody seed, fished out a kerchief, and wrapped it around his hand to stifle the flow.

He ignored the pain. He was very good at that.

Benjamin's face had grown pale, but fortunately he didn't continue to pry into Samuel's actions. "What now, sir?"

Samuel licked his lips and tilted his head toward the sky. Above, the black bird was still circling. "Tomorrow," he said, "I shall plant this seed as a symbol of rebirth. As it grows, so will this town, and I will be remembered forever."

He paused for dramatic effect.

"We will call it Graves Grove."

RACHEL

E.D.E. BELL

The sun always set early in the valley.

Edwin hustled down the dimming street, clutching a parcel in his rough, chapped fingers. He stared at the ground, hoping no one would notice him. It was Sunday night, and he was running late.

The street ended just ahead, and Edwin grimaced at the men standing on the walkway to either side. Mr. Harper paced outside the Town Hall, doing whatever the strange man did outside the Town Hall every night, alone. And across the street Mr. Graves leaned against a post, talking to the Constable.

Edwin grunted. There was no way to avoid them both. He glanced a moment at Mr. Graves, who stood pinching a monocle in his left eye and twisting a lavish scarf Edwin was certain had been intended for a woman. And the Constable—he avoided him at all costs. The man would ask about Rachel. Always, about Rachel. About how she'd gone, and where she was.

Edwin knew where Rachel was.

And he'd never tell them. They wouldn't understand; maybe they'd even send him away. No, he'd never leave this place.

Even if he hated it.

Mr. Harper it was, then. Edwin veered to the left. "Well, hallo, Edwin, it's almost Monday, isn't it?" Mr. Harper said in a sing-song voice, as he tipped his wide-brimmed hat over his broadening grin.

Edwin grunted, with a slight nod he hoped would pass for a greeting.

"I'll be by, you know. Early, too. Spring lamb is our favorite; we wouldn't miss the loin for anything. Be sure and cut it for chops!"

"I always do," Edwin muttered, his eyes planted ahead.

The road thinned as he entered the trees, and his cabin slipped into view.

Too dark, he thought. *Will need to hurry.*

He scraped his boots on the coarse mat and listened for the sound of the rocking chair. Back and forth, it creaked. Like a heartbeat. The only heartbeat that was left of the two women he loved.

It was enough. It had to be.

The chair continued its lullaby as he approached. "Beloved," he whispered, leaning in to give his wife a kiss. The blanket had slipped a bit; he tucked it back around her shoulders. "I'm sorry, but I've got to hurry if I'm going to see her. There's clouds tonight."

He didn't expect her to respond, her blank eyes fixed on the worn quilt which covered the window before her. He turned to leave.

"She needs friends."

Edwin rested his hand in a gentle caress against her drooping chin. "I'll take care of her, Ilana. Always." Ilana gave no answer, except for the rhythmic rocking of the chair.

It was cold in the shed, but there was no time to build a fire. He'd have to make do. The rifle leaned against the stove. He swept a bullet from the tool chest and dropped it into his pocket.

The lamb was waiting outside, tied to a post. It kicked against the dirt as he approached, its tail wobbling against the chill breeze. "Come, child," he coaxed, unwinding the rope. The lamb followed, bleating as it twisted the rope against Edwin's firm grip.

Whispering a prayer, he slipped the rope from the lamb's neck and, using his knee to brace the soft creature against the ground, tied the rope firmly around each pair of legs.

The lamb screamed, writhing against the sudden confinement. Edwin loathed this part. But it had to be done. For her, he would do anything.

Pulling the bullet from his pocket, he pushed it into place. The rifle's stock pressed firmly into his shoulder, and its cool wood grazed his face.

The lamb tilted its face up toward him. Edwin acknowledged the open mouth and the wavering tongue, but he no longer heard the cries. He positioned the dark metal straight against the soft white fur and took one last look into a pair of wide, terrified eyes.

With a zing and a crack, it was done. The head slumped to the ground, the eyes open but unmoving. Edwin breathed, several long breaths.

He leaned the rifle against the outer wall and reached for his blade. Kneeling, he pressed and sawed into the thick, resistant neck until the blood seeped through. Dragging the small animal toward the hook, he hoped it wasn't too late. Edwin couldn't wait another week.

"She's here," he called to the night. "Please, hurry."

It would be a while yet. It always took a while; he didn't know why. But it did, and rather than sit and wait while the carcass bled, better to just keep prepping.

Returning inside, he rested the rifle behind the tool chest, away from view. Edwin rubbed a bar of lye against his hands and then into the grain of the table. It was a solid table at least—a gift from Ilana's father. They were from this place. Edwin wasn't. He used to work for Lord Strathcona himself, and they'd detoured through this small valley entirely by accident. Smitten by the lovely young woman with the wavy chestnut hair, he'd simply let the caravan leave without him, abandoning the riches of his former life for the soft words of a kind woman. If he'd known then…well, it didn't matter now.

He mustn't lose this chance. Back outside, he scanned the forest as the water pumped into the oversized bucket. Lugging it inside, he poured the cool water over the soapy table, the suds flowing to the ground, washing over the blood-stained floor. Hurrying, he cut off a measure of twine, grabbed a sturdy hook, and picked up his blade.

The twine was for tying off the ends he didn't care to contemplate. The hook was for the guts. In his father's old shop, they'd used the offal for sausage. Edwin couldn't see to do it. Instead, he left the plump, glossy innards out, for the forest to take. He slogged outside and squatted over the furry mass.

Edwin yanked, again and again with the hook, concern suffusing his expression as the twilight faded to darkness. Reaching for his saw, he noticed her. He exhaled.

The lamb was more beautiful now than in life. Her long legs gleamed in the darkness, her ears and snout alive and twitching. Her eyes flitted about the dark forest, oblivious to her own glistening remains strewn at Edwin's feet, illuminated by the moonlight. Edwin stretched an imploring hand toward her, then dropped it to his side; there was no apology he could offer.

There was only Rachel.

He glanced wistfully back at the carcass. He hadn't moved with enough haste, and she wasn't quite ready to tie up. Bleeding would have to wait. The meat might suffer, but he had ways around that. He placed the saw onto a mound of dirt.

"I'm ready," he said, his voice quavering.

The lamb took tentative steps forward, first walking, then leaping back and forth in little jolts. She darted into the trees.

Edwin shielded his face as they tromped through the thick undergrowth of the woods. Branches snapped against his hands, and cobwebs caught in his fingers. He wished they'd just take the path, but the little ones never did. When he finally emerged into the field, two large silhouettes loomed against the dark, cloudy sky.

The curling branches of the sycamore tree contrasted the sharp lines of the steeple to its side. The top limbs, where the bark had fallen, glowed almost white, even in the darkness. With a shudder, he forced his eyes from the harrowing tree. He broke into a run as shapes emerged around him. Lambs and calves danced in all directions, radiant and free, their bellowing and bleating combining in a chorus of harmony and life.

Where was she? She had to be here. She must be here.

Rachel.

She never saw him, the way the others did. It didn't matter. He absorbed her sweet expression, a tiny image of Ilana. Her hair swung to each side in two glowing braids. As she danced, her cotton dress swished underneath the apron, so lovingly embroidered. She twirled a nosegay of columbines—oh, he'd have to tell Ilana that—until, with a start, she raced toward him.

No, not toward him. He turned as the spring lamb rushed from behind him toward the little girl. She fell to her knees, letting the flowers scatter beneath the slender hooves. She nuzzled her tiny face into the creature's soft wool.

Edwin gazed, transfixed, as tears streamed down his ruddy cheeks.

Without warning, they disappeared. "No!" he shouted. "No!" Realization dawning, he dropped to the ground, watching in horror as the moon broke through the drifting clouds, streams of moonlight illuminating the tall, geometric, steeple.

He dug his thick fingers into the dirt, where the flowers had never really been. He choked back his tears. He'd seen her. It was enough.

Edwin, stood, wavering, to his feet. Best to be back. There was skinning to do, and he hadn't even bled the creature properly.

It was Sunday night, after all, and Mr. Harper would be by bright and early for his chops.

"I love you," Edwin whispered. "And I will never leave."

FOUNDER'S DAY

MARK ANDERSEN

"Injunction is not even a word," Amelia Le Doux insisted.

I'd been told the old lady was eccentric, but this statement seemed most odd to hear from a town librarian. Especially one as old as she was. Miss Le Doux had to be about seventy, but she still had a lively face and piercing blue eyes. She was trim, and probably stood about five foot two, but I never saw her rise from her chair in the musty-smelling library.

"Ma'am?"

She smiled and patted my knee. "You're a good boy, I'm sure, but you're ignorant. Not your fault, really. It's the times. First came that never-ending depression, and now Hitler and his war. I shouldn't blame you. Well, unless you're lazy. Are you lazy, young man?"

As she sat back in her chair, a strong aroma of her gardenia perfume remained.

"I don't think so, Miss Le Doux."

"Call me Miss Amelia. Everyone does."

"Thank you, Miss Amelia. But why do you say it isn't a word?"

She drew herself to her full sitting height. "What do you mean? Of course it is a word. I use it often."

"I'm sorry, ma'am, but you said it wasn't a word."

"I'm afraid this interview isn't going to go well if you attempt to put words into my mouth. It has always been a perfectly acceptable word. Look it up, young man. The library has a dictionary right over there. It is the third person neuter pronoun." She pointed to another table in the library and glared at me.

It. She switched words on me. I mentally slapped my head.

"I'm sorry for the misunderstanding, ma'am. Why did you say injunction is not a word?"

"Why are you asking about crossroads, young man? We have only one road through Graves Grove. It leads both in *and* out."

Oh, man. This thirty-dollar gig is tougher than I thought.

Come on over to our little town, they said. Room and board for three or four days and thirty in cash. Just write a praise pamphlet about our founder, they said.

I'd been here two nights and I still didn't know what to write. The bombastic mayor was worthless. He hardly knew the founder. The others I'd spoken with were just as useless. When one of them mentioned that an original settler still lived, I'd hoped my problems were solved. But I wound up with Miss Amelia. *Save me from the ramblings of old ladies.*

"Maybe we should just start over." I flipped my notepad to a clean page to symbolize a new beginning.

She tilted her head back to look up at me and down her nose at the same time. "I can stick to the subject if you can."

We'll see about that.

"Miss Amelia. I understand you're the only surviving settler of Graves Grove."

"Since eighteen hundred and eighty. I was seven years old. There were younger children, and of course older ones. But I'm the only one still in this town and still alive."

"And how old are you now?"

"Did they remove mathematics from the curriculum during the Depression? Nineteen hundred and forty less eighteen hundred and eighty plus seven years. How old am I, young man?"

She's a librarian, all right. I did the calculation twice before answering. "Sixty seven, ma'am?"

"Sixty six. You didn't ask my birthday. It's only February, after all."

"When is your birthday?"

"March 22. I'll be sixty seven years old." She announced her age with pride, as though we hadn't just been discussing it. "If that European war doesn't come over here and kill me."

Right. The Nazis had Graves Grove in their expansion plans.

Back to work.

"The town was founded on April 30, 1880?"

"It was. That was the day after we arrived. Old Maddie planted the town sycamore tree. You can see it out that window."

"Yes, I've seen it." It was a huge tree, but with the leaves down, its branches looked twisted and sinister. "You said, *Old Maddie*?"

"Samuel Madsen Graves, of course. I didn't start calling him Maddie until later, when I was grown."

"You were close?"

She leaned away from me. "What are you suggesting, young man? Are you implying that I had an inappropriate relationship with an older gentleman?"

I shook my head vigorously. "No, not at all. Just that you had a nickname for him. Did others call him Maddie?"

She looked up at the ceiling for almost a minute, her lips moving.

"Flossie. She called him that."

I looked through the list of past and present town residents that I'd gotten from the mayor. "I don't see a Flossie on here."

"Her name was Florence. She was one of the Dills. They didn't stay long. Here and gone. Some of them did that. People either love it here or they skedaddle pretty quickly."

"So you've lived here since you were seven?"

"My husband carried me off for a couple of years."

"Husband? I didn't know you'd been married. Your name is still Le Doux."

"The marriage didn't take. That resulted partly from him wanting me to leave the valley and live up in the hills. Oh, he was a handsome, rugged man. But handsome counts for less when the man is uncouth and mean. Are you married, Mister Martell?"

"Not yet. And you can call me Mike."

"Well, you find yourself a good woman, Mister Martell, and you be nice to her."

"Yes, ma'am. I'll remember that. What happened to your husband?"

"Now, what's that got to do with Maddie? Are you writing about him or me?"

I tapped my pencil on the pad. "Good point. What was Sam Graves like?"

"Samuel. He never liked to be called Sam. Little Timmie Norton kept calling him *Sam* until he disappeared."

"Disappeared?"

"Doesn't matter. Samuel was the kindest, most generous man who ever lived. He came from back east: Virginia on the Chesapeake Bay. He bought this valley from a man he met there."

"Who was that man?"

"I don't think I ever heard his name. Maddie always said God sent him here."

"Do you think he bought the valley from God?"

Her mouth tightened. "Really, Mister Martell."

"I heard a group of townsfolk took a trip to see the place Samuel Graves grew up. They found a man there named Onice Graves, but he'd never heard of your man Samuel. In fact, they couldn't find anyone who'd ever heard of him."

"Yes, I know that story. But those people, well . . . they drank. I was amazed they found their way back home, frankly."

I tapped my list of questions with the pencil. "Did Mister Graves build the schoolhouse?"

"Oh, yes. Schoolhouse, this library…" She waved her arm, encompassing the reading room and its dusty shelves. "Even the town hall. He paid to put up the first electric lights. We had a zoo briefly, until all twenty-two animals escaped. The woodsmen claim there's a family of llamas living up on the mountain."

She leaned toward me in another cloud of gardenias and whispered. "They also claim the llamas lie with the lions and eat humans, so what can you believe, really?"

I nodded, but inside I pictured my head shaking over the bizarreness of this old lady's ideas.

"Samuel was quite the philanthropist. How did he earn his money?"

"That's a crude question, Mister Martell."

I shrugged. "I'm writing his life story. I need to know."

"Hummph. Well, he owned the valley. He earned money from selling the land, and he earned money when the Norton boys and their sons harvested trees. But really, it's nobody's business. He had interest in gold mines, I heard. Invested in the railroad. He owned the freight company running wagons in and out of town. Not that his financial affairs were ever of any concern to me. And the bank, that was his."

I thought about some of the other mysteries I wanted to get answered. "I understand he was something of a clothes horse."

Her eyebrows dropped over her nose in a question. "A drying rack? Why would anyone say that about Maddie?"

"Sorry, ma'am. A different kind of clothes horse." I saw confusion in her eyes. "It's an expression. I hear he liked to wear…unusual clothing."

She rewarded me with a huge smile. "He was a fancy dresser, that's for sure. You should have seen his red and yellow suit the day we planted our tree. He even had a top hat, although we called it a stovepipe back then, after President Abraham Lincoln. Samuel was also quite fond of his full Indian headdress. It came from Sitting Bull. He wore it with his buckskin."

"His bronze statue...did the town have it made with several outfits?"

"What do you mean, Mister Martell?"

"I've been here two and a half days, and each day the statue was dressed in different clothes. All in bronze."

"I'm sure you're mistaken. Do you drink, young man?"

"In moderation, Miss Amelia. Only in moderation."

"Hmmph." She crossed one hand onto the other on the table between us.

I made another note on my pad.

"Tell me about Samuel's coyote."

"Dog."

"I heard about a coyote."

She looked at me with studied condescension. "Our town is in the midst of woods running up the sides of the Rocky Mountains. Of course there are coyotes. But Maddie had a dog. It did have a wild look to it, so maybe some of the younger folk remember it as a wild animal. But let me assure you, I wouldn't let a coyote sniff me the way that dog did. Why, when I was sitting down, it would put its snout in my lap and sniff all over."

"Ma'am?"

"My second husband threatened to kill the poor thing, but I prevailed upon him to leave it alone."

"Second husband?"

"Divorced women could remarry, Mister Martell. It was quite common on the frontier."

"What happened to him?"

Her eyes almost teared. "His body was found in a tree halfway up the mountain. His viscera were missing."

I didn't know how to respond to that without appearing to be a nosy reporter, so I fell back on the mundane. "I'm sorry for your loss."

She wiped her eyes with a lace handkerchief. "Doesn't matter. I took my name back again years ago."

"Do you have children?"

"I did." She put her handkerchief into her bodice. "My boy disappeared in aught nine. My little girl was last seen clinging to the back fur of a black bear loping down the valley."

"What?"

"I'm sorry, Mister Martell. I didn't mean to distract you. Maddie never wanted political office, you know. Big Ben Harper was mayor the first dozen years, and then my father took over for twenty. After that, they get confused in my head, even my brother's terms. Small men doing a small job. Not like Papa and Ben. The town doubled in size under Ben and then tripled from that under Papa. Maddie was more of a spiritual leader to us all. He was quite learned and intelligent. Did you know that he could read the Bible upside down and in the mirror?"

"I didn't know that, Miss Amelia."

"I remember a favorite quote of his: *Yeah, though I walk like a shadow through the valley of death, I will fear no equal.*"

"Ma'am, I don't think that's the quote."

She glared at me. "Young man. Can you read upside down and backwards?"

"I don't think so."

"Then don't question your betters."

I noted her quotation on my pad, murmuring, "Yes, ma'am."

The fire in her glare died away, and she returned to her panegyric to Samuel Graves.

"Maddie was generous to a fault. We had a Maypole every year the day after founding day, and he paid for the whole festival." She paused and then peered into my eyes. "We haven't had a party like that since he died."

I gave her a small smile, hoping I'd been forgiven for doubting her quotation. "Big party this year, though."

"Yes, indeed." She leaned in and smiled, showing a glimpse of teeth. "Five years back, we put up the statue. This year, you're writing a book for us."

I tried not to inhale her flowery aroma. "Pamphlet."

Her smile disappeared. "I thought it was going to be a book."

"Not for thirty dollars."

She sat back in her chair. "I see. What else do you want to know for your little *pamphlet*?"

"I saw a lot of posters for missing children."

"It's so sad. Parents don't watch out for their young children."

"Seems like a lot of kids. Why do people stay here?"

Miss Amelia looked at me like I'd asked her why people like to breathe.

"Look out that window. Those mountains are the prettiest sight in the world. The earth in this valley will grow anything. The woods teem with game, and our loggers can't make a dent in the forest, the trees grow so fast. And the water from our river is the sweetest in the world. Why stay, indeed."

I actually thought the water had a sulfur smell to it, but I wasn't going to tell her that.

"Yes, ma'am. I guess I see your point. Still, you lost two children, yourself."

She froze me with her glare. "Things were wilder back then. Animals came into the middle of town. And the winters here can be quite cold."

"Sorry, ma'am. I apologize for any offense. Your family seems to have had bad luck."

"My dear Mister Martell, in this valley, it isn't about luck. It's about survival of the fattest."

"Ma'am? Survival of the fattest?"

"Fittest, young man. I told you not to put words in my mouth. Don't you know your Darwin? Hard times lead to the survival of the fittest."

"I'm so sorry. I must have misheard you."

"Ignorant and deaf. Nonetheless, when you find a young woman who will have you, I insist you let me know. I want to write the young lady a letter."

"Well, thank you, Miss Amelia, but I don't think that will be—"

"I want to warn her about your stupidity and tendency to be rude. Now, if you'll excuse me, I'm tired. Please use the outjunction when you leave town."

In the end, I took advice from my editor back in Calgary. I made up the whole thing and wrote it as a hagiography. The townsfolk loved it.

THE SUMMERFIELD HORROR

MATTHEW HOWE

25 October, 1923

My Dear Dr. Chambers,

While we have never met, I understand you are the physician of the town of Graves Grove. I write to you with the utmost urgency concerning a citizen of your town, a man I believe to be your patient.

A few months ago, I received a letter from a Mr. David Summerfield of Graves Grove. He had been referred to me by a mutual acquaintance, Dr. D. Newman of Vancouver. Mr. Summerfield had become obsessed with retrieving what he believed to be repressed memories of a childhood trauma.

I have some expertise in this new field, and since Mr. Summerfield was unwilling to travel to Vancouver where I could treat him properly, I advised him on a course of self-hypnosis that has proven quite effective for those who show the discipline to adhere to the methods exactly as I prescribe.

I am afraid that something is terribly wrong with Mr. Summerfield. I've included his latest correspondence to me. As you will see, it is quite frightening in its implications. I hope I am not too late and that I am alerting you in time to prevent something terrible from occurring.

Please don't hesitate to contact me with further questions.

Best regards,
Dr. Richard Cooper

19 October, 1923

Richard,

I write because you are the only living soul who may give credence to what I am compelled to say. Though our relationship has been entirely confined to correspondence, I feel a kinship with you. Not only have you been supportive of me since I first learned of your expertise from our mutual friend Dr. D. Newman, but it was your suggestion that I embark on a course of self-hypnosis that has led to my ultimate understanding of a great mystery.

You see, I am supposed to be gone. Not dead. Worse than dead. Gone from this world in a way I can almost not describe.

My beloved mother, dead these fourteen months now, was the agent of my salvation. My memory of the incident is dim, for after I was pulled by my mother's loving hand from the malign embrace consuming me, I fell into a deep trance state and did not emerge for nearly a month. All memories of the incident were gone, or so it seemed at the time.

I have not spoken much of my personal life, but my family relocated to Graves Grove in 1895, a mere fifteen years after the community was founded by Mr. Samuel Graves. I was born in 1899 and since my arrival in this world, have never left the confines of this valley. My father passed away when I was still an infant and I was raised by my mother, Annabelle, a strong woman, wise beyond her years. My father left to us our modest house and a small inheritance which sustained us.

Like all children of Graves Grove, I began my education at the S. M. Graves Elementary School. And like most children, school held little interest for me and our recess play time was the highlight of our day.

Our school was well-equipped with playground equipment, but this was mostly shunned in favor of the tree, that huge, brooding sycamore which, while only having been planted two decades prior by Samuel Graves himself, had sprouted into a specimen of enormous girth and height. The twisting labyrinth of branches begged to be climbed and transformed into pirate ships and mountaintops by youthful imagination, and the massive, twisting root structure curled around the tree's base could become hidden caverns deep beneath the earth.

On that terrible day, it was the roots where I played, my friends and I imagining that we were in search of a dragon and his hoard of gold. I remember crawling through the roots, then a strange blackness taking me. I remember hearing my mother's voice shouting to me, and then I remember waking up in my bed at home, Dr. Chambers, the local physician at my side and my mother flung across me, weeping with joy and relief.

As for the tree, I never returned to it. My mother withdrew me from the school and assumed my educational duties herself. This was frowned upon by many in our community, yet my mother stood fierce and strong against those who insisted that I return to "proper" schooling.

She did not relent until I was ready for secondary school, and it was only later that I understood this was due to the fact that our higher education was conducted in a building across town from the elementary school, far away from that tree.

I led a more or less happy life in our small community. I showed an aptitude for math and was taken in by Mr. Marcus Walters, the town's sole accountant, who educated me in his profession. When Marcus had sufficient confidence in me, he retired and I assumed his practice which included occupying his small offices above Shipp's Hardware Store, whose books I kept in exchange for a reduced rent.

As the only practicing accountant in Graves Grove, my business was a modest success, and I began to think about finding a suitable wife and starting a family of my own when, shortly after my 23rd birthday, my mother fell ill. It was a strange ailment that our noble Dr. Chambers was unable to diagnose. He recommended bedrest and quiet, and while not tending to my duties at the office, I saw to my mother's care.

I spent much of my time reading to her, and even as her mental faculties deteriorated, I hoped the sound of my voice would bring her some small comfort.

Then, as the end drew inevitably near, that terrible and miraculous thing happened. Her eyes, which had been dulled as her life-essence drained away, suddenly brightened. She raised her head off the pillow and met my eyes, and for the first time in days I knew she recognized me.

"I was napping," she said. "And I saw you, in the roots." Her voice was a sharp whisper, fragile and thin, but I sensed her determination. And I realized she was speaking of that long-ago day at the tree.

"I ran to school, to the tree, your friends were there, but no sign of you. And I looked everywhere, called your name but you didn't answer. And then I saw you. I saw your foot among the roots."

She hesitated, as if she was having a hard time finding the words. "I saw your foot, only it wasn't all there. I could see through it. But I grabbed it. And I felt you. And you were cold. Your flesh was frozen and your touch burned me, but I held on and I pulled. I pulled and screamed and I prayed to almighty God and there from among the roots you came and fell into my arms." I recall I began to shiver at this point in her narration because even as she spoke those words, part of me was reliving them.

"I tried to rouse you. You opened your eyes. You looked up at me and for a moment I thought all was well. Before you collapsed unconscious, you spoke."

She took a moment to gather her strength.

"You told me," she said. "You told me what you saw, and it has haunted me to this day."

And then her strength fled. She fell once more into her pillow. The dull glaze returned to her eyes, and she returned to a deep sleep from which she never recovered.

But her words sparked something inside of me. A fleeting vision swept across my mind, just an impression, an impression of gazing upon some unspeakable terror, gone as quickly as it had arrived.

But I knew that the impression triggered by the words of my mother was no phantasm, but the vague shadow of memory.

The next weeks were consumed with the task of caring for my mother in her last days, then making arrangements for her final rest once the inevitable had occurred.

Following the funeral I returned to my life. But her words, that fleeting scrap of vision stayed with me, clung to me. I found myself distracted at work, I found myself losing sleep. My plans for starting a family of my own seemed unimportant. I became obsessed with what had happened that day on the playground.

I spoke to Dr. Chambers, in the strictest of confidence of course, about my obsession. While it was beyond his powers as a healer to treat, he suggested I visit

Dr. Newman in Vancouver. And while I certainly had the means and the time to take such a trip, the notion of leaving Graves Grove filled me with an irrational terror.

I did, however, write to Dr. Newman. He recommended you as a potential solution to my problems.

You know the rest, of course, and I began the regime of self-hypnosis exactly as you prescribed, sitting quietly in the tailor position, closing my eyes, concentrating only on my breath, clearing my mind and thinking of nothing. For several days, little happened. I could feel a vague tingling at the very edges of my perception, yet it never materialized into a memory of any coherence and I feared my attempts would prove fruitless.

It was the afternoon of my fifth day of self-hypnosis when I experienced the first strange occurrence.

I was in my second-floor office when I happened to look out the window. There, glimpsed past the rooftops, was a strange meteorological formation, a slowly spinning vortex of black clouds. From my vantage point, I realized this strange formation must be down near the river, my full view of it blocked by the buildings on Hill Street. While I had never seen a tornado, such as plagues the Midwest of the United States, I thought this was what it must be.

I was about to run to the street and shout for my fellow citizens to take cover, when I realized that there was not a cloud in the sky. The day was clear and bright, the sun shining fiercely.

And then the other piece fell into place. This unusual vortex, I deduced, was hovering near the elementary school. Directly over, I was sure, that malignant tree.

Seized with dread, I hurried out into the street. I walked toward the river until I had a direct view of the school and the tree. That strange apparition was gone, yet I felt a deep foreboding. It was afternoon, recess time, and the shouts and cries of the children came distantly to me.

And then screaming.

I threw all fear away and sprinted for the school. As I approached, I was joined by others who had also been drawn by the uproar.

The screams were those of Miss Mayberry, the second grade teacher and a recent addition to our community.

She was screaming for Timothy Mathers, screaming that he was gone. One moment he had been there, playing among the roots of the tree, and now he was gone.

Others tried to console her, assuring her he had only slipped away to raise the sort of mischief he was well known in town for. Yet Miss Mayberry was inconsolable, insisting that she knew he was gone and would never be seen again.

The other men and I mounted a thorough search of the school grounds and surrounding area and found nothing.

I walked back to my office, crestfallen and not a small bit terrified. I realized then what I know now. Young Timothy Mathers had not disappeared; he had been taken. As I had nearly been taken and would have had my mother, reacting to some strange instinct, not intervened.

My strange vision, that black cloud which heralded the boy's disappearance, I theorized I had been able to see what no other had due both to the experience I had suffered as a child which had left a lasting change in me, and my efforts to revive lost memories.

As horrific as the circumstances were, this strange episode caused me to redouble my efforts. I had made concrete progress, and felt certain that with enough effort, the mystery which consumed me would be solved.

It was a full month before anything else of note occurred. Again, the almost unspeakable terror I witnessed happened in the bright of day. I was leaving lunch and walking back to my office when I spied Mr. Samuel Graves standing up the hill from me, speaking to the mayor.

As I noted earlier, Mr. Graves is the founder of our community and has always been an eccentric character whose origins are shrouded in no small amount of mystery. There is one aspect of his character known to all who have had dealings with him: his flamboyant wardrobe. Mr. Graves never appears in the same outfit twice. He was as likely to be seen in a handsome sack-coat and three piece suit as he was in formal evening wear, which he would don at any time of the day.

Today Graves was wearing a linen suit in a strange, pale blue color and a top hat, utterly inappropriate, of a deep burgundy. I don't know what compelled me to stare at him, but as I did, I felt a strange darkness come over me. It was like a curtain being drawn across my vision accompanied by a strange, hot rushing which seemed to travel through my mind right to left.

When the curtain passed I could see again, but I could see…more. I could see through the reality we occupy to the truth at the core of things.

I saw Mr. Graves as he truly was.

Taller, nearly seven feet, thin to the point of emaciation with large tendons standing out wherever his exposed flesh was revealed. His skin was a ghostly greenish-gray color, strongly textured. His true head was wider and flatter with eyes nearly the size of tea cups, almond shaped, multifaceted like those of a fly which glowed a dull yellow. As he spoke, I could see the teeth in his mouth were sharp, needle like. And his hands, the hands he gestured with, Richard, there were not hands but segmented mandibles of a distinctly insectoid aspect.

Graves, I realized, was not human, or not fully human yet somehow projected his human form into the minds of all who interacted with him. My particular experience as well as my mental exercises had allowed me to pierce the veil he somehow erected.

And then the worst. Graves turned as if disturbed, and those strange, inhuman eyes met mine. The pleasant smile on his face changed to a frown, and I realized he knew that I was seeing him as he truly was.

I nearly fainted, and tore my gaze from him. That black curtain passed my vision again and when it was gone, Mr. Graves was just Mr. Graves again. Only he was still staring at me with that terrifying knowledge in his eyes.

I put my head down and hurried off.

I must tell you, Richard, the next few days were ones of almost unbearable tension. I expected Graves to arrive with the local authorities to arrest me on some trumped up charge, for I had no doubt that what I had witnessed was true.

As the days passed, my relief grew and swept me toward a new conviction. I realized I must cease my efforts to learn the truth, because I knew now the truth would destroy me. This decision brought great solace, and life returned to a semblance of normalcy for nearly six months.

Until this Monday past.

I was taking my exercise, walking to the top of Hill Street, when a darkness caught the corner of my eye. My thought was to look away and ignore it, but some other primal instinct took command and I turned toward it.

It was one of those strange vortexes. It was back where I had first glimpsed it, no doubt over the school, over the dreaded tree. Unlike the first incident, this apparition was smaller, thinner, more tenuous. It faded from view of its own accord after only a few moments.

I took a deep breath to reorient myself and turned away from the sight. I realized I was standing in front of the Constable's office again. Through the front window, I could see a bulletin board on the eastern wall. Pinned to it was a handbill concerning the disappearance of Timmy Mathers. Next to it, a second notice advertised the disappearance of another child. And another, and another. In fact, as I looked with growing horror,

I realized the entire board was covered with notices of this sort.

I don't know how the sheer number of children who have disappeared in this small town goes virtually without comment or action by the authorities. Now, knowing what I know, I can only assume there is some sort of mass hypnosis in action, which dulls the minds and instincts of our townsfolk.

But I had been able to break free, at moments, of that influence and I knew the sight I had just witnessed, that brief appearance of the vortex, heralded another terrible evil. I suddenly knew in the core of my being that within the next few days, another child would vanish while playing among those roots.

And I knew I must act, but before I could act I needed to understand the nature of the threat. That meant turning once again to self-hypnosis. Only I could not go back to the slow, incremental progress I had made earlier. Drastic action which would bring more concrete results needed to be taken and needed to be taken immediately.

Oh, Richard, I cannot describe the effort it took that night to gather the courage to do what I knew I must. I left my house an hour after sunset when most of our town's citizens would be having their dinners and thus be off the streets.

The walk down to the river seemed endless, each step an effort as if I was walking steeply uphill, not down.

The town was deserted, silent except for muted laughter and talk coming from the warmly lit houses I passed.

As I neared the river, the soft susurrations of tiny waves against the rocks grew louder. This sound normally calmed me, but here it only served to sharpen my apprehension.

I entered the schoolyard through an open fence, walked across the grassy play area to the sycamore.

It had grown only larger and more imposing since I had last visited it, the root system curled around its base a maze worthy of the Minotaur.

I nearly ran then, and for sake of my sanity and my life, I wish I had.

Yet I had to know. The memories buried deep inside my mind were clamoring for release, and instinct told me that here, at the place where I had nearly been taken, they would be set free.

I sat down on one of the larger roots. I leaned my back against the bole. It was cold, as if I was leaning on a slab of iron and not a living organism.

I closed my eyes and, as you had instructed me, concentrated only on my breathing.

I do not know how long it was before the memories surfaced, before the darkness behind my eyelids exploded into a scene of horror so potent I can barely bring myself to write of it.

In my memory, I was once again playing among the roots when the sunlight filtering down faded away. I wasn't frightened, sure that a cloud had passed over the sun and that in moments that bright, warm light would return.

But it did not, though the darkness did lighten. Not with the golden hues of the sun, but with a sick, green light that spoke of death and disease. A strange coldness began to settle upon me.

I heard a voice calling, my mother's voice I dimly realized, screaming for me.

But I ignored her and crawled deeper toward the green light which had cast a strange spell over me.

The darkness I had been thrown into suddenly split apart, the world opened before me, and I saw, oh God my dear Richard, I saw through the abyss. I saw the terrible secret the sycamore hid.

I was still in the root system of the sycamore yet I knew I had somehow pierced a veil which separated two worlds.

The roots continued before me, a sprawling field of them enormously vaster than the root structure of the tree at the school. I could not see the trunk of the tree for it was behind me, but I felt its vast girth and weight. The greenish light, I realized, came from terrifyingly bright sunlight filtering through the leaves of this alien tree. The sycamore, I realized, had a twin on the other side of some strange break in reality: another, utterly unearthly growth of vast proportions.

The branches of this arboreal monster stretched away from me for at least a hundred yards, and the branches moved with a liquid animation that could not have come only from the thin breeze blowing.

In the few gaps in the tightly clustered branches and leaves where raw sunlight did penetrate, I saw a most curious phenomenon, that of double shadows. I realized that I was no longer on Earth, and the landscape beyond me belonged to a planet which orbited a binary star, a concept I was familiar with from my brief study of astronomy in secondary school.

A great distance away I could see the structures of some sort of community, though the structures I observed were grotesque mockeries of human architecture, seeming more grown than built. The colors, the angles, the textures of everything were wrong, as if different laws of physics held sway in this hellish place.

Yet the terror I felt was mixed with a profound curiosity and a recognition that I was gazing upon something few men had ever witnessed.

That curiosity fled before the horror when my wandering gaze fell upon the pods.

They were suspended from the lower branches, fat, liquid filled, translucent pods of a nature I could not divine.

Inside each floated a child.

Human children, I realized, plucked from Graves Grove as well as other communities across the face of our Earth where another malign sycamore might bridge the gulf between worlds.

That had been the fate I avoided, to be consumed by this abomination. That was the fate of young Timmy Mathers, and that would be the fate of the next child taken. My terror reached a peak, and I felt my very sanity threatened as I finally understood the evil at the heart of Graves Grove.

I tried to rip my gaze away from the horrific spectacle before me, but was unable to, drawn by some strange compulsion to understand. And as I looked more closely, I realized my initial impression that the tree was feeding on our children was wrong.

The human children the pods held were not alone. Each pod contained not one, but two beings. One human, one…something else. These two beings were pressed into close contact with one another, and as one of those bulbous pods slowly turned from the sickening motions of the branches, I was able to see more clearly and realized that the two entities inside the pod were merging together, their flesh blending, combining.

Below, movement caught my eyes as three beings pushed through a screen of low hanging leaves and entered the space under the branches. The two larger ones I recognized as of the same general aspect as my vision of Samuel Graves. The third was smaller and even more alien in appearance without a hint of human form, nearly completely insectoid though it walked stiffly upright.

A child, I realized. Their child.

I could tell at once how weak and sickly it was, unable to even walk without the aid of its parents, its leather-like skin grayish and mottled. I could hear its breath, a thin, liquid wheezing.

The two beings led their child to a low hanging branch, picked it up, and offered it to the limb. At once, a screen of leaves curled over the creature and in moments formed one of those strange pods around it.

The creature had fallen unconscious, but I sensed the larger ones were waiting. And I realized what they were waiting for.

Me.

I was supposed to have been snatched into the embrace of that horror and placed beside that creature in that pod. I heard a rustling sound and looked away from the pod to see a network of smaller roots suddenly free themselves from the ground and reach for me. One of them fastened around my wrist, another my neck. A third went through my mouth, opened to scream, and down my throat.

At that moment I felt something come into me, some fragment of the tree's power.

Then I heard my mother's voice sharpen, closer now, felt something tug distantly at my leg. There was pain, great pain, and a momentary struggle between worlds over my body. But a mother's love was stronger, and I was ripped free of that evil embrace and back into the world I knew.

The last image I remember was my mother's face, her hair backlit by our earthly sun, looking down at me with such love and relief as I have never known. Then blackness as my exhausted body fell into that dark sleep.

And then my memory was finished.

Back at the tree, I stood. I knew now what our town was. I knew now who our founder was. One of those things who had begun life as a sickly alien creature, part of an ancient, dying race, somehow merged through techniques I could never imagine with a human child to produce a specimen hardy enough to survive, sent here to establish a portal through which more children could be taken.

I had nearly been one of those children, I had nearly been taken to merge with that pathetic creature I had seen and live out the rest of my life on that alien world. And while the parents of Timmy Mathers may take some comfort in the knowledge that their son lives on, though in a strange and mutated form, I have vowed that this horror must end.

I returned home, and I wrote this letter. I plan to post it on my way to my office. I will use a false return address to ensure it is not seized before it reaches you. Because someone must know, Richard, someone must know of the evil that lies at the heart of Graves Grove and perhaps other communities over this Earth.
Someone must stop them.

You alone know the truth. Do with it what you will, but know that even though I march off to a certain death, I remain your friend.

~ David Summerfield

1 November, 1923

Dr. Cooper,

I thank you graciously for your letter, though am saddened to tell you it did in fact come too late. Do not blame yourself, it was too late long before "Mr. Summerfield's" letter ever reached you.

The man who wrote you died a few hours after posting his note to you. He was found at the elementary school, setting explosives which he had stolen from the local hardware store to the town's prized sycamore tree. The man had armed himself with a revolver, and I'm afraid our constable was forced to shoot in self-defense. But the man who died and the man who wrote you was not David Summerfield. In fact, there is not nor has there ever been a David Summerfield residing in Graves Grove.

The man who wrote you was in the grips of a great mental instability, to the point he did not even know his own name or his own family lineage. Many aspects of his account are true, he was our community's sole accountant. And he did have a relationship with a child who disappeared, but the man who died under that sycamore tree was Mr. George Mathers, the father of Timmy Mathers who vanished while playing near that sycamore in 1921. Mathers' wife, Annabelle, who in the letter is referred to as his mother (make of that what you will) did suffer a strange premonition, did attempt to reach and find her son, but was unsuccessful. She took her own life a few months after their son had vanished.

The sycamore sits on the banks of the river, and speculation is that young Timmy fell into the waters and was swept away by the current. Sadly, his body has yet to be discovered.

I can only assume Mr. Mathers' fantasy is a way of reaching closure. I cannot imagine anything more awful than losing a child, especially when that child's fate remains unknown. The "evil" sycamore he speaks of is nothing more than a particularly marvelous example of that noble species. The plague of vanishing children he notes is purest fantasy.

Graves Grove is a quiet community, and I would appreciate you not sharing the details of this case with the wider world. We seek nothing but to be allowed to live our own lives and avoid notoriety of any sort.

Again, I thank you for your concern. I'm coming to Vancouver next week and would enjoy meeting you. Is there a chance you could carve out a bit of time in your schedule? I'd love to hear more about this self-hypnosis method of yours.

With great respect,
Dr. Henry Chambers
Graves Grove, B.C.

Vancouver Gazette
November 14, 1923

DOCTOR VANISHES MYSTERIOUSLY

Dr. Richard Cooper, a well-respected psychotherapist of the West End was reported missing yesterday by his wife Rachael. Dr. Cooper was last seen leaving his practice, on his way to take dinner with Dr. Henry Chambers, a colleague from out of town.

While there were reservations made in his name at the Academy Club, Dr. Cooper never arrived, though Dr. Chambers did and waited more than an hour before contacting Dr. Cooper's wife.

At this time, foul play is not suspected, but anyone with any information concerning Dr. Cooper's whereabouts is asked to contact the Vancouver Police Department at their earliest convenience.

THE SCHOOL TRIP

TRAVIS PERRY

The little boy in a cowboy hat and boots stared up at the tree in the center of Graves Grove. His stare was so intense and his eyes such a striking shade of blue that Mamie Rue, who had been walking to the town public library to return a book, found herself stopping beside him to comment. "Whatcha doing, little boy? Are you lost? I haven't seen you around here before."

He met her gaze directly, completely unafraid. "I am looking at this tree. Uh, no, I am not lost. Even though I am not from here at all. I am from Olney, Montana, USA."

"Oh really?" She found herself smiling. He sounded funny, this little kid—talking without contractions. "I'm sorry, I don't know where Olney is. But I *do* happen to know that Montana is in the United States, and that even borders British Columbia."

"Oh, okay. This is my first time to Canada. My grandmother is Canadian, but she lives in California now. I don't know if I've ever talked to a Canadian before. Other than her." Mamie found herself smiling again. *Well, at least the kid did say the word "don't."*

"Ah, so you think maybe Canadians don't know much about the USA, then."

"Do you?" The boy's eyes widened in earnest.

"Yes, we really do. The movies we watch are made in America, just like the ones you watch. And a lot of the things we buy are made in the USA. So I think every Canadian knows probably more about the US than you know about us."

"Oh, okay. That is very interesting. I suppose you know that this is the United States bicentennial, too."

Mamie nodded. She found herself bending down to match the boy's eye level. He continued to meet her gaze directly. *This sure is some strange kid.* "Can I ask you a question?"

"Of course."

"What are you doing here by yourself?"

"Oh, I am not by myself. I am on a school trip. Like a field trip, but longer."

"Where is everybody else?"

"At the gas station a few blocks from here."

"Shouldn't you be with them instead of talking to me?"

"Why should I be? They said we had a break for thirty minutes to eat and use the bathroom. It has only been about five minutes." He leaned closer to her and whispered, as if they were collaborating in some sort of conspiracy. "Though it is true I should not be talking to you since I have been told not to talk to strangers."

"Oh, yes, that's a very good thing to tell little boys. That and you shouldn't be wandering around by yourself. Though we don't have to be strangers. My name is Mamie." She held out her hand.

The boy shook it. "That is a funny name."

She chuckled. "Can I ask you another question?"

A look of deep confusion crossed the boy's face. "You have already asked me other questions."

She chuckled again. "True enough, I did. But I asked, because—well, it doesn't matter why I asked if I could ask you.

I just wanted to know, why is it you don't use contractions?"

"Because they told me in school that contractions are a shortcut."

"Yes, that's true."

"A shortcut is a lazy way. I am not lazy." This boy—he must have been seven or eight—said this with utter seriousness.

She stood up and tilted her head back in a peal of laughter. After a bit, she looked back down. The way he stared at her, his brow furrowed, completely not understanding what she thought was funny, that compelled Mamie to stop. "I'm sorry for laughing. You're just so, um, *different* from other boys I've met."

The boy nodded. "Yes, I have heard that before." His voice turned distant, and for a moment she wondered if it was because she'd hurt his feelings. But no, that didn't seem to be the case. What *was* true was his eyes were focused behind her, into the town park.

"Um." Mamie Rue took two steps closer and knelt down in front of him. He tilted his head sideways to continue gazing behind her, right past her head.

She said, "So you're looking at our town tree, are you?"

"Yes." He continued to stare past her.

"Would you like to know what kind of tree that is? They aren't very common around here. We mostly have pines, just like you do in Montana."

"Certainly," he said, still staring past her.

"It's a sycamore. Our town's founder planted it. Do you know what a sycamore tree is?"

"Oh, yes." Abruptly the boy began to sing in a very loud, off-key voice. "ZACCHEUS WAS A WEE LITTLE MAN AND A WEE LITTLE MAN WAS HE; HE CLIMBED UP IN A SYCAMORE TREE FOR THE LORD HE WANTED TO SEE; AND AS THE SAVIOR—"

"Yes, that's right." Mamie Rue interrupted the awful singing. "I suppose you heard that song in church?"

"In Sunday School, actually."

"Well, yeah, of course. Is that why you're staring at the tree?"

"No. I did not know what it was until you just told me."

"Then why are you so interested in it?"

"The tree looks angry."

"Excuse me?"

"Yes. I think it is a dangerous tree."

"Excuse me...I don't think I understand you."

"You don't?" The boy looked perplexed. "Should I say it again? It looks like a mean tree. Scary."

"A tree...is mean?" She could not hide her sense of doubt from her expression, but it didn't seem to faze the boy in the slightest.

"Yeah. You know, some trees are nice and easy to climb. I climb a lot of trees. But that one looks scary. Look at the roots. Like an octopus or something."

"It's just a tree."

"Yes, I know. But I would not want to climb it. It is like it wants to hurt me."

"Ah...this is a little creepy."

"Why?" asked the boy, meeting her gaze for the first time in a while. His eyes were so very blue.

"I...uh...it's just a tree."

"Yes. But I think it is not a nice one."

"But trees are not mean or nice. They are just *trees.* And anyway, I've climbed that tree before."

"You *have*?"

"Yes."

"And you didn't get *hurt*?"

She bit her lower lip as she thought about that. Well, yes, she'd scraped a knee a time or two on the tree's bark. She jumped from it once and twisted her ankle. She had a friend when she was about this boy's age, Robbie, who used to say the tree roots led down to hell and that it wanted to take her down there—however, that boy used to say all kinds of strange things. A bit like this boy here.

Though Robbie did disappear one summer. No one knew what happened to him.

"Um, some little things happened to hurt me. But nothing too bad. I mean, I'm still alive, right?" She forced a smile as she said it.

The boy examined her face carefully, as if not quite certain if she were in fact among the living.

"Okay. I suppose so," he finally proclaimed.

"Here, let me walk you over to the tree. I'll keep you safe."

He breathed a deep sigh and then very seriously held out his hand. After a brief hesitation, she took it.

The two of them, hand in hand, walked from the sidewalk where they'd been standing. That particular strip of concrete ran down Graves Grove's main avenue, past the library, right next to the park, and into the shops of the downtown area. They went up over the concrete lip around the large boxed area the tree occupied.

Its roots rose above ground in twisted shapes that almost looked like tentacles, just like the boy had said. But that was perfectly normal for a sycamore, of course. Its bark showed fissures and gray and white patches. Its branches drooped just a bit as if reaching downward—instead of angling upward toward the sun. Mamie could almost understand the boy's reluctance when she actually *looked* at the tree. Somehow, she hadn't actually done that in a very long time.

But she had been around this tree her entire life. As a girl, she'd been a bit of a tomboy and had climbed this thing more times than she could count—it *had* to be safe, no matter how it looked. Right?

They both stopped in front of the sycamore, both staring at it. "Now what?" asked the boy.

"We climb it, silly." The young woman tried to laugh, but found her voice caught in her throat.

"I don't think so," he replied.

"Come on, I'll go first."

"Maybe you had better not."

"Come on, don't be silly! I've done it lots of times before. I don't anymore so much, but for you."

"I'm not silly. Not at all," said the boy, his tone level and his face utterly serious.

Mamie turned back toward the tree and found it had a fissure in the bark she hadn't seen—or hadn't noticed—just seconds ago. I was as if the tree had split down the side, a tall cleft, and perhaps deep, though not at all wide. As if the tree were about to split open from an ax blow by an invisible Paul Bunyan, who had just nicked it on his last swing. Or perhaps as if a door were opening into the heart of the tree itself. "That's strange, I haven't seen that before."

"You mean its mouth opening?"

"That's not a *mouth*, it's just a split in the bark."

"How come it wasn't there before?"

"It was...to...there..." As her voice trailed off, she rubbed her forehead. She looked back at the tree. The fissure seemed wider now. But that couldn't be. "Let me settle this once and for all. This is my home town, this tree has been here almost one hundred years. I'm sure it's perfectly safe—I'll climb the tree and prove it to you!"

"Don't! Please do *not*. That tree wants to hurt you, too!"

"Just hold on, little boy, just wait right there. I'll pull you up after me. But only if you aren't too afraid. First let me show you—I promise it's perfectly safe." She set down her library book in front of the tree, stepped closer to it and reached for a low branch, putting her right foot on a tree root bent high upward. It felt very strange to decide to climb this tree after all these years, something she wouldn't have even imagined doing just a few minutes ago—but at the moment, it seemed to make sense. She felt thankful she was wearing jeans and a blouse so at least she'd stay modest—

"Travis, come here!" bellowed a voice from behind her. She turned and noted a woman in a green dress and curly brown hair shouting at the boy behind her.

"Yes, Mrs. Dunlap," answered the boy, his voice rising in surprise.

"Where have you been? We've been looking for you for the past twenty minutes. The bus is ready to leave!"

"Twenty minutes? Really? I swear I just left five minutes ago."

"It's been twenty-five, but you were supposed to be with the rest of us the entire time. Come on now, let's go!"

Both he and the woman turned back away from the tree and the boy trotted off after her meekly.

The woman, Mrs. Dunlap, cast a single icy glare back at Mamie Rue. The boy didn't look back her way at all.

Mamie let go of the branch and backed away from the tree herself. The fissure in the bark seemed even bigger than it had just moments before. Somehow.

But obviously, that couldn't be.

She snatched up her book in haste and ran to the sidewalk. She forced herself to slow to a walk, but her walking pace back toward the town library was far too fast to make sense. No, she needed to calm down. She was breathing hard for no reason at all. No, nothing at all had happened to make her breathe like that. Not a thing.

RULES

DAKOTA CALDWELL

Just where do you think you're going?" The voice echoed out of the house, filling the air.

With a groan, Curtis slowed to a walk, turned back, and stuck his head through the front door. "I'm going to hang out with Mitchel! Remember?"

"No, frankly I don't!" Curtis's mom appeared in the door of the living room, sewing needle and thread in her hand. "Tuesdays are scheduled as chore days. You have laundry to get done."

"I *know* Tuesdays are chore days." Curtis sighed. "I asked you about it in advance. There's a storm coming through tomorrow, so we want to go goof off today instead. Please?"

"I don't like the idea of you slacking your responsibilities just because you want to avoid getting wet. No, boy, I'm afraid the answer has to be no. Go on, get back to work!"

Curtis let out a long breath and slowly stalked into the house. His mom reigned like a tyrant; that was for sure. Ever since his father had died, years ago, she had set the house on a stringent schedule. Mondays were for shopping, Tuesdays were for weekly chores, Wednesdays were for having fun.

Of course, Curtis had adjusted to the schedule fairly well. It had begun when he was in elementary school, so now that he was a junior in high school, he had more or less accepted the idea of living off a set of rules. The real problem was that Mitchel, his best friend, had a cousin who happened to be coming though Graves Grove that day. Given that not many families with young, adventurous children dared to live in the town, friends were a rarity, which made guests extra special.

Curtis quickly made his way back up to his room, where a large load of laundry awaited him. After folding a small handful of shirts, his gaze drifted out the window. With only a small bit of hesitation, he slid the glass open, unhinged the screen, and stepped out onto the shingles. He cast a single glance backwards before walking up to the edge of the roof and climbing out into their large oak tree. Forgiveness was easier to come by than permission, and he knew whatever the punishment happened to be, it would be worth it.

It took him a matter of minutes to make it over to Mitchel's house. Had he not been careful to take a number of shortcuts, he was quite certain the town gossips would have given him away almost instantly. As he got closer, he broke into a grin at the sight of an unfamiliar car parked in the driveway. Without waiting another second, he bolted for the house. Mitchel flung the door open long before Curtis had arrived, though he had an annoyed look on his face.

"What took you so long?"

"My mom." Curtis shrugged. "You know her schedule. If you dare to even think about breaking it, she acts like the world is ending."

"So...she let you go after all?"

"What planet do you think we're living on? I snuck out!"

"Oh. Okay." Mitchel shrugged. "Come on in!"

Brimming with excitement for the day, Curtis tore past Mitchel and into the house. In the living room, a young girl leapt out of her chair, seemingly startled by the commotion. Curtis drew up short as her presence registered in his mind.

"You cousin is…a girl?"

"Is that a problem?" Mitchel walked around the dumbfounded Curtis and gestured with a wave of his hand. "Curtis, meet Francine."

Curtis found his mouth slightly dry. "Hi. I'm Mitchel. Uh, Curtis! Uh, good to meet you!"

"Dude, what's with the stammering?" Francine stood up and crossed her arms. "Yes, I'm female. Am I the first you've ever seen?"

"Well, the pickings are pretty slim in this town." Curtis shrugged. "You've got Mamie Rue Le Doux, but she's about all. Crazy broad, never stops talking to her lunch basket. You reckon she keeps something in there?"

"What I 'reckon' is that we're taking entirely too long talking and not enough time doing something." Francine started to walk toward the door. "At this point, you may either show me around the town, or you may stay here and chat like the old ladies in my grandma's bridge club. What's it going to be?"

The two boys nearly knocked each other over in their haste to get out the door. While it would still be the same, creepy old town to them, the delight of showing it to someone was unbearable.

In a whirlwind, they took Francine all the way downtown, a breathtaking walk of five blocks. When they arrived, Francine crossed her arms and stuck her nose up in the air. The posture made Curtis extraordinarily annoyed with her. After all, it was just downright rude to act snobbish toward someone else's town!

"This is the best you've got?"

"What do you mean?" Mitchel seemed appalled at the notion that Graves Grove wasn't good enough. "We've got the General Store and Feed Supply building right over there! It has everything you could need for life in this place. You won't find anything like it back where you're from."

"Where I'm from, we have dozens of stores, all specializing in something. We have enough people that one single store can't hold it all." Francine started walking down the street, kicking at the cracks in the sidewalk. "Come on, there has to be something interesting here."

"We've got the town square."

"Yeah, and the statue!" Mitchel lowered his voice. "It changes clothes every night. No one knows how it happens. One day, it'll be wearing a suit and tie. The next day…"

"Have you heard of something called a television?" Francine frowned. "You know, the things our parents rail and complain about because they didn't have it when they were growing up? Get real, this is the nineties!"

"We've got a sycamore!" Curtis's mouth twisted upward. "It's said to have killed hundreds over the years. Young children, innocently crawling through its twisted, bent roots, vanishing without a trace. It's said…"

Francine yawned. "We have hundreds of children go missing *every* year! 'Child predators' are what they're called. You're going to have to come up with something better."

"There's the old warehouse." Mitchel shrugged. "A retail store tried to set up shop here a dozen or so years ago. They wound up going bankrupt and leaving town, but their warehouse is still intact. You can walk through it, check out the old offices, it's pretty great!"

"Hmm." Francine shrugged. "I guess if that's the *best* you have to offer, I could live with it."

A flash of worry cut its way through Curtis's mind. His mom had forbidden him from ever going near the place, for reasons she had never discussed. He had always been curious, though…

"Great!" Mitchel smiled, then frowned. "Of course, we're going to have to clear it with Curtis here first."

"Why would Curtis not be okay with some innocent exploration?"

Curtis started to reply, but Mitchel cut him off.

"Oh, his mommy won't let him go play anywhere that might be dangerous!" Mitchel's voice mocked Curtis. "Isn't that right, Curtis? Mommy doesn't want her little baby getting hurt."

"Hey!" Curtis frowned. "Having rules isn't a bad thing!"

"No, but having ridiculous rules can be, well, ridiculous." Mitchel shrugged. "Come on, I've gone over there plenty of times. You'll be fine!"

Curtis nodded slowly. "I'm already going to be in trouble anyway, so I might as well go with you guys. Besides, even if you hadn't brought it up, I was still going to go."

He could tell Mitchel didn't believe him, but he supposed nothing could be done about that. They tore away at a run, heading for the far side of the town. When they arrived, Curtis couldn't help but shiver.

The building was enormous, by far the largest Graves Grove had to offer. For the most part, it was featureless, though a large bank of windows had once been prominent across the front of the edifice. They had since been broken out, leaving toothy gaps that looked deadly to say the least.

"How do we get inside?" Francine actually seemed interested, which filled Curtis with hope.

"There's a door around the back." Mitchel led the way. "Come on!"

They rounded the building and came to a large, wooden door. It was weathered, and seemed to be bowing inward. The most prominent feature, though, was a set of claw marks that stretched from the top of the door all the way to the base. Mitchel paused, but Francine laughed.

"Oh, this is classic! A broken-down warehouse, scratch marks, what's next? A screaming ghoul?"

"It's probably just a bear." Mitchel shrugged. "We get them around here from time to time. I know the company dealt in food items, it was probably just trying to get at them."

"Well, let's quit standing here and go look!" Francine opened the door and stepped through. "Come on!"

As Curtis stepped inside, he couldn't help but feel a shiver pass down his spine. He was entering forbidden grounds. He had passed the point of no return.

The moment he had gotten the initial heebie-jeebies out of his system, he took a look around. They had come out onto the floor of a huge, open space that seemed to take up about half of the warehouse. The opposite half, though, was blocked off. Broken-out windows indicated the presence of offices, and several doors seemed to allow access into them. Francine ran toward them before either of the two boys had a chance to say a word.

Without waiting for them, she bolted through the nearest door and down a narrow hallway. When they caught up with her, she stood in the middle of an old office, spinning in a circle. A rotting desk had been pushed up against a nearby wall, and several filing cabinets lay on their sides against it. Several pictures hung on the wall, but they were so corrupted by time and water that Curtis could only make out the barest impression of human figures.

"This is amazing!" Francine's voice almost sounded musical. "This may as well be a long-dead civilization, years after the apocalypse carried everyone away! And just think of what the apocalypse might have been! Undead souls, rising from the grave to…"

A loud roar cut off her tirade. All three teens spun on their heels, and Curtis felt his blood turn to ice. The noise hadn't sounded like any animal he had ever studied, which terrified him.

"Was that a bear?" Francine's voice was now shaking. "Is there a bear in this place?"

Before she could answer, a dull crash echoed through the hallway. Despite being far more muffled than the roar, the effect was exponentially more horrifying.

"What was that?" Mitchel's voice was almost inaudible. "Please tell me something knocked over a lamp."

Curtis shook his head. "I wish." He swallowed a few times before continuing. "That came from the door to the warehouse. Something just shut it."

Slowly, almost numbly, the trio stepped back out into the hallway. The door at the far end was still open, providing them a direct line-of-sight to the exit. They saw nothing alive, though Curtis's suspicions were confirmed in that the only way out had indeed been barred. They could hear scuffling noises, and several muffled growls permeated the air.

"Come on." Curtis motioned to the rest of the group. "Let's get the hell out of here."

Deciding to move before he got cold feet, he stepped out into the hallway and started walking away from the open expanse. Mitchel quickly caught up to him and leaned close to his ear.

"Umm… Not to be a downer, but shouldn't we be trying to get *out* of here?"

"We *are* trying to get out of here." Curtis threw his arms up. "If something is out there, we need to go *away* from it before we make our way to the exit! Make sense?"

"Oh. Right."

"Uh, guys?" Francine let out a squeak. "Help!"

Curtis turned to see something standing in the doorway to the expanse. It seemed to fill the entire area and vaguely resembled a human. The posture appeared slightly off, though. It seemed hunched over, and the limbs seemed longer than they should have been. Without a second look back, Curtis broke into a run.

At the end of the hallway, just as he had hoped, a door led into a stairwell. He slammed his shoulder into the doorknob, trying desperately to break through. The creature let out an enormous howl. Loud, thudding footsteps sounded in Curtis's ears, and he let out an involuntary scream as the door stuck. Mitchel joined in the frenzied pounding, and the obstruction gave way. They ran through in a heartbeat and slammed the door behind them.

Acting on his gut instinct, Curtis started running down the stairs. Mitchel and Francine followed closely, gasping for breath. For once,

Curtis felt a flash of thankfulness for his mom's strict training, as he could exert himself far more than either of the other two.

The stairwell terminated in a single, white door. Curtis drew up short as he noticed a number of signs strewn across the floor. The ones that could still be read proudly displayed warnings of biohazards, toxic chemicals, and high voltage. Most concerning, though, was the fact that the signs had been torn to shreds. Claw marks covered the door, making it likely that whatever had been stored inside had either been corrupted, or escaped.

"You could have mentioned this!" Curtis turned and stuck his finger into Mitchel's chest. "Biohazards! Acids! There's something over there warning us to wear protective equipment to guard against viral pathogens!"

"I didn't know about any of this!" Mitchel seemed to deflate. "I've never actually come inside this far. I would just go inside the first door every Friday after school, stay in there for a few minutes, and come back out so you would think I was doing something cool. If I had known…"

A roar shook the stairwell, and Curtis smelled the faint odor of urine as one of the youth lost control of their bladder. The trio made it through the door in record time, though by now Curtis wasn't counting their chances as being very high.

The moment he crashed through, Curtis wound up tripping over a chair and falling headlong across a table. Mitchel grabbed him, hauling him back up, and they kept running. By now, all strategy had gone out the window. He simply sprinted, opened doors, and hoped beyond hope that the route would continue to open in front of them. Crashing noises behind them spoke of the creature's presence, urging them onward.

They ran for a matter of minutes before Curtis tore through one final door and found himself in a small room with no other exits. Mitchel and Francine slammed the door behind him, and Francine fumbled for a lock.

"Quick! Don't let it get us!" Her voice made Curtis's eardrums hurt. "I don't want to die!"

"No one is going to die." Mitchel grabbed her by the shoulders and looked her in the eye. "We're going to make it out!"

As if to defy his words, something hit the opposite side of the door, and hard. It bowed inward, and Francine's eyes rolled up into her head. Both Mitchel and Curtis were too shocked to catch her, and her head cracked against the floor. Mitchel turned to Curtis, white-faced.

"We've got to do something! Look for a weapon!"

Curtis glanced around the room. Several crates were stacked against the far wall, all of which were open. Hardly daring to hope, Curtis dashed over and reached inside. His hands closed on something cylindrical, and he drew it out into the light.

The moment he could actually see it, his heart broke. He held a can of cooking spray, nothing more. He prepared to throw it away when Mitchel let out a yell.

"Look at this!"

Curtis ran over to the crate Mitchel was examining. Cans of soda were stacked in small boxes, a generic off-brand that was quite popular with the citizens of Graves Grove. The interesting factor, though, was the ooze. A blackish-green slime bubbled out of dozens of holes, which seemed to have split open from internal pressure.

Curious, Curtis pointed the cooking spray away from himself and pressed the plunger. Rather than a mist, black scum exploded outward, coating the wall. Horrified, Curtis dropped the can and turned back to the door.

"They were playing with the food supply!" Mitchel's voice squeaked like a rusty bike wheel. "They were going to turn all of us into…that! How much of this actually hit stores?"

"We don't know what their goal may have been." Curtis hoped beyond hope that they were wrong. "It could be…"

With a final thud, the door burst off its hinges. Standing in the light was what had obviously been human at one point. Somehow, though, it had become something different.

It stood over two meters tall, huge and hulking. The hands hung down near its knees, its long limbs looking disproportional to the rest of its body. Long claws protruded from each finger, giving it a wicked grasp. Muscles stood out across its body.

Two features stood out above everything else. The first was the ooze. Sores covered its entire body, from which a blackish-green goop dripped onto the floor. At that point, all remaining doubt vanished from Curtis's mind. Whatever the monster had become, it had been created by the food. The second feature was the face. It had been twisted like a rope in the wind, with the mouth nearly stretching ear-to ear. The nose was hooked and hawk-like, but the eyes were haunting. Whatever semblance of humanity had once been held there was now gone—all that was left was an empty, blank, and hungry stare.

All of this was taken in a single glance. Before Curtis had a chance to do anything, the creature leapt forward and swept its arm out. The blow caught Curtis dead in the center of the chest and launched him across the room.

When he landed, he crashed into a crate, shattering it into splinters. Cereal boxes cascaded down around him, and he felt something wet splatter across his arms. He leapt back to his feet and tried to decide what to do.

The creature had grabbed Mitchel. Long claws sliced into his torso, and blood ran down onto the floor. A moment later, the creature threw Mitchel across the room in the opposite direction. His head hit the concrete wall with a crack, and he fell to the ground, either unconscious or dead.

The creature bent down over Mitchel, then walked back and sniffed Francine. With a slow turn, it fixed its gaze on Curtis. Curtis felt his knees go weak, and he started backing up. He hadn't planned on dying! Why hadn't he just listened to his mom?

Slowly, carefully, the creature walked forward. The splattering of the dripping wounds echoed in Curtis's ears, and the stench clogged his nostrils. It opened its mouth, revealing dozens of yellowing, rotting teeth.

Suddenly a loud ringing sound cut through the air. The creature's head snapped around, and it turned and tore out of the room at a loping run. Slowly, Curtis shook his head, trying to understand what had just happened. It didn't make any sense.

Curtis weighed his options. He could try and carry one of his unconscious friends out of the building and hope the creature didn't come back for the other, or he could run back into town and get help. After a moment of thought, he decided to follow the latter course of action. Someone could bring a gun, and the creature could be finished for good. Satisfied with the idea, he left the room and began creeping back toward the exit.

The entire trip back out filled him with terror. Every pop, every clink of glass, every footstep made him jump. There was no way of knowing what was harmless noise and what was the creature stalking him. By the time he reached the large, open room, the terror had worn off, to be replaced with an intense curiosity. What had happened to create the monster? What had the company been trying to accomplish?

About halfway across the expanse, he drew up short. The door to the outside stood wide open, which only meant one thing: the monster had escaped. Terror flooded him yet again, but this time for the citizens of the town. It would be able to prey on the townsfolk, probably killing hundreds of them before someone managed to kill it. The only way to prevent mass destruction was to warn everyone!

Without another thought, he tore for the exit. The worst sight of the day greeted him the moment he came out, though. The creature was hunched over about four meters away from the entrance, eating ravenously from a large metal bowl. Behind the bowl, looking at the monster with the most longing desire Curtis had ever seen, swooned his mom. She looked up the moment he came out, a horrified expression on her face.

"Curtis! What are you doing out of the house?"

"I could ask the same of you!" Curtis was floored. His terror and curiosity were stripped away, to be replaced by rage, pure and simple. "What are you doing with this…this creature? It tried to kill us!"

"Curtis, you have to understand…"

"What I'm understanding is that you're feeding a monster! How long has this been going on? *What* is going on? I want answers!"

"We don't always get what we want, Curtis. You've been breaking my rules, and now…"

"To hell with your rules!" Curtis roared. "I'm not leaving until you start talking!"

His mom let out a long sigh. "I suppose you deserve answers. You're old enough now."

"I'm 17! Yeah, I'd say I deserve answers! Start talking!"

"This warehouse was owned by the Moonlight Corporation."

"I know that much."

"When we moved here, the company was just putting in the warehouse. Your father needed a job, and they were hiring, so he took the position."

"He died shortly afterward, right? This thing killed him, didn't it?"

"No." His mom set her jaw, working it back and forth slowly. "Curtis, this *is* him. He found evidence that company was doing some highly illegal genetic modifications. He took it to the authorities, but the police around here have far larger problems to contend with. Your father took it upon himself to obtain the evidence against them."

"And this is what happened?"

She nodded. "He came home that day, saying he had taken photos, but he had been forced to leave them at work. He also started complaining about his body itching. The next few days, he got sharper and more basal, and refused to leave the house. Scratched himself and all out furniture to shreds. The fifth day, he left at dawn to go to work. The company pulled out later that day, citing financial failure. Ever since then, I've come here every Tuesday to give him a change from his usual meals of rodents and birds. One of the technicians in town helped me wire the bell into the intercom, so he knows to come."

"And you didn't tell me this why?"

"I didn't want to burden you with the pain!" His mom started sobbing. "I come here every week because he's my love. My husband, the one I will be bonded to until one of us dies. I can't give up hope that, one day, the serum will wear off and we can become a family again! Until then, this is something I need to deal with."

Curtis shook his head. "I don't believe this. This is ridiculous!"

Suddenly, without warning, his father stood up and dashed back into the building. His mom smiled and crossed her arms.

"Look at him run! He always was an athlete, and now even more so. Don't worry about your friends, now that he's been fed, he'll be a lot more docile toward them."

"This is stupid." Curtis turned and stormed back into the building. "I'm going to go get my friends back. When I finish, I'm going back into town, and we're going to destroy that…that…thing!"

As he walked through the expanse, his mom's words echoed through his mind, over and over. It was just infuriating she had kept it from him for so long! He entered the hallway and began absently scratching his arms. Dark thoughts welled up, and he let out a low growl. Yes, once he got back to town, he was going to set things right.

THE JAR
J.S. BAILEY

Graves Grove wasn't the town people expected while passing through from one place to another. Tucked away among the peaks of eastern British Columbia, it looked the sort of place one might find on a postcard or a pretty calendar boasting country scenery.

Bethany Willis thought that postcards and calendars were full of crap. A kid down the street from her had gone missing last week.

Again.

Bethany trudged home from the coffee shop where she worked one Tuesday afternoon, having narrowly avoided colliding with Mamie Rue Le Doux and her creepy-ass pram out on the sidewalk. Mamie was one of the first hints Bethany had that things weren't quite right around Graves Grove when she'd moved here to get away from the city lights five years ago. The woman's kid, Archie, had vanished back in the eighties and, according to the locals, she'd been pushing his pram around town ever since, talking to the picnic basket she'd stashed inside it.

Bethany shivered as she kicked snow off her boots, then fitted her key into the lock and let herself inside her white clapboard house. Nobody had ever been able to figure out where the missing children went, and the abductions had been going on for more than a *century.*

Bethany had considered moving back to the city just to get away from all the weirdness here, but something always stopped her from putting her house on the market.

The moment she stepped through the door, she saw her roommate sitting in her living room armchair, watching her with forlorn eyes that lit up when she drew nearer to him. He looked like an ordinary man wearing black slacks and a light blue button-up shirt, but he was anything but ordinary.

"John, *why* are you still here?" Bethany asked, slinging her purse onto the end table beside her couch. She didn't feel nearly as pleased to see him as he did to see her. Every time she left the house, she prayed she'd come home to find he had moved on to some happier afterlife that didn't consist of her house. "It's got to be depressing just sitting there day after day. Hell, it's depressing just watching you."

John scowled but said nothing. He usually didn't, though he did occasionally sing at the top of his lungs in the middle of the night—usually show tunes, because in life he'd been fond of theater.

"You know I can leave, right?" Bethany said to him. "Sell the house and be gone."

John rose, his eyes widening in alarm. Bethany felt a pang of guilt. No, she couldn't leave. No one ever left this town once they were here. Its beauty cast a spell over its residents and mired them in place like their feet had sprouted roots.

Bethany wished she'd known that *before* she bought the house.

"Please stay," John said, his voice faint as if he spoke from a million miles away. It was the most he'd said all week.

"You know I will," Bethany said with a sigh. "Now I have a favor to ask. I have a date tonight. He's coming here. That means you need to stay out of sight and not pull any of your crap. Okay?"

A spark of something—anger? disgust?—flashed through John's pale blue eyes. Bethany turned away from him and went to change out of her work clothes. It wasn't her problem if her roommate didn't want her to bring a gentleman friend by to visit. The house belonged to her now. She could do whatever she wanted.

CHRIS JONES, who worked for a local logging company, had been seeing Bethany for three months. Chris hadn't visited her house yet, and Bethany didn't have the guts to tell him about John. As far as she knew, only she could see the spirit. If she tried to tell Chris she shared her house with a former resident, he might think she'd lost more marbles than Mamie Rue Le Doux and dump her.

Bethany didn't see John anywhere when she got out of the shower and dried her hair in preparation for her date. He remained out of sight when she started dinner, lit half a dozen candles in the living room, and closed the blinds.

Maybe, for once, he'd behave.

Her heart raced as she checked the clock for the thousandth time. She had made it a point to never have company and honestly had no clue how John would react to visitors.

Or how visitors would react to John should he emerge. But this was Graves Grove, and for all she knew, everyone in town might have a secret ghost in their house. She ought to form a support group.

At six-thirty, Bethany straightened the spaghetti straps on her little black dress and withdrew a bottle of Pinot Grigio from the cabinet. A knock came at the door as she stirred pasta still bubbling in a pot on the stove. Heart fluttering, she hurried to let Chris inside.

Bespectacled Chris, whose stocky build and dark brown beard gave him the appearance of a very young Santa Claus, had bundled up in a navy blue snowsuit that made Bethany feel significantly underdressed by comparison.

"So I finally get to see the old homestead," he said with a wink as he gave her a one-armed hug, the other arm holding a bottle of champagne. "You look awfully cold in that dress. I can take you upstairs and warm you up if you'd like."

She grinned. "In your dreams, Lumberjack. You know I'm a good girl."

"Don't say I didn't make the offer."

They moved into the kitchen and helped themselves to the Italian feast Bethany had set about cooking once she'd gotten out of the shower.

"You did a nice job with the décor," Chris said, nodding at the olive vines cascading from the tops of the cabinets. They dined at the table in the kitchen, which Bethany had done her best to decorate like the Italian restaurants she had frequented while living in Vancouver. She'd ordered plastic olive vine garlands and fake bunches of grapes off the internet and also compiled an Italian opera playlist that played softly from the iPod dock on the counter.

One downside to living in Graves Grove: the nearest fancy restaurant lay a million miles away.

Chris sipped at his Pinot Grigio, looking as relaxed as Bethany had seen him all week. "You ought to take up interior decorating," he said. "I like it."

The house creaked. Bethany jumped. "I have doubts that anyone in this town would pay for something like that."

"You could ask Mamie. She's got money."

Bethany grimaced at the thought of the aging woman wearing her deteriorating gold dress and rhinestone belt around town like a frail ghost of the 1980s. "I'm not going near that place. For all I know she's got her dead family stuffed and sitting around the dinner table." The house creaked again. Bethany glanced nervously up at the ceiling. *You behave yourself,* she thought savagely toward her unseen roommate.

"What's the matter?" Chris asked.

"Hmm?"

"You look worried."

"I'm not worried."

Something fell over in the living room. She and Chris looked at each other, then toward the open archway through which they could see the loveseat and the umbrella stand beside the front door.

A pink umbrella with white polka dots lay on the floor like a beached fish that had just leapt from the waves.

"Does it do that often?" Chris asked, not quite as concerned as Bethany had expected.

"No." Bethany's voice quavered. "Usually it's other things. DVDs. Knickknacks. Sometimes books. It only happens when he's angry."

Chris blinked. "When *who's* angry?"

At that moment, a booming rendition of "Worst Pies in London" from the musical *Sweeney Todd: The Demon Barber of Fleet Street* began to emanate from near the fireplace.

Chris jumped to his feet. "Bethany, what's—"

Bethany groaned inwardly as John continued singing unabated, and gave a sad glance at everything she'd done to make her kitchen beautiful for the occasion. A perfect date, ruined.

Thanks, John.

THE NEXT day, Chris met up with Bethany at the coffee shop when her shift ended. He wore a flannel shirt, jeans, and a stern expression that looked out of place on his usually-jovial face.

"Okay," Chris said as she slid into the booth across the table from him. "Talk."

"I'm sorry I couldn't say anything last night," Bethany said. "He could have overheard us anywhere in the house."

"Who is he?"

"John Bradley. You know, the one who supposedly got hit crossing the street back in 1982? I looked him up in the library archives after I found him living there. Well, not exactly living. You know."

"Ah," Chris said. "That one."

"You know who I'm talking about, then."

Chris folded his hands together and sighed. "I've heard people mention it. Apparently John was so transfixed by whatever clothes Sam the Statue had on that day, he stepped right out in front of a logging truck barreling down the road and never knew what hit him."

"What was Sam wearing?"

"My brother said a tutu. Nobody cared, though. About John. Too mean to like, and always singing. He got kicked out of a theater troupe in Vancouver for disorderly conduct. Kept singing during other people's acts, they said."

They both lapsed into silence. Bethany cleared her throat and said, "I don't want him there anymore. He drives me crazy."

"Why not move?"

"He gets depressed whenever I bring it up. I hate seeing him that way."

"You *see* him?"

"Sometimes. Yes."

Chris ran a hand over his bearded chin. "Has he ever tried to hurt you?"

"He got mad and flung a vase off the mantel when I told him I'd be going away for a week to visit my parents. It hit me in the shoulder." She winced at the memory. "Gave me a bruise."

Chris's face darkened. "You can't let him treat you like that."

"How do you propose I make him stop?"

"Hmm." Chris bit his lip. "I might have just the thing."

TWO DAYS later, Bethany's phone rang. The caller ID indicated it was Chris.

"Hey," she said when she answered.

"Do you have a moment?" he asked.

"Sure, why?"

"Come to my house."

Bethany's heart skipped a beat. "What time?"

"Now, and don't say anything else in case Elephant Ears is listening."

The line went dead. Bethany ended the call and sighed. John stood in the archway between the kitchen and living room with his arms crossed, his eyes calculating.

"IT'S CALLED a spirit jar."

"A spirit jar." Bethany stared dubiously at the small glass jar sitting on Chris's kitchen table. It looked like the kind baby food came in, only someone—Chris, most likely—had painted a squiggly black symbol on the side.

Chris unscrewed the cap. "Yep. People trap spirits in them. My mom has a whole case of these at her house."

Bethany kneaded her temples. *Of course she does. It's Graves Grove.*

Chris went on. "The spirits go inside the jar, you put the cap on, and voila! No more spirits to bug you."

Bethany stared into Chris's brown eyes and saw no humor there. "You realize John can walk through walls," she said.

"I do."

"What's going to stop him from 'walking' right out of the jar?"

"It's a spirit jar. They can't get out unless you open the lid."

"What's going to make him go inside in the first place?"

"That's the mystery of the spirit jar. Spirits are attracted to them like bugs to a zapper."

"You're sure about this."

"Absolutely."

"You're not putting me on?"

"Why would I do that?"

Bethany sighed. "Supposing John actually goes and gets himself stuck in this thing. What do I do with it?"

"Store it in a box, or keep it out on a shelf if you want. Makes for an interesting conversation piece. Want to go try it?"

Bethany hesitated a moment, then said, "Sure."

BETHANY DROVE Chris to her house with too many doubts racing through her mind. Her mother had always warned her to avoid the occult at all costs, and what was a spirit jar but some other form of forbidden magic?

She shifted uneasily in her seat as she turned onto her street. Her white clapboard house looked as innocuous as always. She wondered if John knew what they were up to. The way he'd stared at her when she'd talked to Chris on the phone…

And what would it be like for John? Would being stuck in a jar forever be uncomfortable? What if he hated it in there? Could Bethany be held responsible for a poor spirit's suffering, even if he *had* been an obnoxious theater reject?

Bethany parked in her driveway and shut off the engine. "Maybe we should call a priest," she said, reaching for her purse. "He could get John to move on to wherever he's supposed to go."

"That's assuming John wants to go anywhere. Now don't say anything about this when we get inside. It works best when they're clueless."

JOHN WATCHED from the corner unseen as Bethany and her man friend stomped into the house and into the kitchen. The living were always so noisy, clomping around like a herd of Clydesdales. He didn't know how they could stand it.

The man—Chris, John thought his name was—unscrewed the lid off a baby food jar and plunked it down in the center of the kitchen table. Someone had drawn a squiggly line on the glass.

John recognized its purpose immediately and grinned.

He felt the jar's energy tug at him, but he didn't worry about it. He was John Bradley. Death hadn't put an end to him, and neither would a repurposed baby food jar.

"What now?" Bethany asked, worry evident in her eyes. Bags hung under them like she hadn't been sleeping well. John had always found her honey-colored hair and slim build attractive—much more so than the Graves Grove stock he'd had the misfortune of knowing in life. If only John had been born in a different decade. If only he hadn't been so awestruck by the bronze tutu that the Samuel Madsen Graves statue had been wearing when John stepped in front of the logging truck that swiftly knocked him into kingdom come.

Chris said, "We wait."

MINUTES TICKED by with no apparent change to the status of the jar.

"How will we know he's gone in?" Bethany asked.

"I'll just know. In the meantime can I have—" Chris's thick body went rigid, and his eyes rolled back in his head.

Bethany was too startled to scream. She grabbed Chris's arm as he started to fall, and then suddenly he seemed himself again, standing straight and blinking as if he found the kitchen light too bright.

He held his hands out in front of him, then turned them so his palms faced upward, acting like he'd never seen them before. Then he ran his hands over his cheeks and beard. "Well. This is different."

"Did it work?" Bethany asked, eyeing the jar. It looked like it had filled with fog.

Chris picked it up, capped it, and held it up to his face for closer inspection. "I would say so. Wouldn't you?" He put it in his pocket.

"What are you doing with that? You said I could keep it."

"Did I? Must have been a slip of the tongue. You have to bury these things if you want a spirit to stay put for good." Chris drew in a deep breath and let it out with an expression of contentment. "Breathing. Do you have any idea how good that feels?"

"I—I've never really thought about it. Are you positive John won't be uncomfortable in there?"

Chris's eyes twinkled mischievously. "Quite."

THE SNOW began to melt later on that day, and Bethany and Chris walked down to the river where the great, ancient sycamore tree loomed close to the waters. Squealing children bundled in snowsuits tossed snowballs at each other, seemingly unconcerned that another of their brethren had disappeared in recent days.

Disappeared like a soul sucked into a jar.

"Do you think this town will ever be normal?" Bethany asked, feeling a sudden sense of inner sadness she couldn't quite put a finger on.

"Who wants it to be normal? Normal is boring." Chris pulled the spirit jar out of his pocket, tossed it up into the air, and caught it with the same hand like he was playing with a baseball. He wrinkled his nose. "A lumberjack. I thought you had better taste than that."

Before Bethany could object, Chris gave the jar an overhand pitch. It landed smack-dab in the river with a plunk where the ice had already melted away, and sank out of sight.

"The silt will bury it eventually," Chris said, brushing his hands together. "Good riddance." He hooked his arm through Bethany's in a most un-Chris-like manner. "Let's go get something to eat. I'm famished."

As they walked away from the park, Chris began to sing about the worst pies in London.

LIKE A FLASH
CAITLYN KONZE

Nathan parked the rental car in front of the General Store and Feed Supply. While he ran inside, Melanie got out to stretch her legs. "Graves Grove," the paint-chipped sign had called this tiny town buried in a valley within the Canadian Rockies. Not exactly a name that inspired relaxation. She wondered how Nathan stumbled across it. There were other places in British Columbia to vacation. Like Vancouver. Then again, the whole point was to get away from the brightness and buzz of cities like Reno. *Well,* thought Melanie, *mission accomplished.*

Not far down the street was a bronze statue of a handsome man standing proudly on a stone pedestal. Melanie was admiring the workmanship of the top hat and cane he carried when she heard the sound of something hitting pavement. She turned to see an aging woman pushing an old fashioned bassinet-on-wheels down the sidewalk. A bottle rolled along the ground.

"Hey!" Melanie grabbed the bottle, the milk still warm, and jogged after the woman. "Excuse me, you dropped this."

The woman stopped mid-lullaby, her back to Melanie. "Hi. I think this belongs to you." Still, the woman would not turn. Melanie took a deep breath and reapplied a smile. She walked around to the front of the pram and held out the bottle. "You dropped this back by the store."

The woman's hair was falling out of a salt-and-pepper bun. A hat that at one point in time must have been a vibrant shade of green drooped to one side. Quick as the flip of a switch, the woman's face animated with exaggerated concern.

"Oh, sweetums, your bottle! We can't forget that, can we?" She snatched the bottle out of Melanie's hands. "Doctor Moore says he'd like to see more weight gain by your next check-up. Here you go. That's a good boy."

The lady shuffled past Melanie without so much as a thank you. As the pram was pushed past her, Melanie tried to catch a glimpse of the baby. But there was no child. The bottle was nestled next to an old fashioned picnic basket. Melanie caught a scent that reminded her of Thanksgiving leftovers she had once discovered in the bowels of her refrigerator. In July. Trying not to think about tiny rotting corpses in wicker baskets, Melanie returned to the store.

A bell jingled. Nathan stepped out with two plastic bags.

"Back in the car, babe. The clerk says there's a park down the road that we can eat at."

Melanie's stomach gave a dangerous lurch at the thought of eating, but she didn't argue. Neither of them had eaten since the mid-flight peanuts and pretzels, but a picnic was the last thing she wanted after her encounter with the strange woman.

It was a short enough drive that they could have walked. Melanie's gut had barely settled before their feet crunched across the gravel parking lot and onto lush, preened grass.

"Where do you want to sit?" Melanie asked, eying a patch of level sun-bathed lawn.

"How about over there, by that tree?" Nathan pointed to a large and archaic looking sycamore that cast shade dark enough Melanie wondered if they'd need a flashlight to see their food. The tree was both captivating and repulsive. The trunk twisted and leaned while branches thicker around than Melanie's waist drooped to perfect climbing level. Its roots were so wild and wide-spread it looked as if the tree was trying to extract itself from the ground and crawl away. Although there was a light yet sustained breeze, not one of its leaves so much as twitched.

"You sure?" But Nathan was already striding purposefully toward the wooden beast. Melanie followed. The gurgle of running water grew in volume the closer they came. They chose a raised bit of root to use as a table on the drier side of the tree. Nathan pulled out of his shopping bags two sets of yogurt, string cheese, tea whose flavor Melanie couldn't pronounce, and pre-wrapped BLT sandwiches. She unwrapped one of the cellophane lumps. The sourdough was stained red from a thick-cut slice of tomato. Melanie opened her mouth to remind Nathan, again, that she hated tomatoes when a click made her jump. Her sandwich tumbled down her shirt and onto the ground.

"I love taking pictures of the pretty ones."

Nathan choked on his sandwich as a man stepped out from behind the tree.

Nathan gulped his tea and tapped his chest with a fist. When he recovered, he half shouted, "You can't just sneak up on a guy like—whoa."

The man had circular sunglasses on and wore a long-sleeved shirt, jeans, and gloves even though it was flip-flops weather. In the man's hand was a camera that had a large flash attachment that drooped over the camera not unlike the tree and its branches. He took a few steps closer. What Melanie had assumed were white gloves she now saw was his natural skin color. All his exposed skin, which wasn't much, was just as white. Even his hair and eyebrows were so fair it hardly looked like they were there at all.

"You're visiting." It was a statement and not a question. "I'm a professional photographer. Would you like your picture taken?" he asked Melanie. Then to Nathan, "As a couple?"

Melanie said "No" at the same time that Nathan said "Sure." She gave Nathan a look. He shrugged.

"Come on, Mel. It could be our only chance to take one together."

Melanie mumbled her dissent while Nathan positioned themselves so the mountains were in the background. The pale photographer smiled. Melanie shuddered. Even his teeth were unnaturally white. He took off his glasses and put them in his pants pocket. Melanie tightened her hold around Nathan. The man's eyes barely had any color to them. There was just enough to be classified as blue, but the white-blue of the sky on a cloudy day.

"Say disease."

Before Melanie could ask if he meant "cheese," the camera's bulb flashed. The light was blinding in the shade of the tree. Melanie squeezed her eyes shut until the kaleidoscope of dancing colors faded. When she opened them, the man was pulling a portable printer out of a backpack she hadn't realized he'd been wearing. The man checked his camera screen and made a noise like he just ate something delicious.

"I like the pretty ones."

Nathan put his arm in front of Melanie.

"What did you just say?"

"Two dollars per print. Touch-ups are extra and can be mailed within 24 hours."

"I asked you a question."

The man continued like he hadn't heard Nathan at all. "Cash or check only. Checks can be made out to Arty Arthur Photography LLC. There's an ATM in Grady's general store if you need it."

"Are you deaf?"

Melanie tried to pull Nathan away from the photographer. "Nate, it's fine."

"Did you just hit on my girl?"

"Nathan, let's just leave."

Nathan folded his arms in front of his inflating chest. "Not until this freak apologizes."

The printer spat out a photograph. The pale man held it up to the light and squinted. He groaned and shook his head.

"Too dark." He pointed at Melanie. "You're bright, though. Do you want your picture taken?"

"That's it, you sick sleaze."

Nathan shoved the man. He tripped over his printer and landed between two roots, camera cradled in his lap. Melanie heard a snap when he landed. His shocked expression made Melanie wonder if he even knew what he'd said was inappropriate.

Nathan grabbed whatever rocks and sticks he could find off the ground and threw them at the photographer. The man protected his camera with one hand and pulled himself out of the tree's grasp with the other. He made to grab his backpack, but Nathan pulled back a fist. The man ran.

"Yeah, you'd better run before I catch up and kick your—"

"Stop, Nate! I'm fine. He's gone, okay?"

"You're defending that creep?" The sneer on Nathan's face frightened her more than the tangled tree. Melanie pulled him out into the sun. Nathan's body relaxed under her touch as soon as they were free of the shade.

"Let's just go check in, okay? I'm tired."

After a moment Nathan's face returned to its normal color.

"Yeah. Sure, babe. Hey, look. Free picture." Nathan grabbed the photo off the ground.

"Let me see."

Nathan snorted. "Camera must be broken or something. What a loser."

"I still want a look." Melanie held out her hand, but Nathan ripped the picture in half and put the pieces in his pocket.

"Forget it. It didn't turn out. Let's go."

MELANIE HAD been to bed and breakfast inns before. Bright, outdated but cute, and usually sitting proudly upon well-manicured landscapes and blooming perennials. The Graves Grove bed and breakfast was nothing like that. It was a three-story monster of a house with stone pillars lining the porch which sagged slightly in the middle. Melanie followed Nathan up cracked concrete steps past two lion-bodied cherubs on pedestals guarding the front door.

Nathan frowned. "The website pictures looked a lot better. But hey, nice view right?"

Melanie looked over her shoulder. The inn sat on slightly higher ground than the rest of the town. Not enough to be classified as a hill, but enough to see the park, the huge tree, the statue, and even the facade of the general store. The sun was setting, and a red glow was rolling down the mountains from their snow-capped peaks.

The front door opened. A cheery woman with an ornate hair clip that kept her wild, gray-streaked hair from escaping its bun welcomed them inside as if they were distant relatives. She had loose arm skin that flapped whenever she gesticulated, which was often.

"You must be Melanie and Nathan. I'm Beverly. Come in, come in. So glad you made it safely." Melanie wondered if that meant some people hadn't made it here safely.

"Let me show you around. Over here's the dining room. Meals are at eight, noon, and five. I'll take your bags, dear." Melanie handed the woman her duffel bag. Nathan took her empty hand in his. They followed their hostess up a set of stairs wide enough for four people to walk side by side. "Don't you two look adorable? The Savanna Suite is yours." Beverly winked. "The only room with a private bath. Are you honeymooning?"

Melanie felt her face get warm. "Oh, we're not married."

Beverly stopped so suddenly Melanie had to grab the banister to keep from falling back down the stairs.

"I see." Then she was moving along in her brisk pace, although Melanie thought her voice dropped a few degrees in warmth. "There's a rack in the entry hall with brochures for horseback riding, guided trail hikes, and all that outdoorsy stuff young people are into these days. Not much to do in town but shop." They started up a second flight of stairs, this one so narrow they had to climb single-file. "There's a library with board games down the hall from your room. My word, this gets harder every time." Beverly hoisted herself up the last few stairs and tried to finger comb her rebellious hair back into its bun.

Nathan glanced at Melanie before asking, "Do you know a lot of people around here?"

"Small town, dear. Everybody knows everybody whether they want to or not."

"Do you know a really pale guy with a camera?"

"Oh, that'll be Arty. Such a dear." She leaned in to whisper, "Albino, you know," as if anyone could fail to notice his unnaturally white skin. "Takes lovely pictures. He did the ones for this house, actually, on the internet. Well, here we are. The Savanna Suite. Ladies first. You've just missed supper, so we'll see you at breakfast. Nighty-night."

The room was all warm tans and browns that clashed against the bruise-blue, blood-tipped mountains framed by an open window. The striped curtains twisted and flowed like becoming fingers. Melanie walked to the window to close it, but stopped with her hands on the frame when she saw the view. The sycamore was a black silhouette against a sea of emerald foliage. Melanie felt each heartbeat thick and strong against her chest. She had to grip the edge of the window to keep herself from climbing out and down toward that tree. Longing conflicted with irrational fear. The kind that drives children to wrap their blankets tight around their toes so the monsters under their bed won't chew them off.

Something moved among the roots of the tree. Melanie leaned further out the window. All was still now, but she knew she saw something. It was too far away to be sure, but Melanie thought it could have been either a medium-sized dog, or some kid crawling over the jungle-gym roots.

"You've got to be kidding me!"

Melanie closed the window. "What is it?"

"Just look!" Nathan flung his arm toward the two twin beds and their tiger print comforters.

"I know, tigers don't even live in Africa."

"No! When I reserved this room, the pictures showed one king-sized bed, not two dorm beds!"

"I told you I wanted separate beds."

Nathan looked even angrier for a second, but quickly recovered. "If there had been any double queen rooms, I would have booked them. I haven't slept in a twin since I was in grade school. I hate it when my feet stick out."

Melanie crossed her arms. "How could you think one bed was okay after what we talked about?"

Nathan threw up his hands. "We've been together for six months, Mel. You said you wanted to talk about the next step in our relationship. I thought you meant—"

"I thought I was pretty clear about my convictions."

"Fine." Nathan tossed his bag onto the closest bed. Melanie took it off and put it by the door.

"What are you doing?"

"You think I'm going to trust you to sleep in here after this?"

"What's the problem? There are two beds just like you wanted."

"But you reserved one. Without my permission. That's not breaking my trust, that's shattering it."

"Whatever. We're here now. Our flight isn't until Sunday. What do you expect me to do?"

"I expect you to sleep in the car."

Nathan's face hardened. Melanie wondered what she would do if he refused. Were there other hotels in this town? They hadn't passed any on their way to this place. Thoughts of trying to find a place to sleep in the dark with the creepy photographer still out there made Melanie want to apologize and let things go. Yet if Nathan really did reserve what he thought was a single bed room, he had done it deliberately. If Melanie compromised on that, how many other compromises would Nathan expect this weekend?

When it was clear Melanie had nothing else to say, Nathan picked up his bag. "Whatever you want, babe," he said without inflection.

MELANIE CHANGED sleeping positions with a fitfulness that had nothing to do with the size of her mattress. When she finally fell asleep, every dream she had was filled with the hair-raising feeling that someone was watching her, following her, close enough to breathe into her ear. No matter where she went or how far she ran, she could feel someone behind her. In her dreams she ran. But if ever she slowed, a bright flash of a camera would send her sprinting again.

Melanie woke with a start. It was still dark. Her whole body ached like she really had been running for her life most the night. She fumbled for the lamp on the nightstand.

"The pretty ones, they call to me."

Melanie screamed. Her fingers found the light switch.

Arty was standing at the foot of her bed. His sunglasses were askew and one lens was missing. One pale eye watched Melanie. Melanie dove for a Gideons Bible in the nightstand drawer, but when she turned back to throw it at Arty, he was gone.

It seemed like hours before Melanie's heart rate slowed to normal. She tried to tell herself that she had still been dreaming. But she knew that wasn't true. Arty was here. She grabbed her cell and tapped Nathan's name. No answer.

Melanie eased out of bed and gave herself a moment to calm down. Instead, her goose bumps spread. She wanted nothing more than to jump back into bed, pull the covers over her head, and sleep with the light on. But Melanie knew she wouldn't be able to sleep unless she knew she was safe. Concentrating on forcing one foot in front of the other, Melanie worked her way around the room. It was slow at first, the fear so strong it was painful. She shook so hard she almost dropped her phone twice. But after checking under both beds and behind the curtains, she grew bolder. Wielding the heavy Bible as a weapon, she checked all the closets, cupboards, and even behind the shower curtain in the bathroom. There were no boogey men, no cross-dressing murderers with mommy issues, and no one waiting outside her room with an axe.

She tried Nathan one more time. He picked up on the fourth ring, his voice slurred with sleep.

"Mmyea?"

"Nate?" Melanie paused. What would she tell him? The photographer was here then magically disappeared? She sighed. "I had a bad dream."

The pause at the other end of the line was so long Melanie wondered if Nathan had fallen back asleep. "I'm sorry, Mel. Do you want some company for a little while?"

Melanie tried to swallow the lump developing in her throat. "I think so…I dreamt about that guy in the park. He was stalking me. I swear he was here when I woke up, but…I just think—"

"I'll be up in a minute."

The call ended. Had she made the right decision? Or was this a compromise she would end up regretting?

A flash of light made her jump. She was wide awake now. No dreams. Melanie looked around. The window was open a crack. The curtains twisted in the draft. Hadn't she closed it before bed? She looked out expecting rain or lightning jumping from cloud to cloud in the distance, but the night was so clear she could see traces of the Milky Way, even with the light on.

The door opened. Melanie jumped. Nathan came in and wrapped his arms around her. Melanie tried to keep composed, but tears spilled down her cheeks and onto Nathan's shirt. Her shoulders shook with silent sobs.

"That bad, huh?" Nathan said, kissing the top of her head.

Melanie nodded.

"It's okay. Get in bed. I'll stay as long as you want."

Melanie wasn't sure how long she tried in vain to sleep. Each time she closed her eyes, a flash of light would force her awake. When the darkness retreated enough that she could see the room in the pre-dawn haze, she sat up. Nathan's pants were crumpled at the foot of his bed. One torn half of the picture Arty took lay face down on the floor. Melanie spent a few minutes watching Nathan's deep breathing before she pushed herself out of bed and fished the second half out of his pocket. She brought the two pieces to the window where the light was getting brighter. Nathan had torn the picture so that he was on one half and Melanie was on the other. At least it should have been Nathan. All Melanie saw was a person-shaped swirl of darkness like a picture of a black hole. Melanie was at least recognizable in the other half of the photo, but a small white ball appeared over her chest. At first Melanie thought it was the glare of the sun or a dust mote, but there were streaks of light woven around her body. It was like Arty took a picture on a Canada Day night while someone ran circles around Melanie with a sparkler. Even as Melanie stared, the little streaks began to orbit the ball of light.

"So pretty. I love the pretty souls."

Melanie gasped. Both pieces of the photo fluttered to the floor.

NATHAN YAWNED and stretched. His knuckles hit a wall. He cursed, remembering last night's drama. He had almost taken the rental and driven back to the airport. Screw Melanie and her convictions. But she changed her mind after a few hours. Maybe she was warming up to taking their relationship to the next level. He'd give her one more week. If Nathan didn't get what he wanted after a week, it was time to get it from someone else. Nathan sighed and put on his sweet voice.

"Did you sleep better knowing I was here?" No answer. "Mel?"

Nathan rubbed his eyes and sat up. Melanie's blankets had fallen to the floor. Her bed was empty. For a second Nathan thought she faked the whole thing so she could take the car once he was asleep, but Mel's bag was still next to the dresser and her phone sat on the nightstand. He didn't remember the window being open, though. Nathan walked over to close it and stepped on something. It was the messed up picture that creep took. Or at least Nathan's half of it. He couldn't find Mel's half. Nathan shrugged and closed the window. He thought he saw a brief flash of light by that huge tree in the park before he stuffed his airline ticket in his bag.

WHERE'S MATHESON LAM?

S.R. BETLER

All her life, Madison had understood the importance of first impressions, and her first impression of Graves Grove was this: the day was overcast, threatening rain; the buildings were old and in desperate need of attention; a wrinkled woman in a stained dress pushed an empty, ramshackle pram past, cooing at the picnic basket inside; the statue of Samuel Graves in the center of town was wearing a dapper suit and ascot but no top hat; there were few children about, none unattended. Oh, and there was something in the woods, but no one save the town stray seemed to notice.

It wasn't until her second impression that Madison discovered the sycamore tree in the center of town, with its twisting limbs and peeling bark. Second impressions were important, too, she decided, and it was easier to judge something from a distance, so she hiked up her skirt and reached for the lowest branch.

"I wouldn't do that if I was you."

Madison whirled around to face a boy—about her age—with unkempt black hair and ill-fitting clothes. He looked harmless enough, aside from sneaking up on her. More than that, he was the first unaccompanied child she'd seen since moving to Graves Grove.

"Why's that?" she asked, ruffling her skirt so it would fall back into place just so.

"Sometimes kids go up and they don't come back down." The boy paused, and his dark eyes seemed to be taking her in, traversing the length of her body. They finally stopped as their gazes met, and he flashed a lopsided smile. "You must be new here. Name's Liam."

"Just moved in. I'm Madison." She swept her gaze over the tree, all the way to the top. The sycamore had so much personality in it that it felt almost sentient, and the branches really were just right for climbing. But she supposed, if it was dangerous…

"So what happens to them?" she asked.

"Hm?"

When she glanced down, Liam had his head cocked to one side. *Oh*, she thought, *he's a bit slow.*

"The kids. Where do they go?"

Liam shoved his hands into his pockets and shrugged. "Where's Matheson Lam?"

"Who?"

"Oh, that's right. I guess you wouldn't know." Liam paused to scratch behind his ear, and he ruffled his hair as he continued, "Matheson Lam was one of the first settlers here. He was the town tailor right up until his death. They got him all ready. Put him in his casket, and had a wake and everything. But when they went back to bury him, the body was gone."

"What do you mean, gone?"

"I mean the coffin was empty. No sign of him."

"Empty?" Despite it being unbecoming to a girl her age, Madison frowned deeply, tapping her chin with her index finger. "But where'd the body go?"

"No one knows. It was just…gone." Liam slowly circumnavigated the tree, vanishing behind the trunk as he spoke.

"Dead bodies don't just disappear." Madison raised her voice to make sure he could hear.

"Well, this one did." Liam poked his head around the other side of the tree and leaned his shoulder against the trunk. "I s'pose the kids end up in the same place Matheson Lam did."

"But no one knows where that is."

"Now you got it." Liam tapped his index finger against his temple twice and smirked.

"Okay, so if you don't climb trees, what *do* you do for fun around here?"

"Well." Liam grinned and stepped forward, lowering his voice. "I know this place—"

A long, drawn-out howl interrupted, lingering over the grove, and it took a few seconds for Madison to realize that it was actually someone calling for Liam.

"Sorry, I've gotta go." He ran off toward the western part of town, but he paused just long enough to shout back, "Welcome to Graves Grove!"

THE STATUE in the center of town was wearing dress pants and a ruffle top with flared sleeves, which was well enough, but Madison felt the outfit was incomplete without a bowtie. She was debating where she might find one when something cold and wet pressed into the palm of her hand.

She looked down to find the town stray nosing her, and she knelt to stroke his russet fur.

"Liam says your name is Copper," Madison said as she rubbed behind his ears, and the dog responded by thumping a leg against the ground.

Copper bowed away from her hand and shook his head, ears flopping loudly. He huffed and then trotted off through the park.

"Hey, where are you going?"

Copper didn't answer—of course not, since not even in Graves Grove were dogs able to talk—but Madison followed him to the eastern part of town. He stopped suddenly in the tall grass, sniffed around a bit, turned in place three times, lifted his leg on a bush, and then disappeared into the forest.

Madison stopped in the shadow of the trees. They towered over her, leaves whispering as a warm breeze passed through them, as if they were trying to share a secret. It was mysterious, but somehow familiar, and nothing broke the monotony of small town life quite like an adventure. Madison took a step forward. She raised her other foot, but someone grabbed her arm and jerked her backwards.

"You mustn't wander into the woods," the aging woman scolded, wagging a finger in Madison's face. Her voice was pitchy and hoarse, and there was a wild look in her narrowed eyes.

"You're hurting me." Madison gritted her teeth as she tried to peel off the hand, to no avail.

In response, dirty nails dug into her skin, just for a moment, before the woman finally released her grip. Her eyes slid over to the trees and she whispered, "You mustn't go in the woods. Nothing good happens in there."

At that point, Madison couldn't tell whether the woman was talking to herself or not, but she seized the opportunity to slowly back away. The movement drew attention, and those wild brown eyes locked on her again.

"Promise me you won't go in the woods, girl. Promise me!"

Madison opened her mouth to answer, but someone grabbed her shoulders from behind, and all she managed was a startled gasp.

"We promise, Mrs. Le Doux." Liam's voice was loud in her ears as he pulled her backwards. "We're just gonna go play in the park."

Mrs. Le Doux pursed her lips as if she were about to argue, but instead, she nodded and turned her attention back to the shabby pram in front of her. As always, it was devoid of any signs of life, but it did contain a worn-out picnic basket and a checkered cloth. She cooed at it, nonetheless, as if she were apologizing for their walk being interrupted.

"What was *that*?" Madison asked under her breath as she followed Liam back towards the center of town.

"That's just Mrs. Le Doux. She didn't mean no harm. She's just a little... Well, she's not exactly all there anymore, if you know what I mean."

"You think?" Madison glanced back over her shoulder to see the woman holding a full-blown conversation with the pram's strange contents.

"It's not really her fault, you know. Her son was one of the kids who disappeared. She was just tryin' to protect you."

"She's got a funny way of doing it," Madison muttered, rubbing her aching wrist.

Liam just shrugged, and Madison turned her attention instead to where they were going. There were fewer houses on this side of town, and they were more likely to be abandoned or rundown. It wasn't surprising, given the rumors about the forest, but there was a very sudden, stark contrast with the more frequented streets, almost like someone had drawn a line through town.

"Bet I can get there first," Liam said once the park was in sight.

Madison didn't even have a chance to respond before he took off. With an indignant *humpf,* she hiked up her skirt and took off after him, arriving just a few steps behind him but not nearly as winded.

"I win," Liam said between gasps.

Madison scoffed. "I *let* you win." She crossed her arms, though she couldn't help but smile too.

"Pfft."

They stopped to look around the park. It was quiet, being the middle of the day, with few interlopers passing through. An adult might consider it idyllic, but to a couple of kids, it mustered up the familiar ache of boredom.

"Hey, I gotta go," Liam said suddenly. "Mom gets nervous if I'm out of her sight for too long. I'll catch ya later?"

"Sure. Later."

Liam ran off to the western side of town. Madison still wasn't sure exactly where it was he lived, but as he seemed to be the only other child allowed out without supervision, she was just grateful to have that. Now that he was gone, though, the town felt empty, so she wandered around the park until she found a woman sitting on a bench, humming to herself. The stranger looked nice enough, with round, rosy cheeks and curly brown hair, and Madison was already tired of being her only company, so she skipped up and plopped down on the bench beside the woman. The two didn't talk; Madison simply kicked her feet quietly and watched the birds playing nearby.

After a few minutes, the woman cleared her throat and, not once slowing her crocheting, said, "I see you've met Mrs. Le Doux."

"Oh. You saw that?"

"I did. Happened to be walking by. I'm Ms. Pinker, by the way."

"Nice to meet you. I'm Madison."

"Such a lovely girl." Ms. Pinker paused only briefly to pat Madison's thigh twice and then dutifully returned to her handiwork. "I'm sorry if she scared you, dear, but Mrs. Le Doux don't mean no harm."

"Why is she so afraid of the woods, anyway?"

"It's not so much the woods as the unknown." For the first time, her hands faltered, and Ms. Pinker lay them still in her lap, on top of her yarn work. "I'm sure Liam's told you all about the children by now?"

Ms. Pinker looked sideways at Madison, who nodded solemnly.

"Well, when you don't know something, you tend to be overly cautious." Ms. Pinker resumed her work with a renewed vigor, and the hook danced deftly through the yarn. "Mrs. Le Doux just wants to keep you kids safe, is all. So no more going into the woods alone, okay?"

"Yes, ma'am."

Madison glanced towards the forest, which was little more than a green line in the distance. It didn't look all that dangerous, and she watched as a russet spot emerged from between the trees, sniffing the grass as if he were looking for something. Ever since she could remember, Madison had been playing in forests, and there was nothing particularly special about this one, as far as she could tell.

"Hey, Ms. Pinker?" she asked.

"Hm?" The woman didn't look up, now fully engrossed in her work.

"Do you really think kids are disappearing in the woods?"

With a shrug, Ms. Pinker replied, "Where's Matheson Lam?"

THE STATUE at the center of town was wearing a blazer and dress slacks as Liam sat on the base of it, kicking his feet off the stone. Madison counted to four as she skipped—one leg, then two, then one and one. Ms. Pinker had drawn the hopscotch square, and it was fun at first, but Liam refused to play and the novelty was quickly wearing off. On her way back, Madison paused, allowing a brown ball of fur to pass before continuing her game.

"Hey, Copper, what's up?" Liam asked, reaching down between his legs. In response, Copper shoved his nose into the boy's palm and wagged his tail furiously.

Madison paused to watch. "You think he wants to play?"

Copper barked twice, then ran in circles, tongue lolling from the side of his mouth. He barked again and then ran a few paces away and bent down, butt in the air.

"I guess that's a yes." Madison giggled. "So, what do you think dogs do for fun?"

"I dunno. He naps a lot, and the only other time I see him, he's licking himself."

"Ew, gross!" Madison couldn't help but giggle again, as hard as she tried not to.

"So, what should we do?" Liam asked, rubbing Copper's belly absentmindedly. The hound wriggled happily, grunting as he did so.

Madison chewed her lip as she thought, even though that was something girls weren't supposed to do. "Didn't you say you had somewhere you go for fun? You never did show me."

"Oh, that's right!" Liam jumped up, pounding his fist into his open palm.

Copper grunted a few times before begrudgingly rolling back over once it was clear he wasn't going to get any more belly rubs.

"C'mon, before my mother starts looking for me."

Liam took off, with Copper bounding along at his heels.

"Hey! Where are we going?" Madison asked as she raced after them.

"You'll see! Keep up!" Liam shouted over his shoulder.

Since he clearly wasn't answering anything, Madison tried to guess. They were heading toward the far side of town, as they passed the cut-off line where the unmanicured grass suddenly gained a third of a meter. Maybe there was a rundown house of interest, where they would be kept company by spiders and the spirits of those who had died there. Or, better yet, an old, beaten footpath where they could be travelers on an adventure. Or maybe even…

Madison suddenly realized Liam had stopped, and she looked around for something that made the spot as amazing as she figured it would be. Instead, they were standing in a field with the forest looming in front of them. There wasn't anything particularly spectacular or unique about it. In fact, it looked downright boring.

"*This* is your secret spot?"

"Not here. In there."

Madison's heart skipped a beat when he motioned his head towards the woods. It was the moment she'd been waiting for, and every fiber of her was screaming *yes!* Well, *almost* every fiber.

"You're not worried about the rumor of missing children?" she asked.

"Well, I haven't gone missing yet, have I? And I do this all the time." Liam cocked his head to the side and grinned as he added, "But, you know, if you're scared..."

"I'm not!" Madison crossed her arms and huffed.

"Good. Then let's get going."

Copper ran ahead of them, but they'd only made it a few steps before a high-pitched, squealing voice, sounding very much like a wailing siren, called out, "Liam Gagnon!"

Liam immediately froze, his head sinking guiltily toward his shoulders until his neck nearly disappeared, like a turtle attempting to escape into its shell. He winced as he turned back around.

"Uh-oh," he whispered. "That's Mrs. Harper."

"Who?"

"She's the president of the National Arbor Society and, well..."

"Let me guess, not all there?"

"Something like that."

Before they could say anything else, Mrs. Harper was on top of them. Her long, red nails clacked together as she grabbed Liam by the ear and pulled him back out of the woods. Madison followed of her own accord, though her left ear ached sympathetically.

"How many times do I have to tell you to stay away from the trees?" she asked, releasing Liam's ear as she gathered herself to her full height. She towered over them like a giant, with her lips pursed and chest puffed out, wrists poised on her wide hips. "I guess I'll just have to have a talk with your mother about letting you wander around unsupervised, if that's what it takes."

That wasn't what Madison wanted to hear. If Liam was grounded, that meant she'd lose her only companion. *Besides*, she thought as she stared into the depths of the woods, *I'm so close now.*

"Wait!" she called out, too forcefully, and her face warmed as two sets of eyes locked on her. "I mean, it was my fault. I just wanted to walk in the woods. I'm sorry."

Mrs. Harper looked down her nose, studying Madison, who did her best to look contrite.

"Well." Mrs. Harper sighed, and the rigidity of her pose softened a bit. "You're new here, so I suppose you wouldn't know, but I'm only going to tell you this once: *don't go in the forest.* If I catch you again, I'll have a talk with your parents, as well."

"Yes, ma'am."

"As the president of the local chapter of the National Arbor Society..."

Behind her, Liam rolled his eyes as she listed off her title like she was a noble or dignitary, and it took all of Madison's restraint not to laugh.

"...it's my job to protect the trees, and I won't let you kids hurt them in any way."

"But how—" Madison began, but Liam was shaking his head furiously and waving his hands, so she let the question drop. Even though she was curious what danger they could possibly pose to a *forest,* she supposed the how didn't matter. Instead, she said, "Yes, ma'am."

"Good." Mrs. Harper nodded with a sense of finality. "I'm really doing this for your well-being, you know. Trees are living organisms, and like all of God's creatures, they tend to fight back when they're threatened."

Mrs. Harper nodded knowingly, and Madison couldn't stop the question from spilling out.

"Do you think that's what's happening to all the children that go missing?"

Liam covered his face and shook his head, and when he glanced up, between his fingers, Madison shrugged apologetically at him. She hadn't been able to help herself.

Mrs. Harper's lips pinched into a thin line and her jaw muscles tightened, accentuating her high cheekbones and narrowed eyes. For a few minutes, she stood immobile, just looming, staring Madison down. Eventually, she sighed. "Where's Matheson Lam? Let's just not take any unnecessary risks, mm-kay?"

"Yes, ma'am," Madison answered. She glanced further into the trees, where soulful brown eyes were watching her intently. Copper didn't seem to think there was any danger in the woods; perhaps he knew something the rest of the town didn't. After all, how dangerous could the forest be if a *dog* came and went freely? As if reading her mind, Copper turned tail and trotted—unharmed—deeper into the trees.

THE STATUE in the center of town was wearing a button-up shirt, vest, and bolo tie, and a cowboy hat dipped low over the lifeless eyes, but Madison wasn't particularly impressed. Who wore a cowboy hat and boots without chaps? Or, at the very least, spurs.

She stood at the statue's base, hands clasped behind her back as she studied the outfit. If she had been paying any amount of attention, she would have noticed the crunch of grass and the heavy footfalls, but she didn't. So when someone grabbed her from behind, she let out a high-pitched shriek. The few people who were in the park shot her dirty looks, and she felt a flush spreading up her neck and blossoming across her cheeks.

When she whirled around, skirt and braid whipping with the action, she found Liam, who was doing a lousy job of hiding his laughter. She fought the urge to slug him in the arm, because that would be unladylike. Instead, she smoothed the wrinkles out of her skirt and pretended nothing happened.

"I didn't mean to scare you," Liam said once he stopped chuckling, though Madison noted that there was no apology anywhere in there. "C'mon, we gotta go quickly."

Before she had a chance to answer, Liam grabbed her hand and dragged her across the park. He was in a hurry, constantly checking to make sure the coast was clear, and it was all she could do to keep up.

"Where are we going?" she asked, jumping out of the way of a bench that Liam would have otherwise led her directly into.

"You said you wanted to see my spot, didn't ya?"

"But what about Mrs. Harper?"

"She has her hair done every Thursday at eleven, so as long as we hurry, she'll never have to know."

The short grass of the park gave way to ill-tended pavement and eventually to dirt road and then the wild grass that lurked in the eastern side of town. The trees overshadowed them, menacing in a way, but they didn't stop this time. Holding hands, they charged head-first into the shadows, and Madison was nearly giddy at the thought.

The forest was like a whole other world. The summer air was cool and damp, and the silence was replaced by the cries of hundreds of creatures proclaiming their existence. Even the wind sounded different, the way it rattled between the leaves or whistled through the occasional trunk. There was certainly nothing sinister or strange about it. In fact, Madison thought it was rather peaceful.

All of a sudden, Liam threw out his arm, and Madison bumped into it with an *oompf.*

"Hey, what—" Madison began, but Liam cut her off.

"Shh." He looked over his shoulder and put a finger to his lips. "There's something out there."

Madison hadn't been paying attention, but now she could make out the rustling leaves and muted snaps of something passing through the underbrush.

"What is it?" Madison whispered over Liam's shoulder.

"Dunno. Doesn't sound like a bear, though."

"There are bears in here?" Madison asked, a little louder and shriller than she intended.

"It's a forest. Of course there are bears."

They waited, holding their breaths, as the sound approached. There was a loud snuff, and then a square head with floppy ears poked through the bushes.

They both sighed and laughed nervously.

"What are you doing out here, boy?" Liam asked as he bent down to pet Copper. The dog acquiesced for a minute, soaking up the attention, before he stood, shook, and trotted back toward town.

"Hey, where ya going?" Liam called after him, but of course there was no answer.

"Think we should go back too?" Madison asked.

"No way!" Liam answered without hesitation. "We won't get another chance for a whole *week*, if Mrs. Harper has anything to say about it. She's been watching us like a hawk."

"You're right," Madison conceded. "I wonder what he was doing here, though. He's always in the woods, you know. He comes and goes."

"You wanna take a look?"

"But your secret place . . ."

"We'll swing by on the way back."

Liam shrugged, and Madison grinned and nodded. Finally, the sort of adventure she had been waiting for.

"Follow me," she said, and without giving Liam the chance to protest, she charged into the underbrush. She was smaller and faster and no stranger to being in the woods. In a matter of minutes, she was far enough ahead that he was nothing more than the sound of clumsy steps and sharp mutters behind her.

"Hey! Wait up!" he called.

But she didn't. Instead, she veered left, staying just out of sight but close enough for him to follow the sound of her movements. A few minutes later, Madison stopped, staring out into a large clearing.

"Madison?" a voice called behind her.

"Over here!" she answered as she walked to the far end of the clearing, hugging the tree line.

It was a matter of moments before a sweaty, red-faced Liam appeared in the trees, and he doubled over a moment to catch his breath. As he finally turned his attention to their surroundings, he whispered, "Well, I'll be. I never knew this place was here."

Liam stepped forward and stopped in the middle of the clearing, placing his hands on his hips as he looked around. "Wonder what—or who—made this place. Looks like it must have been used for something at some point, with how the trees just stop, but what?"

He glanced over at Madison, who shrugged. She opened her mouth to speak, but Liam cut her off.

"Let me guess, you're gonna say, 'Where's Matheson Lam?' Right?" Liam chuckled; Madison did not.

In a flat, even tone, she answered, "No, I would never ask that."

"Why's that? It's just an expression folks sometimes use."

"Because I know where Matheson Lam is. I'm right here."

"Huh?" Liam's eyebrows scrunched together in confusion, and his head tilted slightly to the right.

For a moment, Madison felt bad, but the moment was fleeting. Nature had a way of weeding out the slow ones, and who was she to argue with that? Besides, she had given him every opportunity to turn back, to change his mind, and the foolhardy child had persisted. That was hardly her fault.

"Imagine, if you will, a creature who feeds off of corpses," she began as she took a seat on a nearby log, smoothing out her skirt over her legs. "He's a Jikininki, a cursed soul doomed to feast on the dead, and though he's never met another of his kind, he knows he can't tell anyone. The place he used to live discovered the truth, and he was forced to flee. So what was he to do? Start a new life in a new town, of course. But people become suspicious of a person who gets too old, so he 'dies' in one form and takes on another. Children are easy; they don't even have to die. They have a tendency to simply disappear, so who would even notice if the new girl in town were to suddenly go missing?"

Liam's eyes widened and his mouth fell open, but no words came out. Madison had to admit that he was taking the news rather well. Either that or it hadn't caught up to him yet.

"You see, people die all the time, for silly reasons, especially children. They get sick, or they fall from trees, or they tumble into the river." Madison paused to look at the ground before adding, "Or wander into quicksand."

Liam's confused demeanor morphed into terror as the gravity of the situation dawned on him. The transformation wasn't something Madison was keen to watch, but it had been some time since the last corpse in town, and starving wasn't something she was keen to do, either.

His calves were already consumed by the muck, but that didn't stop him from struggling furiously to pull them out. In vain, of course. Madison knew there would be no escape; in fact, she was counting on it. The more Liam struggled, the more his panic grew.

"I'm sorry." Madison offered the words, even though she knew they were inconsequential. It changed nothing, and she doubted Liam even heard, as she turned and headed back into the trees. She couldn't help what she was, but she didn't want to watch, just the same. Liam's desperate screams followed her, but she was sure no one would hear. Not this far into the forest.

As she was leaving, Copper was entering. They both paused, and Madison knew he could hear what no human ear could.

"Shhh," she whispered, touching her index finger to her lips. "You'll keep my secret, won't you?"

The response was a deep, rumbling growl of warning. Madison smiled and skipped as she crossed the threshold between the forest and town. She knew that Copper really didn't have a choice in the matter; not even in Graves Grove were dogs able to speak.

THE STATUE in the center of town was wearing a suit and bowler hat. Madison had been disappointed to find there was no cigar tucked into the front pocket, when the outfit clearly begged for one. Not even so much as a pipe. The statue's clear lack of proper style didn't stop her from playing hopscotch in front of it, with Copper lying nearby in the shade of a tree, watching her warily.

In the distance, someone was calling the same thing over and over, but she couldn't quite make it out. As the sound drew closer, Madison recognized the single word: Liam.

She was bending over to snatch the stone off the pavement, wobbling on one foot, by the time Mrs. Gagnon made it to the park.

Out of breath and red-eyed, the woman approached Madison. She knelt down so they were eye to eye and asked, "Have you seen a little boy named Liam, dear?"

"Not since yesterday morning, when we were playing here, but he said he had to go."

"Oh." Mrs. Gagnon's face fell, and it was clear that she was nearing the end of her denial and approaching reality, but she wasn't quite there yet. Instead, she plastered on a fake, tired smile. "Well, if you see him, you'll tell him to come home, won't you?"

"Yes, ma'am. I'll let him know."

The answer seemed to satisfy her, since she nodded and stood. But she lingered for a moment longer, crossing her arms and tapping her chin thoughtfully.

"Where in the world could that boy be?" she muttered to herself.

Madison shrugged. "Where's Matheson Lam?"

SEEING THEM

RAYMOND HENRI

Most people didn't believe in shadow spirits. Most people never saw them. Scott knew where to look. Doorways. Corners. Behind furniture. And one had to look when the ambient light was so dim they thought they would be hidden. Most people who had seen shadow spirits thought they were something ethereal, like ghosts. Scott was pretty sure they were physical. A tribe of humans living under the radar, out of sight, and without law.

To prove his point, Scott worked a deal where he would watch his nephews and let his brother Adam and his wife, Linda, take a weekend vacation away from Graves Grove. After all, that was where he had first seen the shadow spirits, and the stress level in Adam's voice these past few months telegraphed the need for a break.

The plan involved sleeping in the same room with his nephews George, Paul, and Richard, and sprinkling flour on the floor outside their room. When the shadow spirits came to spy on them, they would only have that room to find any occupants. Therefore, if Scott's intuition was correct, they would leave behind footprints, or some kind of discernable markings in the flour. Not enough flour for Adam and Linda to know. Just enough to collect a marking or two.

George, the oldest sibling at eight years, tended to wind up sleeping in the top bunk to comfort Paul, who was five, so the bottom bunk would be Scott's for the weekend. Richard recently had his crib converted to a toddler bed, and Scott was warned that it was entirely likely that Richard would be kicking at his back before dawn.

Fed, washed, brushed, relieved, read to, and tucked, the three darlings of Graves Grove giggled themselves to silence in the warmth of darkness. Scott mused over how taken the town was with its three young imports. Children were treated like a rare commodity here. But for all Scott knew, small towns were like that.

Linda was Spanish, and the boys looked exotic enough that it could also contribute to their growing fame. They were quite a sight roaming through town, Scott's pale skin and red straw hair contrasting with their shiny black heads and olive tans bringing out the piercing gazes of their large brown eyes.

Scott relaxed and listened to the boys' soft snoring, staring intently at the sides of the open doorway for the chance to spot a shadow spirit peeking in the room. He was careful to keep his eyes closed to slits so as to appear asleep as well. It was hours from his customary bedtime, but rather than entertain himself with a movie, Facebook, or phone games, he had his mission.

He allowed himself the betrayal of a smile as he reflected on the way Richard had chased the town's mascot, a dog named Copper, along the river. Copper seemed to hardly be aware of Richard's pursuit, on his own canine adventure, and Scott walked briskly behind, eating his ice cream with the other two boys. It had been quite a good trip out west so far.

It certainly was an interesting town that became more familiar with every trip. There was an underlying feeling of an inner circle that Adam and Linda were just starting to orbit after years of living here. The boys were more readily accepted than their parents.

And there was that lonely tree. Maple? Poplar? No, sycamore sounded right. Scott wasn't very good with trees. Richard broke off his one-sided game with Copper short of that tree. At first Scott blamed the distraction of the abandoned schoolyard playground, but Richard wasn't even looking at it. In retrospect, Copper seemed to give the tree a wide berth as he passed.

Scott's focus shrank back to the dark room, and he chastised himself for not noticing his eyes had been closed. Perhaps he had even dozed. For how long, he had no idea. Carefully, he managed to open his eyes just enough to peer through ginger lashes. It took a little while, but finally he saw one, peering from behind the left side of the door frame. Scott didn't see any eyes in the shadowy outline, but he could feel their gaze.

Satisfied, Scott mentally told the shadow spirit to stay and watch as long as it liked. In the light of morning, he would take pictures of the prints in the flour and have all the proof he needed. Even if no one else believed him. He would know.

The two of them secretly watched each other. The shadow spirit was cautious not to lean far enough into the doorway to be detected; just as Scott concentrated on not allowing his eyes to open wide enough to appear awake. It did, however, become increasingly disturbing to Scott that the shadow spirit took up this vigil.

The furtive purpose of these dark guests seemed rooted in casual observation. Could they have been extraterrestrial? Scott didn't believe in alien abduction, but none of the alleged accounts ever seemed to mention being randomly watched all night from the shadows. He still believed they were physical. He'd be willing to buy they were mermen from Atlantis keeping tabs. For that matter, followers of Cthulhu made more sense than beings from another world with nothing better to do than watch people sleep.

A sudden shift of movement from beside the chest of drawers shocked Scott out of his reverie. He suffered himself the lapse of his post by closing his eyes in order to concentrate his effort on keeping his breath steady. His pulse was a hopeless involuntary stutter being spurred on by wide-awake adrenal glands. How could he have missed that there were two? It took great effort not to swallow and signal that he was awake.

What would these spirits do if they understood they had been discovered? As important as it felt to maintain the ruse of sleeping in ignorance, Scott could not let these shadow dwellers go about their business without some supervision. There were, after all, three nephews to consider.

Opening his eyes to mere slits once again, Scott peered to the door and dresser alternately, almost hoping that the shadow spirits had retreated for the night. Maybe they had gone, concerned about a close call with detection and getting home early.

An immense pressure suddenly pushed down on Scott's chest, rendering him incapable of breathing. Stuck in a wide-eyed gasp, he could only see black. The shadow spirit held its face fast against his. Fighting for a breath, the other one pulled him quickly off the bed.

With a sudden inhale, Scott's vision returned to normal as he sat alone on the floor with both arms spread across the bedside. He panted. A cold sweat pressed his twisted t-shirt against him. His wide eyes scanned the room for any sign of shadow spirits, but none remained.

Slowly, he stood. George and Paul slept soundly in the top bunk with arms draped over one another. Scott boldly checked around the furniture, toy chests, and closet. Should the shadow spirits be watching him, they would see that he wasn't scared. Alas, they didn't seem to be around anymore…

Neither was Richard! The toddler bed was empty. Horrified, Scott yanked up on the blanket. A stuffed elephant tumbled off the mattress and onto the floor. Dropping to his knees, Scott looked under the tiny bed and swept at the shadows with his arm. Nothing.

"No! God, no!" Scott mouthed and shot across the room, leaning into the hallway, flicking the switch as his eyes tried to focus on the dusting of flour.

The momentary assault of light strained Scott's unblinking eyes, but the need to interpret the markings commanded his full attention.

Tiny little size-seven toddler prints leading out of the room were the only disturbances Scott could see. Fruitlessly, he peered into the corners beside the door frame where the shadow spirit had stood.

Could they be spirits? Had he been wrong all this time?

"Richard?" Scott called out into the hallway, bending an ear. No response.

"Richard!" Scott hollered.

"What's going on?" George asked, half awake.

"Richard's not in his bed. He left the room." Scott ran through the report quickly without looking back as he stepped over the flour and into the hall.

"He probably went with Mom and Dad." George sat up, the hair on the right side of his head a mess.

"They went on vacation," Scott responded without thinking, focusing into each room he passed.

"Oh. I forgot." George was waking up a little more and climbed down from the top bunk as Paul slumbered on.

Scott fumbled around in the dark living room for his phone as George shuffled out of the hallway. Scott had become single-minded in his fearful search for Richard. Activating the flashlight app on his phone, he swept the kitchen, dining room, living room, and mud room. His light stuck on the side door. It was unlocked. Did he forget to lock it? That was one of the major instructions Adam had given—always lock the doors at night. That, and the unspoken instruction of not losing one of the children.

In a twitch, Scott flung the door open and swung the LED light from his phone around.

"Richard?" Scott called out. "Richard!"

George appeared behind Scott. "I don't think he would go outside. It's too dark."

The night air clung to the hair on Scott's legs where the shorts didn't cover and made his sweat-dampened t-shirt feel cold. He stepped out onto the walk off the brick steps and made his way to the street, George in tow. The street lights were on, but he detected no movement within their spheres of light.

If any mark of a trail could be found down the sidewalks, Scott hadn't the level of tracking skill to follow them. He cursed his failings and vowed to find Richard before he became just another worn out story of a missing child in the *Graves Grove Gabbler*. Clutching his thick tufts of hair, Scott permitted himself one good exasperated growl, folding him into a crouch on humbled knees. Adam was going to kill him.

"Maybe he wanted to find Copper," George suggested as he pointed off toward the center of town.

Scott shot up with new purpose. "You stay close to me." He speed walked as George half jogged. Continuing to yell out Richard's name would guarantee Avalean Harper getting wind of the incident and running some permanent record in the *Gabbler*, even with Richard's swift return. That couldn't happen. Richard would be returned and no one, especially Adam and Linda, would be the wiser.

They made their way to the town square. Scott nursed a sharp pain in his side, and George appeared to be just warming up. Looking at George, Scott realized he shouldn't have left Paul home alone, but that could hardly be helped now. George was staring at the bronze statue of Samuel Graves. The clothes were different. That must have meant it was tomorrow already.

"Would he have gone to where we found Copper, or where we last saw Copper?"

George only shrugged in reply. "Maybe he wanted to get more ice cream. Because he dropped his."

That made sense. To catch a kid, you had to think like a kid. The only problem was kids think in scattered directions. Scott stretched his sides and scanned the area for any kind of movement. He could hear Copper baying in the distance. Scott and George raised their brows at each other for only a moment before speeding off in the direction of the hound.

As they made their way to the edge of town, Scott swore he could hear another set of steps. They could have been echoes of their own since they didn't sound like they were coming from behind, but more like beside them. Still, he tingled with the sense that they were being followed. Random over-the-shoulder checks didn't show any sign of pursuit.

A light, not altogether unwarranted paranoia convinced Scott that he saw shadow spirits watching them pass from the sides of houses and shrubbery. He forced himself to focus rather on finding Copper in hopes of finding Richard. The baying started up again and sounded closer, coming from the direction of some forested hills beside town where the houses and roads were sparser.

George ran on ahead.

"Stay with me, George," Scott admonished, admitting privately that he didn't know how much farther or faster he could run. "We need to keep a visual on each other."

George looked back, his head appearing to turn beyond natural limits. "I think I know where he's going." The light glinted off George's teeth in an eerie way as his big eyes peered straight into Scott's.

Scott's legs felt like lead. George's lead increased as the cool grassy earth under their feet became tangled with wild brush and leaves.

"Wait for me, George!"

Scott's breathing became heavy and his head light. His vision lacked focus, and darkness overtook his peripheral vision.

"George!"

There was a moment where Scott could track his nephew's pajamas, but that ended once Scott's ankle smacked into a large rock, sending him cartwheeling onto a mossy log.

Scott struggled to keep his head upright and control his breathing to avoid passing out. He could manage to utter, "George. Come back." But there wasn't much he could do to be heard.

A couple failed attempts at standing solidified his suspicion that his ankle was not ready to take any weight yet. All Scott could do was sit there in his misery of being an ineffectual dumbass. How does anyone have three kids and ever have a chance to see them into adulthood? The mere survival of the human species became a mystery to him.

Slowly recovering, Scott looked back toward the town and then off where George had ran. The dog sounds started again, but were now closer to the side of town in front of Scott, beyond where he could see. Damn dog.

Shadow spirits peered at Scott from behind trees. He counted about five of them.

"Fine. Assholes!" Scott called out to them. "Don't help. Just stand there and watch." Then he dropped his head on his chest. "Go ahead and take me. If you're gonna. I don't want to see my brother or his wife's face when they hear about all this. You hear me? You'd be doing me a favor!"

The sky grew noticeably lighter. Dawn was approaching. That crazy old Mamie Rue would be donning that gold dress and tottering behind her rocket of lunacy soon. Scott gave his ankle another go. Swollen. Tender. But he would make a limping effort to make it back to Adam's house before the town woke up to witness his walk of shame.

As he hobbled, the thoughts of his nephews brought him useless sobs. It was all his fault. He had turned out to be a rotten uncle. With any luck, Paul would still be asleep when Scott returned. However, something told him Paul would be terrified and crying in an empty house.

How was Scott even going to tell Paul about his brothers? Here came the sobs again. Scott quickened his limping pace, looking much like someone rushing the sun home after an all-night bender. No, Scott chided himself. That person would have been more responsible than him.

In the multicolored, cloud-filled dawn, Scott made it back inside his brother's house. The sun had not yet crested, but the rooms that had been dark with possibility of dwellers in the shadows now were aglow in ruddy orange. It almost seemed too happy a place to return after the troubles Scott had faced in the last six hours.

He limped with hands on the hallway walls for assistance toward the boys' room. Wanting to find Paul. Not wanting to find Paul. He stopped just short of the mess of trampled flour outside the door. How stupid had he been? Trying to prove something as silly as shadow spirits being physical only to fail and lose his nephews in the process.

Eyes down in the flour, Scott swung the door open slowly, silently. Raising them with great reluctance, he allowed himself to view the top bunk in hope of finding Paul, not having any idea what to say or do about it. There he was, facing the door and asleep. And just beyond, against the wall, George slept.

Scott's elation whirled in sobs, thudding heartbeats, an ill-deserved smile, and a lean against the doorway for support. Dread wrung at whatever relief Scott could feel as he gazed upon the stuffed elephant beside the empty crib. Suddenly crying came from somewhere inside the house.

Quickly limping to the source of the wails, making full use of the walls for crutches, Scott dared himself to hope, wide-eyed and agape. He swung the door open to Adam and Linda's room. Nothing was amiss, yet he heard crying all the same. From inside the room.

He dropped to the floor and raised his brother's bed skirt. There he saw the contorted and glistening face of Richard.

"I bonked my head," Richard wailed.

"What are you doing under there?" Scott felt exhausted with relief at the sight of Richard and could scarcely muster any sympathy for the kid's injury.

He lifted the bed up enough to grant Richard a more comfortable egress. Once in the clear, Scott held Richard and caressed his head. As they rocked on Scott's knees, Richard kept reminding Scott that he wanted his mother, and Scott kept responded that he was going to be okay. And he sincerely hoped so.

THE GIRL WHO WAS FOUND

AVILY JEROME

The forest beyond the clearing whispered, the wind scurrying through the trees making the dark shadows bend and sway. I leaned back against the sycamore in the center of the park, as though I could distance myself just a little more. The rough bark scratched my back, but it was a comfortable sensation.

Behind me, on the other side of the tree, Louann Sackett squealed as Dean Halston tickled her.

I sighed and watched the others from my class laugh and chase one another around the clearing. They didn't notice me. They never did. I was as nonexistent to them as the ant that crawled across my foot.

It was supposed to be a field trip to experience the history of Graves Grove, but mostly it was an excuse for Mrs. King to let us burn off a little bit of spring fever.

Mrs. King stood and dusted the dead leaves and dirt from her backside. She clapped her hands. "Time for us to head back."

Giggling and flirting, my classmates lined up behind Mrs. King for the walk back to the church where classes were held since the old school had been closed and turned into the park.

"You coming, Bea?" Louann asked.

I jumped. I wasn't even aware she knew my name, let alone cared if I got left behind.

I nodded. "I-I'll c-c-catch up in a m-minute."

I glanced back at the park and its wide green lawn sprawling beneath the sycamore. Even all these years later, it still filled me with terror, even though I couldn't remember why. If not for that, maybe I'd find the nerve to leave this place, once and for all. I lingered by the giant sycamore for another moment.

With one last sigh, I trotted to catch up with my class.

We made a noisy troupe, marching through town. People smiled and waved from shops and offices, but their smiles didn't reach their eyes. It was more like an automatic gesture than anything resembling actual joy.

The bell above the door at Grovey Chops tinkled, and Mrs. Harper strode out. She smiled and waved at the class, but when she saw me, her eyes took on a sympathetic gleam. She'd written an entire piece about me in the *Gabbler*, back when. "The Girl who was Found."

The only one. That's why it was newsworthy.

I was too young at the time to remember it, but it still haunted me. Every moment of my life since that night was tainted by it.

I turned away from Mrs. Harper's prying gaze and back to Mrs. King's retreating form. My footsteps echoed everyone else's, but my heart stayed back under the sycamore, the one place I'd ever felt truly happy. The one place where it didn't seem to matter what had happened or what I'd done. In its shade, I was invisible.

Mrs. Mamie Rue Le Doux ambled past, wheeling her old-fashioned pram. People cast pitying glances her way, and even old Copper let out a mournful whine as she passed, but she never noticed.

Louann slowed down to walk beside me. "I feel so sad for her. My ma said she's been wearing the same clothes for the last thirty-something years. And her baby—he must've been so scared, lost and all on his own."

"I-I s-s-suppose."

Louann looked at me like I was crazy as Mrs. Mamie Rue Le Doux. "He was just a baby. He disappeared in the park. Of course he was scared. Just like Julie's brother. You ought to know all about that."

Julie Knoll's big brother. The reason I would never be accepted in this town. I knew I should feel some sort of remorse, but I didn't. All I felt was hate. Hate because he'd left me behind to take the blame.

Louann scooted back to her friends. Whispered words and furtive glances floated back toward me, but I didn't care. I was used to it.

We arrived back at the church and Mrs. King dismissed us, even though it was half an hour early.

I grabbed my backpack and hurried outside, away from the others and their hateful gossip.

"Bea?"

I whirled around and looked up into the most handsome face I knew. Ethan Raynard.

My heart stuttered, and my cheeks went red hot. "H-h-hello, Ethan."

He smiled down at me, almost shyly. "I was wondering if maybe you might let me walk you home?"

I stared up at him and blinked. He'd hardly said two words to me in all our lives, and now he wanted to walk me home? "Sh-sh-sure," I managed to sputter.

He smiled and took my backpack. "You didn't seem to have much fun on the field trip."

"I d-did."

"You just sat there the whole time. Are you afraid of the park, or something?"

I shook my head. "N-no. I j-just l-like the t-t-tree. I have g-good memories there."

"No one would blame you if you were afraid, you know. My mom said you almost died there when you were little."

So I had heard, all my life.

"You disappeared and your mom thought…you know…"

I nodded. I did know. Everyone knew, even if they never talked about it. My mother thought I'd ended up like Mamie's boy. Like Julie's brother.

Tears stung my eyes. I stared straight ahead and kept walking.

"They say when your mother found you, you were half-buried in leaves. Your lips were blue and you weren't breathing."

"Th-that's what they tell me."

"You really don't remember?"

I shook my head.

"They say you didn't talk for months, and when you did, you didn't say anything about what happened."

That part, I remembered. I remembered people trying to coax me to talk, to tell them what happened. I remembered my dad yelling and threatening me if I didn't say something, and my mom's last words, telling me that I could help so many people if I'd just try a little harder to tell them something I didn't know.

"I'm sorry," Ethan said. "I didn't mean to make you cry."

I shook my head. "It-it's not you."

"Is it because of your mom?"

It wasn't, but I nodded anyway. "She g-got sick the n-next d-d-day. She n-never recovered."

We arrived at my front gate, which hung at an awkward angle from the weathered post because my father couldn't be bothered to fix it.

I smiled at Ethan and reached for my backpack. "Th-thank you for the w-w-walk."

"Sure. Hey, if you're not busy tomorrow night, some of us are going to have a party in the woods at the edge of the park. You can join us. That is, if you're sure you're not afraid."

Was this really happening? The girl who couldn't even spit out a sentence without stuttering being invited to a party? And by none other than the rich, handsome Ethan Raynard?

My heart stalled at the thought of going into the small patch of woods near the edge of the river. But I'd be with Ethan. And whoever else went to the party. If I was going to overcome my fear of the forest, then now was the time. Ethan would keep me safe. "O-o-okay."

"Good. Meet me by the sycamore around nine, then."

I nodded, then hurried up the weedy path to the dilapidated front porch. The screen door slammed behind me as I went in, loud enough to rouse my father from his drunken stupor.

He hollered at me from the couch. "Watch it, brat! Can't a man get any sleep around here?"

"S-sorry," I muttered.

"Shoulda been you, died that day, 'stead o' your ma," he grumbled before falling back to sleep.

The words still stung, no matter how many times I'd heard them. But even he couldn't drag me down too far. I'd been walked home by a boy and invited to a party. The gray fog that shrouded my life thinned, and I felt almost happy for the first time since the night I'd nearly died.

MRS. KING seemed to have given up teaching entirely. She gave us all a stack of photocopied worksheets and told us to practice working independently. She pulled out a romance novel for her own independent study time and sat back in her chair.

Whispers in front of me distracted me from my work. I looked up to see Julie Knoll and Mindy Carlton looking at me and giggling.

I mentally checked myself, trying to determine how I'd managed to attract their notice. I'd brushed my hair. There was nothing between my teeth. My shirt and pants were relatively free of stains and fastened all the way.

Maybe Julie was just jealous that Ethan had walked me home the day before. Everyone knew she was sweet on him.

That must be it.

Or perhaps she hadn't even been invited to the party. That thought was nearly as melodic as Ethan's voice.

Ethan walked me home again that afternoon. "I'll see you tonight, right?" he asked as he lingered by my gate.

I nodded.

He squeezed my hand. "Good."

My heart pounded in time to his footsteps as he trotted away.

I crept in the house quietly, careful not to let the door bang. I made my father a sandwich for when he woke up and hurried up to my room to finish my minimal homework. I had to be perfect. I couldn't risk my father getting mad and locking me in my room tonight.

With luck, he'd get drunk and pass out before I tried to leave.

I sat silently through the leftover spaghetti we had for dinner, then handed my father a beer from the fridge before clearing the table.

He shuffled to the living room and turned on the sports channel.

I replaced his empty beer bottle with a full one.

An hour later, his snores drifted up the stairs to where I stood in front of the bathroom mirror, awkwardly experimenting with my mother's old makeup.

After finding the eyeshadow a crumbly mess; the mascara dried out clumps, and the lipstick a melted glob of pink goo, I gave up and settled for putting on a skirt and my nicest shirt.

I tiptoed down the stairs and out the front door, closing it softly behind me.

Once I got past the gate, I was free. I ran all the way through the darkened streets to the other side of town.

I stopped just before reaching the sycamore to catch my breath.

A shadow moved against the tree trunk.

Ethan.

I took one more deep breath and ventured timidly toward him. "E-Ethan?"

He stepped toward me and held out his hand. "You made it."

I nodded.

"This way." He held out his hand.

My heart stalled. The forest. I was really going to go in there.

"It's okay," Ethan said. "Trust me."

I did.

He led me into the trees.

Each step took us deeper into the shadows, away from the yellow street lights that illuminated the town. I swallowed and gripped Ethan's hand tighter.

The sounds of laughing and talking started as a faint rumble and grew more distinct as we neared the party. After a few more moments, I saw a faint light in the distance.

"We're almost there," Ethan assured me.

All this way, and nothing dire had happened. Maybe, finally, I could lay my fears to rest.

We stepped into a clearing, but there was no party. There was just Julie and Mindy, Louann and Dean.

Ethan dropped my hand.

Julie smirked at me. "Oh, good. Now the party can start."

I didn't have time to wonder what she meant before a burlap sack was thrown over my head. I gasped, but the sack kept me from getting a lungful of air.

Someone grabbed me around the waist. I flailed, but someone else grabbed my hands, and then my feet, too, were captured.

"It's all your fault," Julie said. "You were with him when he disappeared. You could've stopped it or at least told someone what happened, but you didn't. It's your fault my brother is gone!"

"Everybody knows it," Louann smirked. "You probably killed him yourself."

It apparently didn't matter that I was five at the time.

"We're going to make sure it doesn't happen again," Ethan said, all the warmth gone from his voice.

They carried me for what seemed like an eternity, then tied my wrists and ankles to a tree, leaving the bag over my head.

I whimpered. I wanted to beg them to stop, to explain that I had no idea what happened the night Julie's brother disappeared, but no words would form.

They laughed, all four of them in a sinister harmony.

The gray fog that wrapped around my heart was thicker than ever, clenching tighter and tighter, but still I couldn't even scream.

"You didn't really think I was interested in you, did you?" Ethan whispered in my ear.

I should've known better. There was no way Ethan actually wanted to spend time with me. I should've seen it.

I shivered. "Wh-wh-what a-are y-y-you—"

That was as far as I got before eruptions of laughter interrupted me.

"Stupid stutterer can't even finish a sentence," Julie spat.

I pulled at the ropes binding my hands.

Yet, even if I could escape, I couldn't show my face back in town, either. Not if it was true what Louann said and everybody blamed me for Julie's brother's disappearance.

Maybe, if I could find the road, I could hitchhike out of here. Start a new life far away. Away from the town that resented me, the father that hated me, and the friends I'd never have.

The ropes weren't tight, but I couldn't do anything with the five of them standing over me, gloating.

Someone yanked the bag from my head, taking a handful of hair with it.

I sucked in a deep breath and squinted against the glare of the flashlight in my eyes.

Something blocked the light—an arm. Julie's arm. In her hand, a shiny piece of metal glinted in the yellow beam.

A knife.

"This is for my brother," Julie growled.

I felt the shock of my breath leaving my lungs a moment before I felt the searing pain in my chest, followed by the warmth of blood bubbling out.

Ethan took the knife and added another burning hole to my chest, then handed the knife to Louann.

The pain intensified, but I couldn't cry out, couldn't breathe.

One by one, around in a circle, over and over again, they stabbed.

It seemed like an eternity before the pain finally started to fade and the world went black.

AN UNDEAD JANE DOE

ELISE MANION

My entree squirmed. I tightened my hold, locking my fangs into the carotid so the artery wouldn't tear. The thirst-quenching blood flowed over my tongue to satisfy my crippling hunger. When I had syphoned the last drop, I let the shriveled corpse fall to the ground. Alone in the dark alley, I gazed at my kill, and all I felt was...replete.

I closed my eyes and listened to the night. Feeding had been my only priority for the past week. Now that I'd done that I felt alive, like myself.

Whoever I was.

I had no memory prior to waking up under that creepy-ass sycamore tree. I knew I was in Graves Grove, a sleepy little town hidden in the Canadian Rockies, because I'd spent the past week hunting the local fare. Although tasty, the town was stranger than myself.

A ringtone disturbed the quiet night, and I turned around to follow the sound. It was coming from the remains of my dinner. After rummaging through the corpse's pockets, I finally located the obnoxious device and pulled out a cell phone. "A.H." filled the screen.

I clicked "answer" and said hello.

"This is Avalean Harper, Editor in Chief of the *Graves Grove Gabbler*," came an imperious female voice. "I'm returning your call regarding the mummified corpses found across the river. What do you know about it?"

That was the strange thing about my unusual way of eating. Within hours, the corpses would become giant-sized jerky strips. I usually left my refuse where I dined, and I'd never been across the river. Apparently there was someone else in town utilizing the same diet plan.

"Not much, really," I answered, which was mostly true. It wasn't my phone she'd called, and I wasn't her friend, but lying to the *Gabbler* still felt wrong.

When I didn't answer immediately, she huffed irritably into the phone. "Look, missy, if you're covering for someone, I promise to keep your personal information anonymous."

I laughed because even I didn't know my personal information.

"You think six deaths in as many days is funny? This town doesn't need a serial killer to add to its lore. If you know something, tell me," she demanded.

Six nights was all the memory I had, along with six meals. Surely, that wasn't coincidence. I felt no threat from this woman, even if she was trying to intimidate me. However, I still felt uneasy. Who had done this to me, and why couldn't I remember a damn thing?

"Hello? Are you still there?" she squawked in my ear.

"If you want a lead, there's another corpse in the alley next to the General Store and Feed Supply." I clicked "end" and shut down the phone, disabling its GPS. I stuffed it in my pocket and took flight, a cool ability I'd discovered that first night. I'd woken up covered in blood and gore and, in my panic, my body lost contact with gravity. I'd propelled myself behind a truck stop on the outskirts of town, where I'd found my first meal.

Now, I zipped across the river to do some recon. Police tape cordoned off the six spaces where they'd found the mummies, just like Mrs. Harper had said.

"It's like postcoital bliss, isn't it?" The question came from behind me. Startled, I turned to face a young woman dressed like the stereotypical FBI agent in sensible heels and carrying a sidearm.

"Excuse me?" I asked of her bizarre question.

She grinned, showing off her fangs. I wondered if I should have been happy to see another woman like me or preparing myself for battle.

"Feeding," she explained. "It's better than sex if you ask me."

"I didn't," I deadpanned. I gestured toward the mummies. "Yours?"

Now she was the one who looked puzzled. "No, love. Those are yours. I've been cleaning up after you every night."

"You've been following me? Do you know who I am?" Hope mixed with the frustration of losing my identity made me more aggressive.

She held her hands up in a placating gesture. "Your memories will return in time. We believe you're one of Tristan's creations." She smiled as if this should mean something to me. "Come, child, let me take you to The Network." She held her hand out to me. I stared at it as if it were a snake.

"Why would I go with you? Why should I trust you?" I asked.

She smiled, this time without showing fang. "I'm Ann, your Handler."

Warning bells rang in my head. "You've known about me for a week. Why make contact now?"

Her smile faded a bit. "Because new creations still in transition are dangerous. As your Handler, my job is to first keep you from exposing our kind, and second, to teach you our laws. Now that you're a week old, I can assess your abilities. The Network awaits, and you'll find answers there." I opened my mouth to argue, but Ann's tone was firm. "Come." This time, when she held out her hand, I took it.

AT THE ruins of S.M. Graves Elementary School, the sycamore stood nearby like a sentinel, its limbs spread across the night sky, shielding us from prying eyes. Ann made a beeline for a relatively new metal door set into what was left of the crumbling foundation. The door was camouflaged by the rubble.

Ann placed her palm on a security sensor. It pinged before the door opened, welcoming us inside and onto a staircase that led down into the bowels of the school. I was instantly suspicious.

As if reading my mind, Ann turned to me. "No one here will harm you. Please believe me."

I nonchalantly shrugged. She'd promised answers and safety so, for now, I would play along.

In a show of trust, she took the lead, and I followed her down the steep staircase. The treads illuminated with each step we took, but on the last one, the stairwell darkened behind us. Dizziness almost overtook me in the split-second blackout, before a long hallway was lit before us, ending in a cavernous room the size of a baseball field.

"This is The Hub," Ann explained as we passed a reception counter. "Think of it as the launching point to the rest of The Network."

"Hold up," I said, stopping in my tracks. "Where the hell are we? There's no way the school's basement is this big." The Hub was round with hallways leading away like spokes on a wheel. There were too many to count.

"The Network has many Ports of Entry around the world. Graves Grove is one of many in North America."

Stunned, I wondered what the hell that meant.

"All of the newly created who have lost contact with their makers are brought here. Look, it will make sense after you've been debriefed and we piece together what happened to Tristan," Ann said.

"Debriefed? Brought here for how long?" I felt a little weightless, and I fought to keep my feet on the floor.

"You're not in custody," Ann reassured me. "We just need to find your creator."

"Then I'm free to go?" I challenged.

"We know you're not responsible for Tristan's disappearance. However, anything you can divulge, beginning with where you awoke, could help us find him," she explained, evading my question.

We entered another spoke opposite the hallway where we came in. Like the stairwell, there was a momentary blackout followed by dizziness before the rest of the hall illuminated revealing glass doors at the end.

Ann pushed through the doors of a large office full of cubicles. Ringing phones and computers crowded the small space. She breezed past the worker bees to another door marked "Conference Room." It was exactly what you'd expect, only without windows to reveal the outside world.

Ann pulled out one of twenty chairs that sat around an oversized conference table and offered it to me. Once we were settled, she opened a folder that had been previously laid out on the table. "Do you remember waking up?"

"Yes."

She looked at me expectantly. I stared back before she narrowed her eyes and said, "Please describe where you woke up."

"The park, by the sycamore tree's roots." My blood had been everywhere, but I left that part out, not wanting to recall the nightmare of my birth.

She scribbled in her folder before asking her next question. "Was your first taste of blood from a human or animal?"

"Animal, a dog, actually, with soulful eyes. He came right up to me, like an offering."

"It was," she confirmed, not looking up from the folder. "Do you remember your first kill?"

"You don't think I killed the dog?"

A dimple appeared in her cheek as she tried to hide her smile. "No one kills Copper. If you woke in the park, he was probably waiting for you. Go on, what happened next? Who was your first kill?"

When I explained about my panic attack, my flight to the truck stop, and that Copper had met me there and not at the park, she shook her head in disbelief. "You took flight before you fed? That's not possible."

The door behind us burst open, and a young man flung himself into a chair next to Ann. They looked similar, both blonde and blue-eyed. "She's a mess. Why didn't you let her shower before doing this, Sister?" he asked, clearly exasperated with Ann.

I looked down at myself. I was, indeed, a mess. My clothes were filthy and bloodstained. All manner of crud was embedded under my once-manicured fingernails. I only had a few acrylics left on my fingers. There was a rat's nest on my head and my mangled nails caught in the tangles. Since waking, my only concern had been feeding, not basic hygiene.

"Yes, princess, you're a wreck," the man said, as if he'd read my mind.

"Not now, Andrew. You know we need to find Tristan as soon as possible, and she's our only lead!"

Andrew rolled his eyes as he stood up and grabbed my hand. His touch was like a punch to the gut. I closed my eyes and tried to decide if it was thirst or if I just wanted to tear the room apart.

"Easy, honey. There are no humans here to drink from, and trashing the facilities would be unwise," Andrew softy chastised me.

I swallowed my panic and tried to focus on what was most important. "Can I have that shower?"

"You bet," Andrew said with a smile. "I'm taking her to her room where she can get cleaned up, suck down a couple of blood bags, and put on fresh clothing. Then you can *debrief* her, Ann." He yanked on my hand and led me out of the conference room, much to Ann's annoyance.

I WIPED the steam from the bathroom mirror and tried to remember the dark-eyed stranger staring back at me. My hair was slicked back from my face and hung below my shoulder blades. The rest of my curvy body was all pale white skin, with large breasts and a bikini wax that confirmed that my human self had been a bit vain. I looked back at my face and grinned. At least I wasn't ugly. Still naked, I lifted the hair dryer off of its hook and began the tedious process of fixing my auburn hair.

"Get dressed and have some blood before we're all sorry," yelled Andrew from the other room.

I donned the robe hanging on the door and met him in the bedroom. He'd laid out clothes for me but impatiently waved a bag of blood at my face. "Drink it. And when you're done with that one, drink the second. Then get dressed. I'll be back in fifteen minutes."

When he bounced back into the room on time, I was dressed in blue jeans, a white v-neck shirt, and tennis shoes.

"Much better, princess. Now you're ready to face the day," he said.

"Night, you mean."

Glancing at his watch, he admitted, "I haven't been outside in a few weeks, and I've lost track of time. Sorry."

"Why? Aren't you allowed to go outside?"

"Of course I am. But this Tristan thing has got my evil twin's panties in a bunch, so we've all been working around the clock."

"Ann is your evil twin?"

"Honey, if we'd been sharks, she would've consumed me while we were still in the womb," he said, as he closed the door behind me. He handed me another blood bag. "You're still a newborn. Feeding often will keep you in control of the primal urges. We also don't want any tantrums." He sing-songed the last sentence, causing me to roll my eyes.

By the time I drained the bag, we were back in the conference room. I'll admit, feeding this way was convenient, but it lacked the thrill of the kill. Andrew had been correct, though. My impulses no longer controlled me.

I handed him the empty bag without looking at him and flopped onto a chair. An employee identification badge was displayed on the flat screen hanging on the wall. The man pictured wore a suit, and the name listed beside his face read "Tristan Tousignant."

Image after image flashed before my eyes, not on the screen but in my head, paralyzing me. Soft, brown eyes laughing at something I'd said, lush lips smiling before kissing me, indiscernible words spoken softly; my hands sifting through silky, brown hair that hung in his eyes. I felt everything and nothing for a man I didn't know.

Ann caught my attention. "Memories?"

The images of Tristan loving me slowly faded from my mind. "Yes, I believe so," I whispered into the room. Clearing my throat, I pointed to the screen. "This man, Tristan. He knows who I am. He holds all the answers, doesn't he?"

She nodded but continued to study me, saying nothing else.

"How can I help you find him?" I asked in the most businesslike voice I could summon.

Their relief palpable, Ann smiled while Andrew patted my shoulder.

"Tristan Tousignant is the best Handler in The Network. He's gifted in detecting those who possess certain talents beneficial to us. He saw in you the possibility of flight. Not all of us can do that."

"Fly, you mean?" It was good to know I had some defenses in my small arsenal.

"Flight is not possible in all of us, no, but Tristan can also detect potential talents in others," she answered. "Tristan is very gifted. We also believe that he's gone rogue, so it's imperative we find him quickly."

Andrew took over before I could ask what going rogue meant. "In order to fly, one must be able to manipulate gravity." At my blank stare he continued, "Levitation is the ability to move yourself and objects with your mind, defying the law of gravity. All of us who can fly can also call items to us, or push things away. For example, if you were threatened by a gunman, you could disarm him from afar."

"Bullets won't kill you, but they hurt like hell. The Network helps the newly created to discover their talents and master them. We'll teach you to fight, and how to protect yourself and those around you," Ann explained.

Until I knew more about The Network and Tristan Tousignant, I had no choice but to help them search for their rogue Handler. But I didn't have to be happy about it. Suddenly another vision hit me, a woman this time. While the vision of Tristan had been tender, this woman oozed hostility. It only lasted a fraction of a second, but it left me with a feeling of dread.

"What is it?" Ann asked.

"You tell me? Can you see the memories I'm recovering?"

"No, I'm an Emotional Empath, specializing in the newly created. I can only interpret how you feel."

Relieved that I would have a little privacy from Ann, I asked, "Is Andrew empathic, too?"

"Yep, I'm the cool twin. I can also fly. Ann's so jealous," he said before he stuck his tongue out at his sister.

"Yes, but I outrank you," she snapped before she continued with her presentation, showing me the layout of the facility. The Hub was, indeed, the nerve center, and it appeared that the newly created were housed together, while the Handlers lived outside of the facility, in different countries. Tristan's last address had been in Graves Grove, where he'd been scouting for talent.

Had Tristan's affection been a ruse to ferret out my potential, or had we been in love? What did the woman mean, and why did I get the feeling that she had something to do with Tristan going rogue?

FEEDING SOLELY off of cold blood bags for a week made me edgy with the need to kill. Daily exercise only helped so much. I practiced levitation on a magazine, only to set it on fire. Dousing the flames with a glass of water before the smoke detectors went off had been my only excitement.

Andrew had taken to calling me by different pet names. At first I'd been "princess," but by the end of the second day I'd punched him in the nose, spraying blood everywhere. He'd healed after downing a bag of blood, so no harm, no foul. But the name game went on. Today, I was Sugar Booger. My flamboyant friend was going to look great with a broken jaw.

"Hey, SB, time for talent search," he announced as he flounced through the door.

"SB?"

He sighed dramatically. "Sugar Booger is just too long. 'SB' sounds way cooler."

I shook my head. "Fine. Where are we going?"

"Talent. Search," he pronounced slowly. "We'll assess your development while looking for other gifts that may have surfaced in the time you've been here. Come, let's get a move on!" He clapped his hands enthusiastically.

When I just gave him the stink eye, he pulled me off the sofa and dragged me out the door until I walked on my own. There appeared to never be a slow time in the bustling Hub. We wove through the masses until Andrew found his spoke and led me down the hallway to glass doors labeled "Talent Search."

I glared at him. "Seriously?"

"Told ya," he laughed. He opened the doors and addressed a brisk woman behind the reception desk. "Tristan's creation has an appointment with the Handlers."

Ms. Brisk smiled, then glanced at her computer. "They're almost ready for you. Please wait on the observation deck."

The deck overlooked an open arena below where a man appeared to be taming a grizzly bear. My thirst stirred at seeing both predator and man circle each other.

"I feel your thirst. But that's not a real grizzly bear, SB," Andrew whispered in my ear.

I narrowed my eyes at Andrew before the creature stood on two legs, threatening the man with its razor-sharp claws.

"Concentrate, David! Your beast doesn't control you!" the Handler shouted. The bear growled his frustration and fell back onto his front paws, shaking his massive head back and forth.

The man pointed his finger at the bear. The beast whimpered before falling onto its side convulsing, and then shrank into a man.

What the hell?

Andrew smirked. "Shifter. We intercepted reports of a grizzly sniffing around the Samuel Madsen Graves statue. You know the one? It changes clothes every so often. Impressive magic, that. Still thirsty?"

"No, I've suddenly lost my appetite," I said before something occurred to me. "Andrew, if Ann is my Handler, why am I always with you?"

He was about to give me one of his smart-ass answers when a group of Handlers applauded the pair in the arena. A well-dressed man stepped from the group and spoke into a microphone. "I think that's enough for today. You did well, David. Rest and feed, and then we will meet you in an hour to go over your results." The speaker turned to me and asked, "Are you ready?"

I shrugged.

He raised a gray eyebrow at my lack of enthusiasm, but Andrew quickly answered, "She's ready, Chancellor," before escorting me off the deck and into the arena, where Ann was already there studying a file. She was always studying a file.

We stopped a yard or so in front of her. With a benign smile on her lips, she closed her beloved file and turned toward the crowd above us. Andrew had already joined the men on the deck, quick bastard that he was. He struck a pose before waving at me with the tips of his fingers. It was hard not to grin.

"I've already documented her flight skill, her duration in the air, and speed. It's all in your packets," she explained to the crowd above.

While Andrew had been my companion night and day, Ann had made me feel like a test subject. Contempt lanced through me before I could stop it. If Ann felt it, she didn't comment on it. No need to give them any more information than they were giving me. I still needed them to find out why Tristan created me and then left me alone. Emotional hurt pushed through the contempt, and I couldn't hide it. Though she raised an eyebrow, she still didn't comment on my feelings.

When I finally took a calming breath, she asked, "Ready?"

"Yes."

"Have you practiced your levitation skills?"

"No." I'd almost set the room on fire, but she didn't need to know that.

Placing a pencil on the table, Ann instructed, "Please concentrate on the pencil."

I stared at the pencil. About sixty seconds went by before I looked at her in question.

"Concentrate. Push the pencil toward me."

Swallowing my irritation, I focused until the pencil flew from the table, sticking her in the upper arm.

"Holy shit!" I hadn't meant to stab her. I moved to help her, but she waved me off with an elegant hand.

"I know it was an accident, but I think we'll continue with the rubber ball."

For the next few hours, Ann stood next to me, out of the line of fire, while I mastered dribbling with my mind. I was about to try a dunk shot when pain tore through my abdomen and doubled me over.

"She's done for the day, Ann," the Chancellor declared over the intercom. "You did very well, Jane."

Who the hell was Jane?

"You're officially a Jane Doe. We have to address you as something other than 'Tristan's Creation.'"

I didn't share the humor in his voice.

I WAS so bored. The less I had to do, the more I wanted to hunt to quench my thirst. I grew more agitated by the minute, and cold blood bags weren't cutting it anymore. Spotting the forgotten cell phone on the coffee table, I thought about randomly dialing someone from the contact list and setting up a meeting for dinner, but the battery was dead. Damn it.

The black screen was blank, just like my past. No memories of people I knew, or places I'd been. No emotion. No attachments. I was a void in my own existence. That blank screen represented my loneliness. Pent up anxiety sent a tingling charge through my body. My hands shook with it. I wanted to scream. And then the locked screen opened up.

Startled, I almost dropped it. When my grip tightened, the battery gained a fifteen percent charge. Remembering the small fire I'd doused, I focused on the battery symbol. A pleasant tingle ran up my arm and, before my eyes, the battery turned from red to green, and thirty percent full. I was charging the damn thing with my mind!

Craving the hunt, I needed to get out of there. I focused on the electronic locking mechanism next to my door and wondered if I could manipulate it. Ozone sizzled for a moment before the door popped open. I was free. Of course, I'd always been free of my quarters, having been issued my own room card, but knowing that I could exit the facility to fulfill my craving had me off the couch and rushing out the door.

I sped down the hallway and entered the always busy Hub. No one noticed as I searched the cavernous space for the spoke that would lead me to Graves Grove. Once I found the hallway, I ran until I reached total darkness. I stopped and held my breath. Stepping through the threshold, I found myself in dizzying darkness for a split second before the stairwell lit before me. I floated up to the same doors I'd entered two weeks ago. I gave the security panel a glare, felt the electric charge build and then... Pop! The door opened at the same time the alarms went off. I took flight into the soft, early evening. Freedom never felt so good.

My feet hit the ground across the street from the old Graves Manor. A woman pushing a run-down pram was speaking gibberish. I knew the pram contained nothing but an old picnic basket wrapped in a checked cloth. Mamie Rue Le Doux was an old woman lost in her life's memories, but her sad presence didn't stir my appetite. I could've gone for her aging butler who was standing on the front porch, but there would be no sport in that.

Ignoring the inhabitants of Graves Grove, I closed my eyes and concentrated. Fear and blood were redolent in the air, luring me to an L-shaped motel on the outskirts of town. Light glowed from only one room, its door unlocked, revealing a murder scene. Though I craved the blood that covered the walls, carpet, and ceiling, the corpse was nothing more than unappealing refuse. I studied the carcass of the young woman, her butchered flesh ripped to shreds. Her long hair and manicured nails were still perfect.

A flashback of me waking under the tree covered in my own blood hit me like a hammer. The corpse and I had a lot in common. We'd both been murdered.

The mixture of anger for the loss of the woman's life and disappointment over the wasted food made a strange emotional brew. Blood spatter still dripped down the walls of the defiled room. The cretin that had done this was still close by. Then I heard a toilet flush.

A grim smile spread across my face. I closed the door behind me and sat down next to his kill, waiting for the bathroom door to open. The surprised look on his face was as delightful to me as I knew his blood would taste. I flashed him some fang.

He gripped a long, serrated knife. Blood remained under his fingernails and along the sharp tines of the blade. I could feel his need to kill again. It was just as strong as mine, confirming that I was a true killer. The difference between us was that I was never wasteful.

"Shall I run?" he inquired.

"Only if you want to."

His eyes flashed with excitement before he raised his empty hand to his ear and tapped it with an index finger. "I have her," was all he said before the door banged open and the same Handlers from The Network I'd seen on the observation deck rushed me. They had me gagged and restrained before I could react. Ann entered the room, gun drawn.

"Has Tristan made an appearance yet?" she asked the serial killer.

With deference, he answered, "No, ma'am, not as yet. But he won't be able to resist this." He motioned to his handiwork with sickening pride.

"Get Jane out of here quickly and quietly. I want this wrapped up ASAP," she commanded. "It's time for Tristan to answer for his behavior."

I fought for as long as I could, but the drug-soaked gag pulled me into a familiar black void. I was nothing and nobody. I prayed I'd find Tristan on the other side.

FAIRY TROUBLED

CATHRINE BONHAM

It was the height of summer. Normally at this time Jenna would be walking around in flip flops and shorts that tested the bounds of decency. Instead, a northerly wind was blowing through the Canadian Rockies, forcing her to wear a sweater in the middle of July.

No. This wasn't Ohio. The Piper family moved to the town of Graves Grove two days ago, the move unfairly causing Jenna to miss out on getting her driver's license by mere months.

"Come on, Jenna," said Emily, her younger sister.

Jenna was rummaging through a plastic tub full of hats, belts, and shoes. "In a minute. I need to find my boots."

Emily's twin, Edward, stuck his head in the door of the girls' bedroom. "Hurry up! I want to see the statue."

"Okay, I'm hurrying." Jenna reached into the tub and pulled out a tan boot with a white wooly lining inside. "One down and one to go."

The twins stood in the doorway, matching green coats hanging open. Red hair tucked into matching green ski caps. Jenna had never understood her siblings' desire to wear the same clothing. Perhaps it was because they weren't actually identical, that they felt the need to assert their twin-ness.

"I had a lovely dream last night about fairies." Emily picked up one of Jenna's sweaters off the floor and held it up to herself, testing the look in the mirror on the closet door. "Did you have a good dream, Jenna?"

"No, I couldn't sleep because of your stupid night light. You're nine years old; if you can't sleep without it, go back to sharing with Eddie."

"But I don't want a night light either," Eddie whined.

"Well then," said their mother, coming into view, "I guess you can always share with Jenna and let Emily have her own room."

Eddie's eyes widened, and his nostrils flared. "No!"

Their mother tousled his hair to show she was only joking. "Are you coming, Jenna? You don't have to if you want to stay home."

"Found it!" Jenna pulled out the last boot and held it up in victory. "I'm coming." She slipped both boots onto her feet, pulled back her own hair—more the color of rusty clay than the bright ginger of her siblings—and pulled on her favorite purple hat. "Okay, ready."

THE STATUE stood in the town square and was, according to the plaque, of the town's founder Samuel Graves. The Pipers had glimpsed it briefly as they drove into town two days ago. Yesterday they had all walked past it, and Eddie had declared that it wasn't the same statue they drove past the day before. Their father said he was imagining it.

"I'm not," insisted Eddie. "Yesterday he had on old-fashioned clothes, and today he's dressed like a professor." The clothes, though made of bronze, did seem to bring to mind an academic persona. A jacket with patches on the elbows, a bowtie, and thick-rimmed glasses.

"These clothes are old-fashioned, sweetie," said their mother.

"But they weren't these clothes. Yesterday they were older and fancier, like George Washington."

Their mother, eager to get him to drop it, turned her family's attention to the General Store and Feed Supply. "I bet they sell ice cream there. Who wants to go see?"

Eddie was stubborn, though, and would not stop pestering their mother until she assured him they would come back tomorrow to see the statue again.

SO HERE they were. Even from a distance Jenna could see something was different. The statue had a bronze hat that had not been there yesterday. In addition it wore a long coat and a scarf wrapped three times around his bronze neck, with ends hanging all the way to his bronze feet.

"See, I knew it would be different!" Eddie yelled.

Jenna was floored. If it had changed since yesterday, there was no reason to doubt it had changed once before.

Their mother studied the statue. She held her right hand up to her left eye. Then she moved it over her right eye. Then back again. "Well, that is just the weirdest thing," she finally conceded.

"It's actually the least bizarre thing that happens here," said a voice from behind them.

Jenna spun around to face a boy about her own age. He had spiky blond hair, no-rim glasses, and a red windbreaker.

"You seem unconcerned that a statue is apparently changing his clothes," said her mom.

"You'll get used to it. I'm Mortimer Kerstin." He held his hand out to shake. "You must be the new family."

"I'm Anna Piper," said her mother, giving the offered hand a pump.

Jenna took his hand and felt a smile break across her face. She stared into his blue eyes and felt completely welcomed. Maybe this move wasn't the worst thing ever. "I'm Jenna," she added, letting go of his hand as an afterthought. Out of the corner of her eye, she noticed her mother looking around frantically.

"Where's Eddie? Did either of you see where Eddie went?" her mother asked.

Emily shook her head. "He was right beside me."

"Eddie!" yelled Jenna.

"Eddie, this isn't funny. Come back," their mother called, worry building in her voice.

"He can't have gone far. I'll help you look," said Mortimer.

"Oh, thank you," said her mother. "I'm sure having someone who knows the town would help a lot."

The four made their way down Main Street looking down alleys and occasionally calling Eddie's name. As they approached the park, Jenna spotted a flash of green run underneath a large sycamore tree. Its twisted root formations, thrusting up from the earth, dominated the landscape. "Eddie!" she shouted.

Eddie stuck his head out from behind the tree to look at her, then quickly returned his attention to studying the branches.

Their mother marched up to him. "Don't even think about it!"

"Think about what?" he asked, his eyes still scanning the full branches.

"Climbing the tree, that's what. Why did you run off?" Mom grabbed him by the shoulders. Jenna was unsure if she meant to hug him or throttle him.

"I was chasing the fairy." He looked right at Jenna and scowled. "I've lost it now, thanks to you."

Jenna crossed her arms. "A fairy? Come on, Eddie, I know you can lie better than that."

"Mom, let me explain."

"No. There will be no explaining. I told you to stay together. What if someone had taken you? Now I have to seriously reconsider if you are ever leaving the house again."

"But Mom!"

"No buts. Emily, you too."

"Aw, I'm not the one who ran off." Emily stomped her foot.

"We're going home now." Their mother grabbed the twins' hands and dragged them behind her.

Jenna sighed and started falling in line. "Jenna, you can stay if you want," said her mother, turning back.

"What?" protested the twins in unison. "Why does Jenna get to stay?"

"Oh, um, okay, Mom," Jenna said, mildly surprised. "When should I be back?"

"Whenever you're ready." Her mother nodded in Mortimer's direction and mouthed, "He's cute."

Jenna's face grew hot, and her stomach fluttered. She prayed Mortimer hadn't seen that.

She watched her mother pull the twins down the road. "So, anything to do in this town?"

Mortimer pulled a digital camera from the pocket of his windbreaker. "I still have to snap my daily picture of the statue for my website."

"Okay, it's a start," she said. "I'm sorry you had to see that back there. Mom's being paranoid. Back in Ohio we used to run around all the time. She's just worried because this is a different country."

"It's fine. Actually, she has good reason to be worried. There are a lot of missing kids from here. I had an older sister who disappeared." He didn't face her; only started walking back through the park as he continued talking. "One day I'm the youngest and then I'm the oldest. Though technically I'm the middle child, I guess."

"I'm so sorry," said Jenna, keeping pace with him.

"Don't be, you had no way of knowing until I told you. Besides, this was years ago, I hardly remember her anyway." He paused to watch an old woman in a faded green hat and scarf push a ratty-looking black pram down the lane and into the park. "Living in the past too long turns you into a ghost more fully than dying does." He watched her for a while longer, then they continued in silence until they returned to the statue.

"I can't believe Eddie said he was chasing a fairy," said Jenna, breaking the silence. "I might accept that from my sister, but my brother is usually a much better liar."

"All the more reason to think it's true, then."

"You believe him?"

"You just moved to a town where bronze statues can change their clothes, and you don't believe him?"

"Fair point. So if you're such a believer, go ahead and tell me about fairies."

"I know they're not sweet little girls in flower dresses, with butterfly wings. Fairies are evil and should be avoided if spotted. They say a child who's been touched by a fairy will die young."

"Who is they?"

"My grandmother, actually. She's seen them. She also said if the fairies choose someone, there's nothing you can do to save them."

"Oh, please. You're just trying to scare me."

"Trust me, if I wanted to scare you, there are a lot better stories I could use to do it. All of them true." Mortimer stood back from the statue of Samuel Graves and lifted his digital camera. He snapped a couple pictures and then turned back to Jenna. "Can I show you something?"

MORTIMER TOOK her to his house and pulled out a box of old photographs from a tall cupboard in the living room. "My grandmother and her older sister took these photos when they were children."

Jenna pulled out the top photo. It was of a young girl in pigtails and a jumper staring up at an overexposed corner of the shot. In the bright corner a human figure with shimmering dragonfly wings could barely be seen.

"This is fake." Jenna let the photo fall back into the box. "It's like the Cottingly photos—it's fancy photography. That can easily be done with a double exposure."

"The skeptical will always find a reason to not believe," said Mortimer. "Look at this one." He handed her a photo from lower in the box. "The first one was my grandmother. This one is her sister."

The photo was of an older girl. Her hands were held out in front of her chin, and on them sat a naked feminine shape. Hair flying around its head like flames, reflections of light showed where the wings began and ended. The frightening thing, though, was the girl's face. A bizarre combination of events must have turned the camera into a temporary x-ray. The face of the girl was a grinning skull, the features of her real face appearing as a negative just over it.

"My great-aunt Harriet died that year from polio. She was only sixteen."

"People die. It's sad, but it isn't weird." Jenna handed the photo back. "I should get going, my mom will be wondering where I am."

Mortimer reached into his pocket and pulled out a phone. "Here, let me give you my number."

"Sure." Jenna pulled out her own phone and hit the contacts button.

JENNA WALKED up to the front door of their three-bedroom, one-story fixer upper. The paint on the front had once been a blue-gray color, but was now more gray than blue.

Inside, Jenna found her mother sitting at the dining room table, typing away on her laptop. "Where are the twins?"

"In their rooms." Mom looked up from the computer with a mischievous grin. "So how'd it go with Mortimer?" Her mom pushed out the chair next to her with her foot.

"It was fine, he showed me some pictures." Jenna toyed with the idea of sitting down, but then decided against it. "This is a really weird town." She slid the chair back into place beneath the table. "I'm going to check on the twins."

Jenna opened the door to the room she shared with Emily. Finding it empty, she removed her hat and coat and left them on her bed. Then she crossed the hall and knocked on Eddie's door. "Eddie, Emily, are you two in there?" When she received no answer, Jenna pushed the door open and entered the room.

Eddie was staring at a thing in the corner. A bright thing. Jenna held her hand up to shield her eyes from the light. "Eddie, where's Emily?" she asked.

The bright light jumped up and flew over Eddie's head. "Close the door before it gets away!"

Jenna reacted quickly and slammed the door behind her. The light was too fast, though, and flew out before the door closed.

"What was that?" asked Jenna, her heart racing and her mind whirling.

"A fairy!" Eddie jumped to his feet. "Hurry, we have to catch it. It's the only way to find Emily." He opened the door and stepped into the hall. "Come on, what are you waiting for?"

"Where is Emily?" she asked, trying to process what she had just seen.

"This way, I see the light in Mom and Dad's room." Eddie sprinted to their parents' room, and Jenna followed close behind. The light darted toward a window, but finding it closed, swooped under the bed.

Jenna dropped to her stomach and peered beneath the bed skirt. Now that it wasn't zooming around as a blurry streak of light, Jenna could clearly see the female shape of its body. Gossamer wings sticking out from its back were nearly transparent save for flecks of refracted light. Its hair was still in the air, swaying about its head as though immune to gravity.

The creature turned to face her, its features little better than a skull with a rubber mask stretched over it. The fairy hissed at her and then jumped into a hole in the floorboards.

Jenna looked across to her brother, on the floor opposite her. "The basement!" they said together.

The two jumped to their feet and ran through the house to the basement door.

They passed their mother, still typing at the table. "What are you up to?" she asked. When they didn't answer she yelled after them, "No running in the house!"

Jenna yanked open the door and preceded her brother into the basement. The light was off, but it didn't matter. The fairy's glow lit up the room brighter than the old forty-watt bulb ever could. It floated about the ceiling looking for an exit.

"We have it trapped now," said Eddie, but then the ball of light zipped over their heads and up the stairs.

"The door!" they cried together. They hurried up the stairs, Eddie leading the way, and ran into their mother at the top.

"What is going on?" she asked.

"The fairy is getting away," said Eddie, pointing past her shoulder. "We have to follow it."

"Enough of this fairy talk, Edward." Their mother held her hands out to stop him as he tried to push past her. "Where is Emily?"

"They took her, the fairies. We have to hurry."

"Mom, listen to him. There was something down there, didn't you see it fly up the stairs?"

"The only thing I saw flying was you two running through the house." She finally stepped aside. "You are obviously tired of being cooped up. Tell your sister to come out of wherever she's hiding, and we'll go out and do something."

"But she isn't hiding," said Eddie, starting to get worked up. "She's missing. I'm not playing, it's true."

"Emily, come out here," their mother called. "It's not possible; I can see both doors from the table. I'd have known if she left the house."

"It was so fast, Mom! We were in my room playing a board game when all of a sudden these lights flew in and surrounded us. They kept circling Emily, sitting on her head and pulling her arms. Then she was gone. One fairy stayed in my room. The same one from this morning. It's like she was taunting me."

"Eddie, where did Emily go?" asked their mother, grabbing Eddie by the shoulders and staring into his eyes.

"I don't know, Mom, I don't know," he said, tears pooling in his eyes.

DAD WAS home from work, and an officer had already been over to take a statement; he hadn't sounded hopeful of finding Emily.

Jenna had called Mortimer right away, and the two of them went down to the park to see if she was by the same tree Eddie had run to. "How could they have taken her? It's physically impossible." Jenna placed her hands on her head and sat on the ground, her back against the tree.

"It almost sounds like the stories of changelings. The fairies take a human child but leave one of their own behind."

"But she got away. We let her escape and now we have nothing." Jenna stood up and started walking, no destination in mind. She just felt the need to keep moving—to pretend she was doing something to help.

"Do you think they were after your sister the whole time?" asked Mortimer, trailing behind her.

"She said she had dreams about fairies last night. I guess it's possible."

"I was thinking, maybe Emily is the one who was supposed to follow the fairy this morning. It wanted her attention, but it got Eddie's instead."

"So you think the subtle approach failed, and they tried a more direct approach."

"Exactly." Once again they were standing in front of the statue where this whole day began.

A little blue-haired woman walked out of the hair salon, where large, painted letters declared the name Grovey Chops. "Hello, Morty," she called from across the square. "Are you taking pictures for your block?"

"It's a blog, Grandma," said Mortimer to the woman crossing the street. "I took those this morning."

"I know it's a blog, sweetie." She held out one arm until Mortimer took the hint and leaned in for a hug. "What's the fun in being old if you can't mess with people?" She released Mortimer and turned her attention to Jenna. "So who's your friend?"

"Jenna Piper, ma'am," she said, extending a hand to shake.

"So formal, dear. Come here, you get a hug too." The old woman opened her arms.

At first Jenna felt awkward hugging someone else's grandma, but the embrace was warm and reassuring.

"Grandma, maybe you can help us. Jenna's little sister is missing."

His grandmother held her tighter. "Oh, you poor dear. I'm so sorry."

"She was taken by fairies," said Jenna.

"Fairies!" The old woman released her. "Oh, we haven't a moment to lose, dear. Quickly! Back to my house."

THE HOME of Mrs. Ophelia Kerstin resembled a thrift store where nothing was for sale. Too neat to be a hoarder and too eclectic to be a collector, Mrs. Kerstin fell neatly into the category of survivalist.

"Jenna, you take the salt," she said, handing Jenna a canister. "Mortimer, grab that birdcage. No, not the gold one, dear, the iron one." She turned back to Jenna. "When your sister vanished, did they leave a changeling behind?"

"I think so," said Jenna. "There was one in the house, and my brother was very adamant that it not get away."

"Oh, what a good boy." Her eyes lit up and she clasped her hands together. "How did he catch it?"

"I'm afraid he didn't. I let it get out." Jenna hung her head.

"Don't beat yourself up, dear. You couldn't have known. How old is your brother?"

"Nine—the same age as my sister."

"Twins. Yes, we can work with that." She reached up into a cupboard and pulled out a box of dog treats. "Mortimer, take one of these and stand out front. Whistle until Copper comes to you."

"The town stray? What do you want him for?"

"His nose, dear. Bring him to Jenna's when you've got him." She took the iron cage from him and grabbed Jenna's hand, pulling her to the door. "Come on, we need some things from your house."

ANNA AND Jacob Piper were near tears when the little old woman explained that she needed to take their remaining two children out after dark with only her grandson, an old mutt, and a can of salt for protection.

"We are already missing one child. I am not letting Eddie leave this house after dark," said their mother.

"But don't you see? Eddie can sense the changeling. If we catch it we can trade it back for Emily," begged Jenna.

"No, Jenna. I have half a mind not to let you go either," said their father. "The Mounties have already tried bloodhounds, and they couldn't find her. What good is that old dog going to do?"

"Dad, I don't know about the dog, but we need Eddie. Come with us and keep an eye on him if you want."

"Please, Dad," said Eddie, coming into the room. "I can help. I said the statue changed and no one listened. I said I saw a fairy and no one believed me. I know I can find Emily, please listen now."

Dad ran a hand through his hair. "I still don't believe it was fairies. But if it keeps Emily from spending the night outside in this weather, we'll go look for her again."

Their mom sat down on the couch and crossed her arms. "I'll stay here. You know, in case she comes home."

COPPER WAS a rusty-colored mutt with floppy ears and a long muzzle. Without any direction, he jumped up and sniffed Eddie all over.

"Shouldn't he be sniffing something of Emily's?" asked their dad. Eddie giggled as the dog's wet nose explored his face.

"No, Dad, we need the dog to find the fairy, not to find Emily," said Jenna.

The dog stopped sniffing, got down, and took off running. They followed him to the park and watched him sniff around. He made his way down to the riverbank. There he sat panting happily.

"Okay Jenna, pour a handful of salt. When you see a fairy, throw it on her. Eddie, you have to tell us when we get the right one. It must be the exact fairy that stayed behind in your room."

Jenna nodded and poured the salt. Various lights started dancing in and out among the river reeds.

"Those are some large fireflies," their father remarked.

"Not fireflies," said Jenna. The dancing lights came out of the reeds and began swirling around them. They were beautiful from a distance, but as they came closer she could make out their deathlike faces.

"Fairies," finished Eddie. He appeared mesmerized, and his eyes followed them as they went around and around. Suddenly he pointed straight out at a fairy who wasn't part of the circle. It hovered a little outside, watching. "That one!"

Jenna saw it. She couldn't time her throw to fall between the other fairies. Her handful of salt would be wasted if it hit the wrong one. Then she had an idea: instead of throwing the salt, she raised the handful to her lips and blew a stream of salt granules directly at the changeling. The grains hit her right in the gut, and her light dimmed. She hovered in a limping fashion before falling to the ground.

Mrs. Kerstin opened her iron cage and rushed to the fallen fairy. She slipped the opening over the fairy on the ground and left it. "There, now we wait. The fairies can't touch the iron, so none of them will be able to free her. They'll be forced to get Emily to lift the cage for them and then you, her family, will have to convince her to stay."

"Are these things behind every disappearance in Graves Grove?" asked their father.

"Oh no, fairies only come for children who are about to die naturally. They are a bit like banshees. They foretell death, they don't cause it."

"But Emily is a healthy young girl. She isn't about to die."

"Are you sure?" asked Mortimer. "There are all kinds of conditions that can eat away at a person before they're ever diagnosed."

"Emily!" shouted Jenna. Her sister appeared out of nowhere, standing in a halo of light.

"What have you done?" asked the young girl, running up to them. "The poor fairy." She reached out a hand to pick up the offending cage, but her father stayed her hand.

"Emily, sweetie, where have you been? We were so worried about you."

"I have to let her out. Can't you see it's hurting her?"

"Emily," said Eddie, reaching out to her. "I was so scared when you disappeared. Why did you leave me?"

"They wanted someone to play with them. They said if I came then I would have fun all the time and I…" She paused, and Jenna heard a sniffle. "I wouldn't have to be afraid to die."

"Come here," said their father, picking her up. "It's going to be all right."

Jenna felt a hand on her shoulder. She turned to find Mrs. Kerstin. "It's over." She nodded to the caged fairy. "You can let it go now."

Jenna squatted and looked at the little fairy through the cage. Very gently she lifted the iron cage until the fairy had just enough room to crawl out. The spiteful little creature flew into Jenna's face and gave her an evil grin, then darted away and flew up into the branches of the sinister-looking sycamore tree. The park became bright as day as more and more fairies filled the branches. They sat there, leering at the family as they walked away.

AS SOON as they got back home, Jenna's parents rushed Emily to a doctor. It took two second opinions and Mrs. Kerstin urging them once more before a blood test discovered the early stages of leukemia. Now two months and one bone marrow transplant later, they were all home.

Today the statue was wearing a pinstriped suit and a long trench coat. Mortimer was taking his daily photo of the statue's latest getup. "When did you get back?" he asked, putting the camera in his pocket.

"Last night. It was a long drive through the mountains," said Jenna.

"How was the operation?" asked Mortimer, glancing at her side.

"I'm fine, it wasn't that bad, really. I'm just glad I was a match." Jenna turned and sat on the statue's pedestal. "I'm still a little tired though. But it looks like Emily will be fine. We did it, we saved her."

"Oh, you didn't save her. You bought her more time." Mortimer turned and sat beside her. "That's all you can do. Everybody dies."

"Do you think that's why they took her? Did they want to stop us from giving Emily more time?"

"Yes and no. Less than fifty years ago most people died at home. Now people die in hospitals. I think they needed to keep her close by so that when she died, they could get to her."

Jenna covered her mouth with her hand. "That's awful! What could they possibly get out of a little girl's death?"

"Folklore says that the fairies were banished from Heaven for refusing to take sides in Lucifer's rebellion. What if, when a child dies, they could use that somehow to feel Heaven again? Like a drug."

"I can't believe that. I think they wanted to save her. What if this whole thing was to get our attention so that Emily would get the help she needed?"

"It's possible. But I was thinking. What if you were the one they wanted?"

"Me? I'm not sick!"

"That day when Emily went missing, before I introduced myself, I took your picture. I've been so afraid to show you." Mortimer reached into his pocket and pulled out his camera. The LCD screen on the back was already displaying the picture in question. It was Jenna and her mother standing in front of the founder's statue. Behind Jenna's head was a bright light illuminating it like a halo. A stark white grinning skull was imposed over her face.

"How old do you have to be," asked Mortimer, "before you're too old to die young?"

THE TREE WHISPERER

JOHN TURNEY

The sycamore tree, growing in the park near the riverbank in Graves Grove, had lived in my memory since...well, before my first memory. I've both hated and loved that tree. And feared it.

Standing under it in the spring as the leaves unfurled, in the summer in its cooling shade, in the autumn as it changed into its beautiful foliage, and in the winter with its bare limbs like black snakes reaching for the lowering snow clouds comforted me. That's why I loved it.

But who can forget the disappearances? Every family in town had experienced a loss. Every class a few schoolmates. Every hockey team, a winger or a center. No generation had passed unscathed. At every wedding or every funeral, people whispered of the missing. That's why I fear it.

You see, I'm one of the few who the tree sucked into its dark soul and returned alive. Returned at all. As survivor of the sycamore, the town of Graves Grove shunned me. Since then, the tree's consciousness lived in me, and that's why I hate it.

And now I'm going to kill it.

I put on my runners, grabbed my sharpened axe, and departed my log cabin. My home. It had been built in the bush by some mountain man. He married into the Blackfeet tribe. A Siksika girl. He settled here to hunt beavers and deer in the 1830s, some fifty years before Samuel Graves arrived. The only thing Graves and his followers found was the log cabin and the belongings. No sign of human life. Or death. It's rumored that they found two plates of an unfinished meal. Moldy and decayed…yet there.

Somehow, that cabin had never deteriorated. In fact, during my two decades living there, rooms have been built. Repairs made. By themselves. Overnight.

First time it happened, I woke in the morning to find a brand new porch with a roof covering and three rocking chairs.

Standing at the door, I scratched my thatch of hair and said, "Dag. I got me a new porch and three rockers. But I only need one." Ma always said I was the observant one. "I need me some coffee." A double-double.

Sometimes, two of them rocking chairs started rocking back and forth all by their lonesome. I've refused to sit in them chairs. Funny thing, they never rocked when Avalean Harper visited to do an article on the self-rocking rocking chairs for the town newspaper. I think she's the only Grovian who hasn't been witness to it. Makes her mad. I think it's funny.

But I digress, heh.

With my axe on my shoulder, I strode up Main Street keeping my gaze focused on that tree in the old school park. Though it has no eyes—naturally, for that's the way the good Lord designed trees—I still felt its malevolent gaze upon me.

I passed the "Welcome to Graves Grove" sign and marched a couple of blocks, never taking my gaze from the tree. Then I glanced sideways and saw I was still passing that welcome sign. Despite walking for a minute or two, I hadn't moved forward a bit. I felt like such a puck bunny.

"So you want to play mind games, heh," I said to the tree.

I stopped in the town square and stared up at the statue of Samuel Graves. Today the statue wore a bronze frontier uniform, complete with bronze raccoon cap. Looks more dignified than last week's clown outfit. If that Harper harpy was a real newsbunny, she'd find out who kept changing the statue's outfits.

"Why did you have to plant that Newf tree, you hoser?" I yelled at Graves.

The statue refused to answer. It doesn't even blink. Though some people said it does.

My shout must have carried far and broad, for Avalean Harper and Agnes Borkman raced out of Grovey Chops, the hair salon. I pictured them as two mutton chops. Moses Mackenzie pulled up in his truck and parked in front of the postal. He unfolded out of the pickup like human origami. I didn't see his pink faced girlfriend, Maggie. She was probably stealing flowers from the graveyard. Clancy Harrington, the butler at the Tudor mansion, strutted out of the General Store and made his way over. Grady Gravis and several others hurried from the Feed Supply. Others found their way to the town square. Everyone whispered questions about what was going on. We were having a regular hi-yu.

Mamie Rue, dressed in her shabby harvest gold dress and pushing that worn-out pram, sang an out of tune lullaby to the picnic basket she kept in it.

"Baby of mine, cry while you sleep. Never again to make a peep. Have no worry, don't you see. Sleep forever underneath the tree." Same words as always. Same screech.

Copper, the russet mutt, weaved a path through the forest of human legs and stopped at my feet. "Well, Copper, old boy," I said and bent over to pat his head. "You a good puppy."

Copper walked over to the statue, hiked its leg, and peed.

"Well done. Go on now, take off," I told Copper. "You've done your job quite right."

As the dog disappeared back into the leg forest, a town's constable pushed his way through the crowd. I watched his head and shoulders bob above the hi-yu. We called him Timmy because he loved Timmy Horton donuts. "Excuse me. Pardon. Sorry," he said in a continual flow of words. Timmy wore a red tuque with a white ball of wool on its crown.

"What's up?" he asked when he stood in front of me.

"I'm going to cut down that tree for once and for all," I answered.

He remained silent a moment, his eyes revealing his concentration of thoughts, then laughed. "You're way too."

"No he's not," Clancy said. "He's got him an axe."

For emphasis, I waved the steel head in front of Timmy's face.

"That blasted sycamore has done more harm," I said to the constable, "to this town than a team of hosers eating Kentucky birds. I'm going to cut it down and let the river take it away, heh."

"I shan't allow it," said Timmy. "It's public property and under the control of the town."

"Bugger off, Tim. No more children have to go missing."

I marched through the park and over to the tree.

Half the crowd followed with cheers of support. The other half followed with jeers of detraction. I couldn't have cared less. That tree was coming down. Today. Now.

Resting the axe against my legs, I spat into my hands and rubbed them together. Picking up the axe, I took some practice swings and then stepped up. I sighted where I wanted my first cut, reared back, and swung that axe with all my might. I anticipated the impact of steel biting into wood, that vibration flowing up the axe handle to my arm and then my shoulders. The first satisfying whack.

Instead I missed, floundered more than a few steps, and fell face first into the river. Sputtering, I came out of the water. I wiped the wetness from my face. I couldn't believe it. I missed. I searched the ground around the tree. Where did my axe go?

My supporters yelled at the other half.

"Who stole his axe?"

"I bet that Maggie took it!"

"Where did that axe get to?"

My detractors yelled at my supporters.

"He didn't have an axe."

"Maggie's at the graveyard, she couldn't have taken it."

"I never saw no axe."

The two sides stood seconds from engaging in fisticuffs when I screamed, "The tree took my axe!" I pointed upward. One of its top branches, at the fork of several branches, clutched my axe.

Everyone shut up. Not a pie hole moved. Every head turned their gaze upon the tree. The evil tree that stole children. And axes. Don't forget the axes. A slow grumble started in the center of the crowd. No one knew who began. However, in seconds, everyone hurled curses at the sycamore.

I charged out of the river, swearing at the trunk. "I'm going to kill you," I yelled at it. "Cut you down. Tear out your roots. Burn you into a heap of ashes. And scatter you on the waters of this here river."

It must have been a sudden gust of wind, but a branch swept down and smacked me in the chest. I flew backwards into the water. I emerged a second time, spitting river water out of my mouth. No wind blew. The sycamore's branches remained as still as the dead.

Grady Gravis raised a fist. "To the Feed Store!" The rest of the hi-yu took up the chant. "To the Feed Store. To the Feed Store. To the Feed Store."

I stood in the waist deep water, shivering, hands to my sides. I raised one eyebrow at Grady's thought process. The tree tosses me into the water twice, and Grady incites the crowd to go to the Feed Store. What a hoser.

With the area deserted, except for Copper lying on the steps to the postal eating a discarded donut, the situation had devolved to the tree and me. Man versus the spooky tree. Man against haunted deciduous. Man against the scary sylvan. Man against…

Something bumped my leg under the water. Startled, I reached down and pulled out a branch, its bark a sodden black hue. Water dripped from it, forming little ringlets on the surface of the water. I tossed it out into the middle of the river, and it floated. Not downstream. But where it had splashed down. How could it float against the current? Something else struck my legs under water and wrapped around my legs and waist. The tip of a root emerged from the water and, I swear, it stared at me like a snake ready to strike.

The first branch now floated upriver. Toward me. A log diverted from the middle of the river toward the bank. Toward me. Its bark resembled crocodile hide.

Despite the branch getting too close for comfort, the log was the problem. It could do damage. It raced toward me. I had my hands out to push the log back out into the middle of the river when a bough from the first branch snatched one of my hands and wrenched it away. The log rammed into me, knocking me under the water. The roots that had my legs yanked them out from under me.

The murky water surrounded me in its chilled embrace. Looking upward, though the water stung my eyes, a watery image of the tree leaned over the water. Something moved, and I glanced downward to see more roots emerge from the river bottom.

The tree was trying to kill me!

I floundered, only in control of one arm. I tried to raise to the surface, but the log refused to move from overhead.

I kicked against the roots ensnaring my legs. When they loosened, I found my footing and stood. I managed a gasp of fresh air, when the log smashed into me again and knocked me under water. I jerked my arm free from the arborous grasp and came up for air.

"Get out of the water!" Constable Timmy said, standing at the river's edge. He pointed upriver. I followed to where he pointed and spotted a log jam coming downstream. Toward me, again. Wall to wall trees floating in the river.

No. They were moving faster than the current. I would be pulverized or drowned.

"Take my hand!" Timmy yelled.

I stretched out my hand to take his, and just as our palms met, the roots dragged me further into the river. I reached into the water and grabbed hold of a root and pulled it and twisted it this way and that. The root resisted my efforts, creating a curtain of splashing water. More roots snaked across the water toward me.

I heard shouts of, "Burn the tree! Burn the tree!"

I spotted a stream of people with flaming torches exiting the Feed store. Grady led the procession as they headed for the sycamore. When Grady reached the tree, he shoved his torch against the tree trunk. Others thrust their torches against the tree.

The roots released my legs.

With that moment of freedom, I looked upriver.

The log jam pushed downriver at an alarming speed. I had to get out of the water immediately.

A wind—I'll never know if the tree created it or if it rushed down from the surrounding mountains—stirred up the branches and knocked aside the tree's tormentors.

I had just scrambled out of the water when Grady crashed into me. We both went into the water. I surfaced, spitting mad and sick and tired of being thrown into the river. Nasty, grimy river water. Cold, gross—

"Get out of there now!" Timmy yelled.

The log jam picked up speed.

Grady's head poked out of the water. His eyes had a glazed look and a bleeding gash decorated his forehead. I grabbed him by the collar and ran against the pull of the water. Making headway proved to be a slow process.

"Here." Timmy held out his hand again.

I grabbed it, and he pulled us from the river just as the front of the log jam swept past. And then stopped. And floated against the river flow.

Those whom the tree had knocked aside had regained their feet. They stared at their smoldering torches. Murmurs and curses against the tree filled the air like the hum of electricity.

I stepped between the sycamore and the crowd. In my mind, it whispered something ugly. It said the regrettable was about to burst forth. What, I didn't know. The tree never said. But I had to stop it.

I waved my hands for attention. "Listen. Hey, listen up, will you? I hate this tree. It's been the scourge of this town since old man Graves planted it. I tried to kill it today. But I realize it can't be killed."

"Why should we listen to you, heh?"

"Yeah, you survived the tree. My boy didn't."

Mutterings of agreement swirled through the crowd.

"Look, I tried to kill it. But it fought back. It fought back. It nearly killed me. This tree will do whatever it takes to survive. You continue this madness and people will get hurt bad. Real bad. Just…just…go back to what you were doing and forget this ever happened."

Copper marched straight up to the tree and yelped at it for a good twenty seconds. He stared at it for several more. He hiked his leg and marked his territory at the base of the tree. But not on the tree. Copper never lifts a leg against the tree. Kind of reminds me of the Bible story where David dumps the water as an offering after his men braved occupied Bethlehem to fetch it for him. After scratching at the grass with his hind legs, Copper marched back to his spot in front of the postal.

With a few chuckles, the crowd dissipated.

I felt a hand clap me on the shoulder. I turned and saw Timmy standing beside me. His face lit up with his toothy smile.

"For a complete hoser, you done good," he said. "Getting the crowd under control like that was something else. So tell me, how did you know the tree was going to get hurtful? Did you just make that up to get folks to leave?"

I glanced over my shoulder and stared at the monstrosity. I met Timmy's stare.

"No," I said. "I didn't make it up. The tree…told me."

"So you've become a tree whisperer," he said in a mocking tone.

"Yeah. I guess I have. It's talking to me and what it has to say isn't nice. Graves Grove is in for some serious bad."

THE NEVER-ENDING CIRCLE OF LOVE

MATTHEW HOWE

Yeah, I was one of those kids. You know, the losers, the misfits, the ones who stood out in a crowd and caught all the crap from the good-looking and the popular.

I'll be honest. It bothered me. Oh, sure, I put up a good front with the eye-makeup and blood-red lipstick, the hair dyed jet black, the punk t-shirts and all those endless birds I flipped, but inside it hurt. Because inside I wondered if maybe they were right, all those kids who picked on me. Maybe I was just some freak loser. A lack of self-confidence, no matter how well you hide it, is like rust. It eats away from the inside until one day everything collapses.

So that's where I was, in a state of advanced emotional rust, when I met Chad.

It was in the library, where I hung out a lot after school. Mostly nerds hung out in the library, and nerds left you alone. That was one of my survival rules.

I knew something was different the second I walked in. Everyone was gathered in groups, talking and looking at the east corner of the main floor where there's a little display of graphic novels and some comfy chairs for reading.

Well, all that had been pushed aside to make room for lights and a camera. Someone was filming something.

I'm the curious type, so I walked over to have a look. Maisie Chambers was standing by the Fiction A-E shelf, watching the goings on. Just that morning, Maisie had called me a "walking freakshow" and "the girl most likely to eat a baby." But this new turn of events was so shocking that she seemed to have forgotten that, not to mention all the years she'd piled shit on me, and actually spoke to me like a person.

"Can you believe it?" she asked. "Someone's shooting a TV show!"

"In Graves Grove? Why?" I asked.

"Ghosts," came the reply. But not from Maisie. I turned and I saw him. Chad. I'd like to say that a beam of sun through the high windows hit him in the back of the head and lit him up like an angel, but that didn't happen. He was just standing under the crappy fluorescents. Didn't matter. He was still a god.

Maybe 21, 22 years old, just a few years older than me. Almost two meters tall, thin, but you could tell he was muscular. He was wearing Doc Martens, skinny jeans, a black t-shirt and a black denim vest over that, even though it was hot as hell in the library. The vest had been hand-decorated with all sorts of patches for punk bands and obscure horror movies. I'm proud to say I knew most of them.

Chad's face was lean but sculpted. His hazel eyes blazed under his cap of brown hair. He was, honestly, the best-looking guy I'd ever seen.

And he'd just spoken to me.

"Ghosts?" I managed.

"We're with the show *Ghost Wranglers*."

"Never heard of it," Maisie said. She was looking at Chad like he was covered in dog shit. I could read it in her eyes: *great, another freak.*

"That's because it hasn't been on yet. This is the pilot."

"Oh, like the first show of the series," I said.

"Exactly." His smile lit up the room. "You know what a pilot is, cool."

I don't know what happened to me. Near I can describe it is the first time my older brother Billy, who is the wimp of all wimps, went hunting whitetail. He was up in my dad's tree stand and got a nice 8-pointer in his scope. Then his brain froze as he wondered if he had the guts to take the shot. Classic buck fever. His finger, though, his finger pulled the trigger without him even realizing it, and that buck was his.

Same thing happened to me, some primal instinct rose above my natural shyness, broke out of the coat of rust, and I stuck my hand out. "I'm Lisa," I said.

He shook it. His hand was smooth and cool in mine. I felt a tingle go up my arm like he was charged with electricity. "I'm Chad."

"What do you do on the show?" I asked.

"I'm a utility," he said. "I do a little bit of everything, carry the cases, set up the lights, reload the camera, dump the footage to the drives."

"Wow, that sounds like a lot," I said. I noticed Maisie staring at me like I'd grown horns. She backed away slowly and vanished around the shelf.

"It's hard work," he said.

"But is it fun?" It sounded like the best thing in the world to me.

"Sure. We've got a great crew, and I get to travel and hear all sorts of interesting stories. Hey, let me ask you something."

"Shoot," I said. I don't know how, but I was keeping the self-confident facade up.

"I was going out to get the crew some coffee. Is there good coffee in this town?"

I was going to tell him that you couldn't eat or drink in the library, then I realized they were TV people. Rules didn't apply to them. How cool was that?

"Good news is I'm the biggest coffee snob in town," I said. Which is true, by the way. "I know just the place."

"Okay, where is it?"

I took a breath, then a leap. "I'll show you," I said.

WE TALKED all the way up Hill Street to Shipps Hardware store. It was easy talk. The facade I'd put up in the library was crumbling, but it was a good crumble. Because what was underneath wasn't shame and terror, it was, well, me. It turned out I was a person who could carry on a conversation with a drop-dead gorgeous guy I'd met two minutes ago and who actually knew who *The Misfits* were. Chad wanted to know all about the town and, as it turned out, I knew a lot about the town. Eighteen years, you pick things up.

I pointed out the statue of Samuel Graves. "See that?" I asked.

"Yeah?"

"Town founder. Samuel Graves. He was known for his elaborate wardrobe."

"Wait," Chad said

"Wait what?"

"We came in last night. I saw that statue. Graves was wearing a tuxedo."

I nodded. The statue of Graves was now wearing a cowboy duster and what looked like blue jeans. "Yep. Statue changes its outfit every day."

"How?" he asked.

"No one knows."

"Impossible."

"This is Graves Grove. Weird crap happens. All the time."

"I like it. Maybe we can work this into the story. Tell me about this Graves guy."

So I did, the whole story of our town's mysterious founder, as we finished the walk to the hardware store, and I opened the door for him.

"I thought we were getting coffee?" he asked.

"We are."

"This is a hardware store."

I slapped him on the arm. Can you believe it? I, Lisa Foster, misfit of all misfits, queen of the outcasts, slapped a good-looking guy on the arm and laughed at him. Not a mean laugh mind you, what I'd call an... amused laugh. "I know it's a hardware store, silly, but like everything around here, it has a secret."

I led him inside.

"Is there a gimp in the cellar?" he asked.

"*Pulp Fiction*, the classics. Nice," I said. "No, no gimp. But this." We reached the back of the store. A *Mr. Coffee* machine that looked like it dated to the Jurassic sat on a rusting TV table. It held a pot of coffee. Next to it, paper cups and a bowl with a sign taped to it. "Coffee - 25 Cents."

"The best coffee in town?" Chad asked. "At the hardware store?"

I poured a cup, stuck it under his nose. "Smell," I said.

He smelled, and his face lit up.

"Mr. Shipps imports the beans. Roasts them and grinds them himself at home. Then puts out a pot for customers. Plus, he's the only place in town that doesn't serve coffee in styrofoam cups."

"I hate styrofoam," Chad said.

"No kidding. Now how many do we need?"

He thought. "Me, you, Deke and Paul."

I poured five.

"Why five?" he asked.

"Because after you finish this one, you'll want another. Trust me."

WE WALKED back to the library. On the way down the hill I saw Copper coming our way. He's the town mutt, cute as can be, but always in a rush, like he was late for class or something.

I knelt down. "Hey, Copper. Here Copper." Copper paused as if considering. Then he looked up at Chad, decided three was a crowd, and sped off.

"Cute dog," Chad said.

"You like dogs?"

"Naaa. I prefer cats." I didn't know what to say to that, unsure how anyone could prefer cats.

"So what else do you know about the town?" Chad asked. "Weird stuff, I mean." He grinned. I looked around and spotted Mamie Rue Le Doux. Graves Grove has a bunch of eccentric types, but she might be the nuttiest banana of the bunch. If that makes any sense.

"That's Mamie." She was down near the constable's office. She was in her warm weather getup, fraying gold dress and a rhinestone belt. She had a death-grip on the broken-down baby carriage she'd been pushing around town since before I was born.

"What's with the baby carriage?" Chad asked.

"Oh, her baby disappeared down by the river, long time ago. They never found him."

"By the river?"

"By the tree, to be exact. That big sycamore where the elementary school used to be. A lot of people think the tree is haunted. You know, in the 1920s the local accountant went nuts. He stole dynamite from the hardware store and tried to blow it up."

"Wow," Chad said. "Exciting."

Chad's cellphone buzzed. He checked the text. "They're almost ready to roll."

"We better hurry," I said.

"Naa, these are all second unit interviews. We'll only use a little of it. And Chris isn't even here yet."

"Chris?" I asked.

"Our producer who's over at the Historical Society doing research. No worries. Deke's not the brightest bulb in the basket, but he can handle this stuff."

Back at the library, no one seemed to mind when I hung around for the rest of the shoot. I even ran back up to Shipps when they ran out of coffee. I also policed up all the empty cups to keep the library staff happy. Not that they noticed, they were star-struck.

We interviewed Mrs. Hoffman, the librarian, and old Dan Jefferies, who was approaching ninety years old but was still sharp as a tack. All the questions were about ghosts and hauntings, anything weird that had gone on in Graves Grove. They had a lot to say.

It was a small crew. Paul was the oldest, a tall, thick guy who looked like he'd seen a lot of crazy shit in his day. He was the cameraman and also handled the lighting. Deke was in his mid-twenties, long hair, pale skin, drooping eyelids. He talked like a California surfer and yawned a lot. He was normally the sound guy, but also directed what he called "second unit." Chad kind of did everything else. "A glorified PA," he told me, as if that meant anything to me.

"Don't let Chad sell himself short," Paul said as he focused the camera. "He could do my job, Deke's job, anyone's job. Guy's got more skills than he lets on. Don't know why he even puts up with this shit."

Chad just smiled, kind of shy. A new side of him. It only made me fall for him that much harder.

WE "WRAPPED" around six. I helped them get the stuff packed back into the minivan they'd rented.

"Where's a good place to eat around here?" Paul asked.

"Best restaurant in town is the diner," I said.

"Coffee any good?" Chad asked.

"Not as good as Shipps. But not as bad as the muck they serve at the General Store."

"Diner it is," Paul said. "Hey, should we buy Lisa dinner for helping us out and stuff?"

"Great idea," Chad said. "Can you come?"

I almost told him I had to ask my parents. But I stopped myself. I wasn't going to ask my parents if I could go, I was going to tell my parents I was going. Or I was going to lie. Yeah. Lying sounded like the plan.

"Sure," I said.

PAULIE'S DINER was pretty crowded, but we found a corner booth in the back. I slid in first and almost melted when Chad slipped in next to me. We got our menus and ordered. As the waitress left, Chad nudged me.

"Hey," Chad said. "That lady is stealing mints."

I didn't have to look. "Pink cheeks? Curly hair? Late fifties, maybe?"

"Yeah," Chad said. "How'd you know?"

I looked over at the register. The diner had a bowl of those after dinner mints next to the register for customers to take on their way out. A woman who fit my description was spooning them into her coat pocket. After a second, she glanced around, picked the whole bowl up and dumped it in. "Maggie Pinker," I said. "Another one of our town's weirdos."

"You have a lot of weirdos in town?"

"Beside me, yes."

"You're not weird," Chad said. "Drop you in Williamsburg, you'd fit right in."

I'd heard of Williamsburg. Some really, really hip part of New York City. Wow.

I played it cool. "So what's this story you're following? I heard you taking about a ghost."

"Yeah, the Deakins Ghost. Back around 1940, a haunted well on the Deakins Farm."

I'd heard of it. Back just before the war, Farmer Deakins started hearing voices from the well. He claimed it was his long dead twin brother. More than a dozen people came out to visit, and all of them heard the voice. Some of them even saw a hazy figure floating above the well. It was warning Deakins not to join the army. He did. Became a paratrooper and died jumping into occupied France on D-Day.

"It's a good story," Chad said.

"One thing this town has, lots of good scary stories."

Deke perked up. "Like what?"

"Well, there's the statue that always changes clothes. Chad saw that. There's been a lot of…" I don't know why, but I lowered my voice. "A lot of people, kids I mean, disappearing."

"Woah, that sucks," Deke said.

"Then there's the spirit cow of Knob Street."

"A ghost cow?" Chad asked, eyes lighting up. I could see he dug this stuff.

"And the demon of Loon Lake."

"Demon?" Deke asked.

"Yeah." This was one of the more obscure legends. I only knew about it because I'd seen a story while going through back issues of the *Graves Grove Gabbler*, our local paper, for a school project. The local priest had a vision about the demon, knew the exact spot where it lay, and demanded the mayor build a giant Tesla coil to disrupt the lines of magnetic force that were feeding it. A few weeks later they had to call the men in the white coats to take him away. Another Graves Grove nutjob. "Supposedly the whole town was built to worship this demon. It sleeps under Loon Lake, but even asleep, it can work strange magic. It's the demon's power that brought wealth to a lot of the old time big-wigs in town, like Graves. Some people even think that's where all those missing kids go, a sacrifice to the demon."

"Why kids?" Deke asked.

Paul snorted. "'Cause they're virgins, dummy."

Deke shook his head. "That's all BS, dude."

"Excuse me?" Paul said.

"The whole virgin sacrifice thing. That was the church, man, they got everyone convinced you had to sacrifice virgins to Satan and demons and stuff just so that would make it harder on the devil worshippers. Virgins are hard to find, bro. Even in those days. But if you look it up, you'll see most demons feed on life force. Innocence, guilt, don't matter, man. And here's the thing." He leaned closer. He smelled like incense. "I did all this research. Most of the sacrifices were like volunteers. 'Cause when you allow a demon to feed on your life essence, your soul is rewarded in the afterworld. An eternity of decadence. Who wouldn't dig that?"

We all looked at him. His face did this strange transition, his lips thinning, then twitching, then he lost it. Laughing. "Oh shit, man, I totally had you. I had you."

We all laughed along with him. "I shoulda known it was crap when he said he did research," Paul said. "Only thing Deke researches is where the best weed in town is."

Deke perked up. "Where is the best weed in town?" he asked.

"I don't know," I said. "I don't touch that shit."

Chad looked down at me. "Really?"

I took a second. Had I just blown it? "Really," I said.

"That is so cool," he said.

I met his eyes and I almost drowned in them.

And then the voice of doom.

No, not my mother who I'm sure would have embarrassed me mercilessly. Worse.

"There you are." It was a low voice, silky, smooth, and absolutely brimming with cool.

We all turned to look, like someone had rung a bell. She stood in the doorway. She was in her late twenties. Blonde. The face of an angel. Athletic body mostly thin but padded in all the right places. Glowing blue eyes.

The producer. Chris. Only Chris wasn't Christopher. Kris was Kristen.

"I've been looking all over town for you." She walked over to the table. Her eyes fell on me. "Oh, hi."

Paul introduced us. Chad, I couldn't help notice, was too busy staring at Kris. "Kris, this is Lisa. She's been helping out."

"Found us some awesome bean water, man. Like Seattle level good," Deke said.

Kris held out her hand. I took it, shook. Her hand was warm, skin smooth, her grip firm. I could sense how strong she was. This was a gal who worked out. "May I join you?"

Chad practically shot from the booth. He grabbed a chair from an empty table and dragged it over.

Then he sat in it. "You can have the booth, Kris. I know you like the booth."

She turned those eyes on him. "Thanks, Chad," she said, and got in next to me.

Now it was Chad who was practically melting.

The waitress brought our food. Too bad. I felt kind of sick.

We sat and I did my best to pretend everything was cool. But it wasn't cool. I was crushed. What had I been thinking? That Chad, this awesome guy who worked for a TV show was going to fall in love with some drippy loser who lived in a haunted backwater? It was just a stupid schoolgirl fantasy. Chad was obviously in love with Kris.

It was obvious, the way he laughed too loud at her jokes (which were always funny, goddamn her), the way he wouldn't take his eyes off her, the way he lunged over the table when she asked if someone could pass the ketchup.

So yeah, it sucked. Until I started to notice something else. Kris. Kris didn't seem to notice the vibe he was sending her way. Or didn't care.

Kris, I realized with growing excitement, just wasn't into him.

I read the blog once about the Never-Ending Circle of Love. The theory goes like this: everyone is standing in a big circle. Everyone is in love with the person in front of them, who is in love with the person in front of them, and so on and so on. The trick is to get the person in front of you to turn around.

That weird instinct rose up in me again. I didn't want to quit. I wanted to fight. I was going to get Chad to turn around.

Which is what led to all the horror and screaming and...well, we'll get there when we get there.

WE FINISHED dinner, and on the way out to the parking lot, I asked if I could help out the next day, after school. Kris wasn't sure, but Paul and Deke talked her into it. Why wouldn't they? Those cases they lugged around were heavy, and an extra set of hands had to be welcome.

Kris said she might be able to find some money to pay me. I told her not to worry about it, I was enjoying it.

But in truth, a plan was forming. It was simple. Get close to her. Find out everything I could about her. A girl like Kris had to have a boyfriend. Or a girlfriend. Or whatever. I had to get her talking about her significant other, in front of Chad, to shut him down. Make him realize he didn't have a chance with her, and maybe understand that the girl for him was right here in Graves Grove.

And if my plan didn't work, I could always feed her to the goddamn sycamore.

THEY WERE shooting at the General Store the next day, and I swear I got there five minutes after the final bell rang. I did whatever I could to help out. I made sure I was super-helpful to Kris, doing my best to engage her, hoping she'd let something slip that I could use to reality-check Chad.

I got nothing.

She was friendly, funny, professional, and gracious. But a stone wall on her personal life.

Which sucked, because while a tiny piece of me was wondering that if she happened to mysteriously disappear, would anyone look harder for her than they had for all those kids who'd vanished over the years, the other part of me was really starting to like her. This was a seriously cool girl. This was the kind of person every girl wanted to be.

After the General Store we went to the office of the *Gabbler* to interview the editor, Mrs. Harper. As the team set up, Kris asked to see the back issues of the newspaper. There was some event going all the way back to the turn of the century she was interested in.

Mrs. Harper, who I could see was flattered beyond belief (and who'd broken her "every Thursday at 11" visit to the hair salon so she could have it redone that afternoon) showed Kris where the stacks were (yes, stacks. Microfilm hasn't made it to the *Gabbler* yet. Not to mention scanning and digital archiving) and set her loose. Which was weird, because whenever someone had to do a research project in the stacks, Mrs. Harper watched them like a starving turkey vulture watches a wounded squirrel.

I helped the guys set up, throwing looks back into the archives every once in a while. The copy machine was out of order, so Kris was just taking iPhone photos of everything she was interested in.

The interview went fine, for them. Me? I got nothing. Kris was a wall of grace and professionalism, goddamn her.

I'll admit it. I was getting desperate. And a little angry. I finally meet a guy who seemed to like me for me, and he had to be in love with this angel.

I realized I had to up my game. Do something big. So when they said they were going out for a quick bite after we wrapped, I begged off and said I had homework.

I did have homework, but screw that, I was on a mission.

After they headed off for the diner, I sent my parents another in a long string of lie-texts, telling them I'd be out until around 10.

Then I grabbed my bike and pedaled across town to the Grove Inn where they were all staying.

What I was planning was pretty crappy, but I had to act. Who knew how long these guys were going to be in town for, and with Kris around, Chad barely seemed to know I was there.

I had a secret weapon. An awful secret weapon. But I was sick of being the one who always lost. And I'd kind of gotten all caught up in this game. So I went for it.

See, I'd worked at the Inn over the summer, cleaning rooms. I knew the layout of the place.

I also knew Mrs. Kozalski, who had the night shift, always fell asleep in her office. That left the registration desk wide open.

I have to say, it was easier than I thought it would be. I biked up to the Inn, parked out back, crept in through the service entrance, and down the main hall to the front desk. The registration ledger was right there, and I flipped through it 'til I saw what room Kris was in.

202. Perfect.

Back outside, I scaled the elm in the back yard, crawled out on one of the bigger branches, and made the jump to the roof without a sound. Freaking Batman.

Then I crept across the roof to the dormer outside room 202 and waited. I didn't have to wait long. Must have been a short dinner. The minivan pulled into the front parking lot, and I heard them talking and laughing as they went up to their rooms.

I got low and crept as close to Kris' window as I could. My idea was simple. When was a woman most likely to make contact with a significant other? Right before bed, right? She'd come home from dinner, get the phone out, make a few personal calls, then hit the hay. I'd be there to intercept it. If I could just get a name, I could weasel something out of her the next day. Find out who this significant other was, then get her talking. Talking a lot. With Chad present.

Okay, dumb plan. I know. But like I said, I was desperate.

I listened carefully as she came in, said goodbye to the others, closed the door. Then nothing. Just the sounds of her shuffling around the room. The little knocks as she threw her possessions down on the table. A squeak as she sat on the bed.

Come on, I thought. *Call. Call someone.*

Then I heard it. A buzz. I recognized it right off. She'd just gotten a text message. I was praying it was: *miss you sweetie, call me right away.*

As quietly as I could, I crept around the edge of the dormer so I could peek into the room.

Kris had her back to me, her phone in her hands, reading some message.

She nodded. Hit a few keys. Making a call. She lifted the phone to her ear. "Okay, Chad. It's on. Your dreams are about to come true."

Oh, shit.

"Meet me outside. Now. And tell Deke we're going."

She hung up, then ripped open the closet and yanked out a bag. She zipped it open, looked inside, I couldn't see, closed it, grabbed her jacket, and went out the door.

I crawled along the roof, quietly until I could look down on the back lot to get a sense of where they were going.

As I watched, Chad and Deke emerged from the Inn and stood out front, waiting. Both of them carried duffle bags as well. Kris came out a moment after.

But they didn't get in the minivan, they circled around the back of the Inn.

I shrank back, hiding in the shadows.

Kris dug in her bag, found something. A flashlight. The beam stabbed through the dark. She walked to the woods bordering the Inn's yard, swung it back and forth. "Here," she said.

My heart sank. Her beam revealed a path. I knew where that path led. To a rocky lookout high over a scenic lake. It was a popular spot for couples on the weekend, if you know what I mean. If they were going up there at night, then it looked like maybe Chad had won and was going to get his wish. Maybe he'd drugged her at dinner, used hypnotic suggestion, but something was up. The look on his face told me everything. I've never seen someone so excited.

Well, except for Deke, because he was tagging along, too. That was kind of weird, right? If those two were going up to the lookout to do what I thought they were going to do, why was Deke going with them?

Call me crazy, call me sick, but I was going to find out.

As soon as they were a ways down the path, I climbed down the tree and went after them.

I followed, quiet and slow. I wanted to turn back a hundred times. I didn't want to see what I knew I was going to see. But I had to. It's hard to explain. But I was riding a freight train. What's that they say about teenagers and their raging hormones? My hormones weren't only raging, they were breaking dishes and throwing TVs out hotel windows. Punk rock chaos, all the way.

Which, I guess, is why I did what I did.

After maybe half an hour I began to close on them. They'd already made it to the overlook and gotten busy. I could hear them up ahead, low moaning sounds, see a soft, warm glow. I was grossed out, but I had to know.

So I crept closer. They were out in the clearing on the overlook. The overlook was a big chunk of rock that poked out over the lake, the water maybe thirty meters below.

There were some trees between me and them. I snuck even closer, peered through the leaves, and I saw them. First Deke. Laid out on a big rock. Naked except for a white cloth wrapped around his waist. He was grinning like an idiot. And he was surrounded by candles.

That was kind of a surprise.

Then Kris stepped into view. She was wearing a long, translucent robe. And paint. Lots of paint. Her body was covered in paint, all these weird symbols. Chad was right behind her, dressed kind of the same, paint and all. It was some kind of crazy freak sex show you might see on HBO if my parents would let us get HBO.

Only it wasn't moans I'd heard, it was some kind of weird chant Kris was doing.

And then I heard a low rumble, from the distance.

And then I saw the knife Kris was holding. It wasn't just any knife. It was old, ancient. I could see how dull and pitted the steel was, except for the edge which glowed like a laser. She was chanting over it. Chanting over Deke.

"Are you sure this is the exact spot?" Deke said. "If we get this wrong…"

Kris shushed him.

"I want eternal debauchery," he whispered.

Chad leaned down to him. "It's the right spot, these are the exact map coordinates, the professor confirmed what Kris found in that old paper, now shut up."

Deke shut up. He leaned back, a huge smile on his face.

Kris chanted over the knife.

That weird rumble grew louder. Mixed with it, a kind of sloshing noise. Like…

Oh, shit. Like water. Like something coming up from really, really deep in the water. Like a big fish, or a whale.

Or a demon.

The path to the lake. Loon Lake. This was Loon Lake. The goddamn demon of Loon Lake. In a flash, I knew. It was real. The demon was real, and these idiots weren't here to film a reality show, they were here to summon the damned thing. They hadn't been trying to solve the mystery of the Deakins Ghost, they'd been looking for an excuse to get at Mrs. Harper's archives and locate the convergence of magnetic force or what the hell ever it was you needed to summon a demon.

Kris ended her chant as the rumble grew. She switched to English. "Oh master, Agaraoth, heed my call. Take the sacrifice of this willing servant as our offering. Drink of his life essence, and use his power to rise from your watery sleep and reclaim what is yours."

Chad picked up the invocation. "Let the two of us, your faithful servants, be your guides and your familiars on your earthly trek. Bestow the glory of your grace and power upon us."

The rumble was even louder, and I heard something else, kind of a roar, like a million pissed off lions.

Kris and Chad spoke as one. Kris raised the knife high. "For yours is the power and the glory and may you reign a thousand..."

Then Kris stopped chanting. She dropped the knife and started screaming. And why not? She'd fallen off the overhang behind her. Well, not fallen, exactly. I don't remember doing it, but I'd lunged from my hiding place and, well, sort of pushed her over the edge. Her scream didn't last long. It ended on a high note, a roar, then a kind of horrible crunching sound that I wish I could forget ever hearing.

Chad spun on me. "Lisa? Lisa, what did you do?"

"Oh, shit!" Deke said, sitting up. "You pushed her. You pushed her off the freaking cliff, man!"

Chad was furious, sputtering. "You stupid little bitch. You stupid loser, freak bitch, *what did you do?"*

"She was trying to summon a demon," I yelled back.

"In case you missed it, I'm trying to summon a demon," he said. He reached down, grabbed the knife where Kris had dropped it. Uh-oh.

"Guys, what do we do?" Deke was panicking.

Chad eyed me, holding the knife "We can still do this. We've said most of the invocation. I know the rest, but the killing blow, it has to be a woman, Lisa."

"Hell, yeah," Deke said. He laid himself back down, adjusted his loin cloth.

"Lisa, I need you to kill Deke," Chad said.

"And fast," Deke said.

"Kill him? Why?"

"Because if you do, the Great Agaraoth will be freed from his prison and once again rule this sphere. We will reign as king and queen, immortal, all powerful. You and me, Lisa. Together. For eternity."

I have to admit, that didn't sound so terrible.

For me, anyway.

"But what about them?"

"Who?"

I pointed south. "Graves Grove, the rest of the world."

Deke spoke up. "Eaten or enslaved, take your pick."

The rumbling was louder.

Chad took my hand. Held it in his. "We'll rule, together. The world will be ours." He fell to his knees. "I'm sorry I called you a freak, Lisa, you're not a freak. You're the coolest girl I've ever met. I know you've been picked on, I used to get picked on. But those people, the ones who tormented you, you'll watch them burn."

Maisie Chambers. Burning. That sounded…all right.

"Guys, do something," Deke said.

"Please, Lisa. Do it for me." I felt something in my hand. Something warm that suddenly squirmed to follow the contours of my palm. I looked down. The knife.

And I felt it then. The power. The knife wasn't just a knife, it was a connection point between worlds or something. I could feel the vibrations of a thousand other dimensions pulsing in that thing. And I saw a vision. I saw Chad and me, laughing while cities burned. Kissing while continents sank into a fiery abyss. Dancing while the world screamed.

The rumbling was louder. I stood up.

"Would someone just please stab me?" Deke screamed.

Chad took my face in his hands. "Do it for us," he whispered. Then he leaned forward to kiss me.

Look, since you haven't been eaten by a demon or enslaved you can guess what I did next. Before his lips touched mine, I did stab. Not Deke. Chad. I stabbed Chad, the man I thought I'd loved, right in the heart.

There was no resistance as the blade went in, no blood, because the knife seemed to absorb it. Only a weird popping sound. His eyes widened. "No." He staggered back toward the edge.

"Maisie's an asshole," I said. "But she doesn't deserve to burn."

And I pushed him. Off the goddamn cliff.

He screamed. Like with Kris, it cut off pretty fast. And there was a roar. Then that crunching and…forget it. I don't want to talk about it.

Deke jumped up. "What did you? What did you do…" He ran to the edge, and I didn't have to push, because he jumped. He didn't scream on the way down, he was shouting. "Wait, Agaraoth, wait, I'm coming, my master…"

More crunching. Then that roar got loud. Really loud. I looked down and I saw something coming out of the water.

I turned away.

I only heard the slosh, but I felt it, felt the air moving as something huge pressed up out of the water behind me, towering over the overlook. I felt the air grow warm, and you know the way you can tell if someone is standing behind you in the dark? I felt that, only magnified a billion times.

But I didn't look. Wouldn't look. I was just praying I wasn't too late. That I hadn't screwed up and summoned the thing by accident anyway.

There was a sound, a squishy squirming sound like a million wet snakes being stirred in a basket. I didn't want to know what was making that sound.

I heard a breath. A single, huge breath that sounded like the gasp of a steam engine. Then another sound, like a hurricane only wetter. And then I felt that huge presence suddenly vanish behind me.

I counted to five, turned, and peered over the edge.

The surface of Loon Lake was a swirling whirlpool, a reverse tornado made of water. As I watched, something big, black and squirming vanished down that whirlpool. I didn't see much of it, but I saw its eyes. I'll never forget its eyes. Its thousands of glowing eyes.

And then it was gone.

I just stood there, a long time, watching as the waters of the lake calmed.

Then I took a look around. The candles were still burning. I snuffed them out.

They'd left their duffle bags and clothes strewn around the overhang. I picked it all up, I hate litter, and carried it back to town. I tossed it all in the dumpster behind the Inn, got on my bike, pedaled home, kissed my mom and dad, and went to sleep.

When I woke up next morning, everything was different. I don't know how to explain it. I'd lost my first true love, but I'd saved the world. Kind of by accident, but I'll still take it. As I walked up to school, past all the knots of jocks and popular kids, I knew. Inside. That if it wasn't for me, they'd all be demon food.

I bumped into Maisie Chambers by the front door. I saw her get ready to say something mean. Then she looked in my face. The insult dried up in her throat.

"Good morning, Maisie," I said.

"Morning, Lisa," she managed, then hurried off.

Something had changed. The rust was gone and everyone, with that weird teenage radar, seemed to know it.

Annie Watson asked if she could sit with me at lunch.

Billy Madsen offered to share his English notes with me.

I got picked third for the kickball team in gym. Third. What the hell.

I walked home with a couple of other kids going that way.

When I got back to my room, I saw a text. It was from Paul. He wanted to know if I'd seen any of the others on the crew. I texted back. Nope. Weird, right?

Then I went in the bathroom and took all my makeup off. The lipstick, the eyeshadow and liner. All of it.

Because what the hell, maybe Chad had turned out to be a demon-worshipping douche-bag who was trying to destroy the world, but he'd shown me who I really was. What I really was.

Cool. Cool as hell.

Lisa, the demon slayer.

SHADOW HAUNTINGS

SEASON 12, EPISODE 14: THE MURDER OF ARCHIE LE DOUX

MACKENZIE FLOHR

GRAVES GROVE
2017

Slowly letting out a deep breath, I attempt to calm my nerves. I can see a russet mutt running towards the park in the distance after what appears to be nothing, barking happily along the way. I turn and exchange glances between my camera crew and my investigative colleague, Jeremy Godfrey, who are too distracted taking bets on how long it will take Jeremy to freak out on camera again to notice the dog's odd behavior.

My heart is racing, and sweat is forming on my palms. It's not hot outside, and I've been on hundreds, maybe thousands of investigations before. However, something's not right. I don't know how or why, but I can feel it.

My attention turns to a woman with graying mouse brown hair curled into a messy bun with ringlets at her temples, wearing a shiny harvest gold A-line dress with a frayed hem and rhinestone belt. She pushes what looks like a moth-eaten pram, its wheels squeaking and thudding like a gurney in an asylum. It sounds like she is talking to the pram, but what she is saying is incomprehensible.

Yes, I conclude to myself. *There's something very wrong about this place.*

My name is Gavin Presley. I'm the lead investigator for the paranormal group, *Shadow Hauntings*, located just outside Vancouver, British Columbia. I've been seeking answers about the dead ever since I was freshman in high school. Those personal experiences still haunt me to this day.

It all started with residual green flashing lights, which would fill my entire apartment nearly every night for a few seconds around midnight. I thought I was going crazy so I even invited some friends over, not disclosing to them what I had seen, until they saw it themselves when we were chatting one night on the balcony. I never was able to figure out where they came from.

Shortly afterward, I became an insomniac. It would be a school night, two or three in the morning, and I would be tossing and turning in my bed, unable to sleep. I kept feeling like something was watching me, and every now and then I would catch what sounded like papers rattling in my room and someone typing on my computer keyboard. A few times I purposely left Microsoft Word open, hoping I would wake up the next morning to see a message from whatever was trying to get my attention—only nothing ever appeared, until one night.

I had a dream where I had been on a paranormal investigation, and a demon had followed me home. I jumped awake with a start, feeling like something had scratched me. I reached behind my shoulder and felt something stinging. Then, as I looked in front of me, I screamed. A man hung from the ceiling, surrounded by flames. The smell of burning flesh filled my nostrils, and I swear I could hear the entity say to me, "Beware of fire," before it vanished.

A month later, the building containing my apartment burned to the ground. Bad wiring is what had been stated on the official report, but my mind was convinced otherwise. I made it my mission in life to find out what it was that I saw, and if possible, to someday see it again.

So, here we are, after filming eleven paranormal seasons, about to investigate a small town called Graves Grove. The town is shrouded in mystery, unsolved crimes, and intrigue. It's located in British Columbia, where there have been reports of the residents hearing children laughing on the grounds where an abandoned school stands in sagging ruins, and a bronze statue of the town's founding father changing attire with no explanation.

We'll be starting with our walkthrough of the town with Mrs. Avalean Harper, Editor-in-Chief of the town newspaper, *Graves Grove Gabbler*, and president of the Graves Grove chapter of the National Arbor Society. I've been warned not to overstep my ground; that she's an authoritative figure, and if she yells, her voice carries across town.

When we first greet Mrs. Harper in the Constable's office, her appearance is intimidating. She is a very heavy set woman with large buttocks that stick out and over accentuates her body's girth in a non-flattering way. Her brown eyes feel piercing and look accusing. Her short hair has turned completely gray. I imagine in an alternate universe she would have been a terrifying disciplinarian.

Once the camera is rolling, I reach out my hand in introduction.

"Hello, I'm Gavin," I start, feeling my hand getting crushed during her handshake. I gesture with my free hand. "And this is Jeremy, my co-investigator. Please, tell us about this place."

"Certainly." Mrs. Harper smiles. "Graves Grove was established in 1880 by a man named Samuel Madsen Graves, claiming to be from the Chesapeake Bay area of Virginia. No one knows of his true origins or even if that was his real name, for when some followers later went to Virginia to pay homage, no one had heard of his existence.

"It is said he arrived in Graves Grove with a small band of followers from the east. Some believe he may have created a new identity for himself in order to flee a previous crime in the United States; others believe he was just looking for a place to start his life over. Samuel remained in Graves Grove until his death in 1930, passing away in his sleep. Some believe he still wanders the area where he planted a sycamore tree himself when the town was founded in 1880, while others believe all of his secrets, including his identity, have been lost forever."

"I see. We'll make sure to check it out during the night hours. What's with all the photographs?" I ask, looking around, rubbing my hand over my sore one. The walls are plastered with photographs of children.

"These are all the children who have been reported missing since 1895. The Constable refuses to take down any photograph of a missing child until he or she is found."

"Wow," I utter, mesmerized. The photographs have to be layered over each other at least a centimeter thick, and I find the different dress attires pictured over the years fascinating. Some of these children have been dead for over a hundred years, yet their photographs remain on the wall as if time has never passed.

"No one knows why so many children went missing over the years. There have been theories, but none of them have been proven true."

"How many children have been reported missing?" I question.

"At least three hundred, maybe more."

"And the children were never found?" I ask.

"No," Mrs. Harper responds.

"Seriously?" I say with disbelief. I glance over to the camera and speak. "Tonight during our investigation, we're going to find out what happened to these children."

"One of the most particular cases was the disappearance of Mamie Rue Le Doux's one-year-old son, Archie," she begins, handing me a photograph of a young boy—apparently she has fully prepared herself for every eventuality in this interview. "The *Gabbler* covered the case. Mamie gave birth to the boy in the summer of 1984. In the fall of 1985, she and her husband, Virgil Le Doux, mayor at the time, decided to go out for a picnic in the shade of Samuel Graves's sycamore tree. Young

Archie was jumping in heaps of fallen leaves and climbing over sycamore roots while Virgil and Mamie were discussing their grocery list. They got into a heated argument. Mamie decided to leave, shoved the list into the picnic basket, and placed the basket in the pram. When she turned for Archie, he was gone."

"What happened to him?"

Avalean shrugs. "The boy was never found. Virgil ended up passing from grief. Mamie is still alive, living in the Tudor style home built by Samuel Graves, alone, except for her butler, Clancy Harrington. No one dares to go there. Rumors have been spreading that tormented voices can be heard from the house at night. Mamie walks around town every day, wearing the same clothing she wore that day, pushing the pram and talking to it as if she were talking to Archie like nothing ever happened."

"Jesus!" I exclaim, handing her back the photograph. "I saw that woman earlier outside." I brush my hands through my short brown hair. "If there's anything we accomplish tonight, it's to end this woman's endless suffering and find out what happened to her son."

I TAKE a seat against the trunk of Samuel Graves's sycamore tree. I want to show respect, but at the same time, if he is still here, I can think of no other way than literally sitting on him. I set the sb7 spirit box, which allows shadow people to communicate with the living using real words.

"Samuel Graves, are you here with us tonight?" I begin. "I've been informed this name may be an alias. Can you tell me if that was your real name?"

"Shh," Jeremy says, putting his hand out, his eyes wide. "Did you just hear that?"

"Hear what?" I ask.

"Dude! I swear I just heard a child laughing," Jeremy says.

I decide to change my focus. "Is one of the missing children here with us right now?"

We wait, hearing just static sounds coming from the sb7 spirit box.

"Can you tell us what happened to you?"

"Die," a robotic voice answers.

"Die!" Jeremy gasps. "It just said die!"

"Who killed you?" I question, undeterred.

"Man."

"What?" I say, looking up at Jeremy for help, unable to understand.

"I think he's saying man?"

"How did you die?"

"Bwanwet."

Jeremy's wide eyes gleam in the moonlight. "Blanket! Dude, it just said 'blanket!'"

"Can you show me what happened?" I ask.

After asking that question, a cool breeze sends a sudden chill down my spine. A white outlined image of two people appears before me like an echo of the past. They are clearly arguing amongst themselves.

"Archie?" I can hear a man calling nearby, getting the child's attention. "Yes, Archie, it's me. You know who I am. It's your friend, Clancy. I work for your Mom and Dad. Come, here. No, no, don't drop your blanket. Come on over here to me. I'll make you the hot chocolate you like so much!" The tall, angular man who appears has one eye on the newly-appeared child while the other is focusing on the parents.

The ghostly diorama continuing like a grainy movie, Clancy reaches out his hands towards Archie, grabs him, and wraps him in his blanket before heading back to the house. When he reaches for the door, he notices the boy is limp.

"Archie?" Clancy questions, carefully unwrapping the boy from the blanket. The boy's face has turned a bluish-gray, and he is no longer breathing. Clancy had been cradling the boy so tightly he accidentally suffocated him.

The next scene horrifies me—Clancy places Archie's body in a hole in the wall alongside a small trinket box, then bricks it up.

The vision fades, and the chill night returns around us.

Jeremy and I glance down at the spirit box, then at each other. We don't need to utter any words—nothing at this point would feel sufficient.

The next morning after the investigation I relay what we saw to the Constable, who launches an investigation into the house and Clancy, the butler.

A FEW days later, my crew returns to Graves Grove to go over our findings with Mrs. Harper and the Constable. It is hard not to notice the yellow-black law enforcement tape now barricading off the Tudor styled home belonging to Mamie Rue Le Doux.

Stepping inside the Constable's office, I shake his and Mrs. Harper's hands and take a seat at the desk.

The Constable folds his hands together and sighs. "Before we begin," he starts, looking up at me from his paperwork, "on behalf of the townspeople of Graves Grove, I want to thank you and your crew for coming here and assisting in the case of Archie Rue Le Doux."

My eyes grow wide. "Did you find him in the house?" I ask.

The Constable sits back in his seat. "After you informed me of your findings, I'll admit I was skeptical. However, I decided to go ahead and obtain a search warrant and start my own investigation of the house of Mamie Rue Le Doux. Skeletal remains of a young child were recovered from the basement of the site. I'm still waiting for the DNA analysis results to come back from the crime lab to confirm the remains belong to Archie."

"My God," I answer.

"Also found in the basement was a box containing photographs from a series of disposable cameras of several children, including some who have been reported missing. Were still investigating how he obtained these photographs, and if there may be a connection between their disappearances and Archie's murder. Clancy is now awaiting trial in the county jail."

Clancy was tried and convicted of first degree murder in the death of one-year-old Archie Le Doux after DNA confirmed the identity of his skeletal remains. Clancy is now spending life in prison in the Graves Grove county jail. Rumors have spread amongst the townspeople that Clancy may have killed more children, but disposed of them elsewhere. The bodies of the other missing children have yet to be found. That mystery remains unsolved.

THE CANADIAN COTTINGLY

CATHRINE BONHAM

Aaron Kessler, formerly of Vancouver, pulled the roll of film from his pocket and tossed it lightly, catching it each time as he contemplated the shop front before him. He had been all over Graves Grove, looking for anyone who knew how to develop and print the roll of film from the Brownie. His search had led him to the *Graves Grove Gabbler.* Apparently they possessed the only other camera in town.

Behind him stood the famous statue of town founder Samuel Graves. Today the ever-changing statue was dressed in a dandy getup; a ruffled shirt topped with an elegant opera cape.

A bell jingled as he entered the office. A young man turned to greet him with an outstretched hand. "Avery Harper, how can I help you, sir?"

"I have a roll of film I need developed. The man at the General Store thought you might be able to help."

Avery looked uncomfortable, as if he wasn't sure he could help. Then he came to some sort of internal decision. "Yeah, I can develop it, make prints too if you want."

"Really, how much would you charge?"

"No charge, actually, but I have a condition."

"Name it." Avery looked around the room and then spoke low so his sole coworker couldn't hear. "I want to be a real reporter, but Mr. Harlow uses me like an errand boy. If there's anything newsworthy in these pictures, I want exclusive rights to the story."

"I'll be honest with you, Avery: my daughters took these photos. I doubt there will be anything of interest on this roll. But if you happen to find something good, you have my permission to use it. Ophelia would sure get a kick out of being on the front page."

"Thank you, sir; I'll get the prints to you tomorrow morning." Avery held out his hand and Aaron, rather than shake it, deposited the roll of film into it.

THE NEXT morning Aaron was savoring the warmth of the rising sun hitting his closed eyelids. He rolled over and felt the empty space beside him. Lillian—always the early riser. Then a screech reminded him why his wife had to get up so early.

"I'm in the paper!" shouted five-year-old Ophelia. "Father, I'm in the paper." Her little steps hurried up the stairs. Heavier steps followed. Lillian trying to wrangle the child, no doubt.

The bedroom door burst open, and a small blur with blonde pigtails landed on the bed with a bounce. A paper landed in his lap. "Look, look I'm in the paper."

He sat up chuckling. Avery must have been desperate for a story. Maybe he named Ophelia the most beautiful child in Graves Grove. "Hang on, Sweetie, I don't have my glasses on."

Lillian handed him his glasses from the bedside table. Instead of clearly seeing her pleased expression at having her child on the front page, her expression was one of concern. He looked down at the paper in his lap. As was always his habit, he made note of the paper's date: July 9, 1950. Next his eyes roved down to the Headline. In bold, large letters were the words:

GRAVES GROVE. THE CANADIAN COTTINGLY.

The picture underneath the headline was of Ophelia, standing in front of the town's famous sycamore tree and gazing up at an image in the corner of the photo. The image was brightly lit, and within the light source was a human form. Hazy lines blurred from its back as though they might be wings.

Aaron dropped the paper and looked at Ophelia. "Fairies?"

She nodded vigorously. "I told you there were fairies. Aren't they pretty?" She pointed down at the picture. "See this one? Her name is Plum."

Then there was a knock on the front door. Aaron leapt out of bed and turned to his wife. "Stall whoever that is. I am going to get dressed, and for God's sake, where is Harriet?"

FINALLY, DRESSED and composed, Aaron descended the stairs. In the sitting room Lillian had laid out fresh pastries and coffee for their guest.

Avery Harper sat in an armchair. An open notebook sat on his lap, and a pen rested limply in his right hand. "Ah, there he is," said Harper, standing up. "I want to thank you, sir, for that roll of film. Even as fakes, those pictures are still amazing."

Aaron stood in place, relief oozing out of him. So Avery didn't believe the fairies were real. Oh course they weren't real, how could he have ever thought? No, fairies—bah. His spirits were higher already.

The sound of the back door snapping shut came from the kitchen. "Father, you wanted to see me?" said Harriet.

He turned as she entered the sitting room. Harriet was a beautiful girl of sixteen, her long, blonde hair held back by a light blue ribbon that matched her flared skirt and flower-printed blouse. "Harriet dear, this is Mr. Harper from the Gabbler. He developed the roll of film you took yesterday."

"Pleased to meet you, sir." Harriet extended her hand.

Avery took the offered palm and, rather than shake it, flipped it over and placed a gentle kiss upon the back. "The pleasure is all mine, Miss Kessler."

Aaron frowned. He then placed an arm on Harriet's shoulder and sat her down on the sofa away from Mr. Harper and next to himself. "Now, Harriet, I want you to understand. You aren't in any trouble. In fact, I'm quite proud of the way you've taken to photography. You've shown exceptional skill without any training at all."

"Thank you, Father," she said with a smile.

"But we do need to know one thing about the photos. How did you do it?"

Shrugging, Harriet said, "It was easy. I pointed the camera and looked through the viewfinder, and then I pressed the shutter. The Kodak brownie is the most user-friendly camera. At least that's what it said on the box."

"No, dearest, the fairies. How did you fake the fairies in the photographs?"

Mr. Harper was leaning in to hear her answer. She looked up at her father. "Oh, but those weren't faked. I happened to have the camera ready when the fairies showed up out of nowhere."

"Now Miss Kessler, I understand you may want to try to milk this as the Cottingly girls did, but honestly it's been done before. And, in fact, the pictures you two manufactured are of a much finer detail than the ones from 1917, but that makes your skill that much more impressive. The better story is for you to take the credit and tell us how you did it. In this day and age it could lead to exciting opportunities."

"But I didn't fake them. They were really there." Harriet stood up and faced her father. "Don't you believe me, Father? Why would I lie about this? You think I'd rather you thought me a foolish child who plays at pretend, instead of an honest adult?" Her petition given, she brushed past Aaron and marched out the front door. She reached back in and, grabbing the doorknob, gave it a yank. Harriet was gone, leaving nothing but a childish slam in her wake.

"Well then, fairies it is," said Avery Harper, putting his pencil up behind his ear.

"Wait, I have an idea." Aaron walked into his study and rummaged in his desk drawer until he found it. He reentered the sitting room and presented Avery with a new roll of film. "When Conan Doyle doubted the story of two little English girls, what did he do?"

"He had them do it again."

"Only unlike Doyle, this time we'll be watching them."

THAT AFTERNOON Aaron presented his daughters with the new film and assured them he wasn't angry. "In fact, I'd love it if you'd show me your fairies."

"Oh no, they would never come out if you were there," said Ophelia. She waved her hands towards herself. Aaron took the hint and bent down to one knee. "They're scared of men."

"Oh, are they now?"

"Yeah, it's the hairy faces. You remind them of gnomes."

"Oh no, do you think I should shave?"

Ophelia reached up and brushed her hand against his well-trimmed mustache. "No, I like the hairy face."

"Well, good. I guess I'll keep it then."

THEY GAVE the girls a good head start, stopping for a time in front of the statue of Samuel Graves. Today he sported a long coat over a front button shirt and tight fitted pants. Bizarrely his right arm was extended and his left arm was held close, as though he were a magician, bronzed in the very act of casting a spell.

Aaron and Avery continued down Main Street and into the park. The girls ran past the towering sycamore tree and down near the river. They looked as if they were playing and having a good time. But there were no fairies flying about. Harriet pointed the camera and clicked the shutter a few times, then she turned it in their direction.

Aaron pulled Avery down into the roots of the sycamore tree. "We've been spotted."

"What should we do?"

"Hope they forget they saw us." Aaron stood and peeked around the tree. Harriet and Ophelia were gone.

"We lost them. Now what?" asked Avery, wiping tree bark and moss from his trousers.

"They're good girls, they'll be back once they finish the roll. Even if we don't watch them take the pictures, it won't be for naught."

"Well, I guess it's still a good story either way. Keeps the suspense building. Still would have been good to know how they did it though."

BACK HOME Aaron was busy reading the rest of the paper. Suddenly there was a knock on the door. "Lillian!" There was no sound of hurrying footsteps. No sound of the door opening, no sound except another knock on the door. "Lillian!" he called again. No answer. He folded his paper and stood with a huff. "Where could she have gotten to?" he wondered aloud.

He took his time walking the two meters to the front door, hoping whoever it was appreciated his getting up to do it himself.

As a fourth knock echoed on the wooden door, he yanked it open to reveal an older woman standing before him, a copy of the morning's paper clutched in her hand.

"Is this the house where the girls live? The ones who took these pictures?" She held up the paper for him to see.

"It is," he confirmed. "I'm their father, what is this about?"

"Your children are in terrible danger."

Aaron widened his eyes. "What makes you think they're in any danger?"

"The fairies have chosen them. Anyone the fairies touch will die young."

Aaron winced. While that didn't sound good, it was easily debatable. "Now, I'm sure that's not true. The girls who took the Cottingly photos are both alive and well, enjoying their old age."

The old woman, who could easily have been a contemporary of the aforementioned girls, snapped, "The Cottingly photos were fakes. Pure hoaxe, and anyone who fell for them was a fool. But I've seen the real thing. Unearthly sprites who dance in the moonlight and prance about indecently, driving mortals mad."

"Look, Mrs—" He stopped and restarted. "I mean, Miss."

"No, it's Mrs. Forgive me. I was so worried about the girls. My name is Mrs. Wies. I was visiting your lovely town when I happened to read this morning's paper."

"That's wonderful. Well, thank you for your warning, but I'm expecting company, and I'm sure you have other things to be seeing to."

"But what about your girls? I haven't had a chance to warn them yet."

"Thank you very much for your concern, Mrs Weis, but my daughter Harriet is very responsible, and I'm sure she and her sister will be just fine. In fact, they should be home any time now."

"Oh, but I really must speak to them. The fairies are tricky and liars. They will promise them things, but the girls mustn't believe them."

"Where are you staying?"

"At the Graves Grove Inn, room 17."

"All right, as soon as the girls get back I'll personally bring them over to see you."

"You promise?" She raised her eyebrows, as though she knew he had no intention of keeping his word.

"I promise, Mrs. Weis. As soon as they get back."

"Well, all right then. As soon as they come back."

Aaron nodded his assent and closed the door as soon as Mrs. Weis turned to leave.

THE GIRLS didn't come back. Night fell, and Aaron and Lillian grew more and more worried.

At a quarter after nine, Avery stopped by. "Do you have that film for me to develop?"

"No, the girls never came back. I've already been to the police, and all they did was add the missing children reports to a stack of them, already knee high."

"You think the Graves Grove goblin got them?"

"There is no goblin out there stealing children. I'm going back out to look for them."

"I'm right behind you," said Avery.

"Lillian, stay here in case they return."

His wife nodded. "Yes, someone should be here when they come back." She un-crumpled a handkerchief she had been clutching and dabbed at her eyes. Then she sat back down on the sofa.

The two men made their way down Main Street, past the statue of founder Samuel Graves, still in his long magician's coat.

"The blasted sycamore is in all of the photos," said Aaron. "I suggest we start there first and then head out into the woods."

"I agree. That sounds like the best plan. Aaron, have you thought at all about what you will do if we find them? I don't want them to be punished too severely over this. You wouldn't have sent them out again if not for me."

"Honestly, I'll just be glad to have them back." They came to the park and stopped. It was as if the great tree had been strung with Christmas lights. The sycamore was alight with tiny people, their bodies shimmering and glowing.

Beneath the tree stood a woman clothed in mists and standing before two still figures, one kneeling over a smaller one lying on the ground. Harriet kneeling above the still form of her sister.

"Get away from them!" Aaron screamed. "What have you done?" He tried to run up to his daughters but was blocked by the specter standing in silhouette between him and the girls. "Leave my children alone," he said to the spectral lady.

She stepped forward, and Aaron was shocked to see the lady wasn't a specter at all, but Mrs. Weis. Her eyes were closed and an unearthly glow emanated from the back of her head like a halo. The woman's head dipped, just enough that the men could see a small figure clinging to the back of her skull. At first it appeared to have its hands in her hair, clutching it the way a bareback rider would clutch a horse's mane. Looking closer, they could see the streaks of blood from where the creature's claws dug into the woman's scalp.

Aaron approached her with the intent of shooing away the beast. "Stop," said Mrs. Weis in a commanding and unnatural tone. "Do not come any nearer, or harm will befall this mortal."

"What do you want with my daughters?" he asked the fairy.

It sent Mrs. Weis's body toward the girls. It studied them with her eyes. "Innocence," it replied. "There is a war in this world, between forces many of your kind fail to comprehend. The machine of war requires fuel. That fuel is innocence." Mrs. Weis looked up and right into Aaron's eyes. "You understand that, don't you? War. How it eats up and devours innocence. How you leave home a young daddy to a baby girl and come back an aged father to a young woman you barely know."

He did know, all too well. The fighting in Europe had eaten him alive and spat him back out into a world he could no longer comprehend. Into a family that no longer needed him, or knew him. Back to a daughter who no longer threw herself at him when he walked into a room, glad, just to know he was home.

"In this war you speak of, which side are you on?" Avery asked.

Aaron looked over, shocked he was still there.

The fairy riding Mrs. Weis looked over, and with her mouth answered, "It depends on your perspective." The fairies in the tree grew brighter. The wood of the sycamore turned almost black in contrast to the intensity of the light.

"This is a nexus. A place for all sides to rest and refuel. Choose a side, man of war."

Aaron glanced at Avery. "Any chance they're talking to you?"

Avery shook his head. "I'm only twenty. I never got a chance to enlist."

Only twenty, so close to Harriet's age, just a boy yet. Aaron stepped forward, taking a stand as the adult present. "I think we've all had enough war for several lifetimes. Why don't you leave and take your army somewhere else?"

"We are bound to the nexus. It calls us and others of our realm. But we can make a deal with you, man of war. Choose a daughter for us to take, and we will protect the other from becoming consumed."

"You don't know what you're asking. I can't give you one of my children."

Mrs. Weis smiled and waved her fairy hordes into the sky. They lifted off from the tree and circled Mrs. Weis in great cyclone of light. "The decision has been made!" she shouted.

Then the park fell into darkness. Every fairy was gone. Mrs. Weis lay on the ground by the still forms of his daughters. Aaron ran to them and saw on closer inspection their chests rising slightly with each of their shallow breaths. He lifted Ophelia into his arms and looked back towards Harriet. There was no way he could carry the both of them.

And Mrs. Weis too. She lay there on the ground gazing upward with unblinking eyes. Avery knelt by her neck. He moved his fingers a couple times, obviously not trained for this kind of thing. Finally he shook his head and stood. "I'm not a doctor, but I don't think she has a pulse to find." Avery ran a hand through his hair. "What just happened? And do I dare write about it?"

"That's your call, I'm just worried about getting my girls home. Can you take Ophelia?"

Avery started holding out his arms to accept the younger girl when Harriet made a noise. She groaned and made a sobbing sound as she tried to rise. Avery bent over and helped her, allowing the weakened girl to lean on him.

Aaron shifted Ophelia so he could hold her with one arm. "Harriet, thank God you're all right. I thought..." He paused, unwilling to say aloud what he had thought.

"It's okay, Father. Do you believe me now?"

"I do. You are not a child."

"Right, I'm sixteen, I can make my own decisions." Suddenly her knees buckled under her. Avery caught her and helped her stand again. She leaned into the newsman's shoulder and said quietly, "Please take me home."

AT THE house, Avery helped Harriet to sit on the sofa. "Here," she said, pulling a black cylinder from a pocket on the front of her dress. "For your story."

"Thanks, but I don't know if there is going to be a story."

"I understand if you don't use them, but I'd like to see how they turned out."

"Okay, sure." He pocketed the roll of film.

Aaron passed the still sleeping five-year-old over to her mother, and walked Avery to the door. "Can you stop by the constable's office and let them know about Mrs. Weis? I don't think she should lay there all night."

"Yes, no problem. What should I tell them about her death?"

"You're the newsman. Make something up."

Avery nodded. "I'll see you tomorrow, sir." After he left, Aaron closed and locked the door behind him.

As Lillian carried their youngest upstairs to bed, he held out his hand for Harriet. "Are you ready to go to bed?"

"Yes," she said, taking his hand. He pulled her up and she leaned into him. "Daddy."

Aaron stopped. This was different. She hadn't called him that since before the war. "Yes, sweetheart?"

"I don't know how much time we have, but I want you to know it isn't your fault. I am responsible for my own choices."

"Whatever you say, sweetheart." He held her close and cherished every step they took together up the stairs.

THE NEXT morning a furious knocking on the door dragged Aaron down the stairs, his bathrobe open and only the left slipper on his foot. It had been an uneasy night for them all.

The opened door revealed Avery standing there in the same clothes he had worn the night before. A stack of prints were in his hand. "I know who the fairies are taking."

Aaron had thought about it all night. His worries had left him tossing and sweating throughout the long night, and only one conclusion had eased his conscience. "It's obvious, isn't it? They took Mrs. Weis."

"No, she wasn't an innocent. This photo was on the roll your daughter gave me."

Aaron took the offered print and felt his heart fall into his stomach. It was an image of Harriet, her hand held out with an ethereal sprite resting on her palm. But instead of her beautiful face, a grinning skull looked back at him.

THE FAMILY BUSINESS

J.S. BAILEY

Tammy Kallenberger jerked awake as the white and yellow Volkswagen bus slowed and made a bumpy turn.

"Are we there yet?" she asked, blinking at the sight of bald peaks towering above them on all sides as they stretched into the azure sky.

"Not yet, Tammy Girl," her older sister Jean said from the driver's seat. "We're just stopping for gas."

"Ugh. It feels like we left Winnipeg years ago."

Jean parked the bus next to a set of faded gas pumps. "Aw, grow up. We'll be at Wilkes Lake in five hours, and then we can kick back and fish for two whole weeks with no one to bother us."

"You mean you'll be fishing. I'm going to work on some programming." Tammy tried not to let her irritation show. Grow up? *Why* did Jean always have to make it sound like Tammy was still a child? She was twenty-eight, for crying out loud, and Jean had just turned thirty. She supposed it was just the maternal side of Jean showing through—after all, Jean had practically raised her since their parents were eaten by a Jikininki all those years ago.

Jean hopped out of the bus and strode to the gas pump with her credit card in hand. Tammy watched her idly as she shifted to get more comfortable in the passenger seat she'd occupied for days. Despite the fact they'd had the same two parents, Jean had grown into a stocky, brown-haired woman who could bench press a dump truck if needed, and Tammy had somehow ended up a geeky, willowy blonde.

Jean put her hands on her hips and appeared to be assessing their surroundings while she waited for the tank to fill. Tammy decided to follow suit and opened the door to join her when an electronic squeal emanated from behind her seat.

Tammy and Jean exchanged an alarmed glance before Tammy dove back into the bus and yanked her backpack off the floor. Setting it on her seat, she unzipped it and tugged out the custom-made device she'd cobbled together from half a dozen pieces of equipment she'd rescued from various dumpsters.

It had been off when she'd put it in her backpack prior to leaving Winnipeg. Now its screen glowed with at least ten alerts.

"What is it?" Jean asked, leaning in for a better look.

Tammy felt her stomach sink toward her feet as she read the glowing green lines of text. "Well, there's ghosts here, for one," she said.

"Every town has ghosts. We can't stop and get rid of all of them; we'd never get done."

"And fairies."

Jean wrinkled her nose. "You're kidding me."

"Jean, I'm not done. The amount of stuff this is picking up is crazy. We've got vamps, demons, at least three shifters, a Jikininki…"

"Shit."

"They're all within a five-kilometer radius of here. What the heck is this place?"

"Graves Grove, the sign said."

"It's like a nexus of some sort." Tammy looked away from her screen and peered up and down the quiet street. Traffic was practically nonexistent, and an old lady sat on a nearby porch knitting a brightly-colored scarf that was already at least eight feet long. Most of the houses were turn-of-the-century clapboard, and paint peeled from many of them. Kind of cute in an old-world way, really, but it made Tammy's skin prickle.

Jean hung up the nozzle and tore her receipt from the dispenser. "Tammy, I think it's going to take us a little longer than five hours to get to Wilkes Lake."

THE TWO women checked into a seedy, L-shaped motel. Tammy touched up her makeup in the spotted mirror while Jean lay out their equipment on one of the twin beds.

"I guess the question is, where do we begin?" Jean said, running a hand over her short hair. She slipped off her brown Carhartt jacket and draped it over the back of a chair, revealing the Bachman Turner Overdrive t-shirt she wore at least three times a week.

Five minutes earlier, the detector had picked up a banshee, but it moved out of the detector's range as soon as it had appeared. Tammy had been somewhat relieved. Banshees were the worst.

"We could go after one of the demons first," Tammy said. "I'm usually pretty good with those."

"Tammy Girl, I'm still having nightmares from that last demon we snuffed. I say we go after the Jikininki. Maybe it's the one that killed our folks."

Tammy tried not to let her shoulders slump—somehow Jean always ended up making all the decisions. "If you think that's best."

"Of course it's best. But first I'm going to see if this town has a decent burrito place. I'm starved."

THEY OPTED to walk since Graves Grove appeared so small, and it felt good to stretch their legs after being cooped up in the bus for so long. Tammy inhaled the crisp mountain air but coughed as a faint whiff of sulfur entered her sinuses. She narrowed her eyes at a teenager who skulked past them on the sidewalk, but the detector emitted no additional squeals.

While they walked, Tammy switched to the satellite map overlay on the detector's screen so she could see precisely where each monster was hiding. They walked past a house containing four ghosts, and a church housing a vampire. The Jikininki it picked up earlier had vanished from view just like the banshee.

As they approached the first restaurant this side of the street, Tammy switched off the detector, not wanting to incite too much curiosity in the townsfolk. "This is a burger joint," she said as Jean reached to pull open the door.

"Too hungry to care."

At once, a reddish-brown dog raced past them on the sidewalk, nearly knocking the two sisters over. "What in the—?" Jean started to say as she regained her balance. "Stupid dog!"

The dog halted about ten meters away from them and gave them a look of apology before hurrying onward.

"Chill, Jean, maybe he's just hungry, too," Tammy said as her own stomach rumbled.

Jean squinted after the dog. "I don't know. You ever see a dog that looks like it's on a mission?"

Tammy laughed. "It probably just wants to find a good Nylabone. Come on, let's go in and eat."

The restaurant was clean and tidy and had been decorated in bold colors and chrome fixtures like one of those 1950s American diners. Vinyl records hung on the walls, and an "Out of Order" sign hung on a jukebox sitting near the door. Why were all jukeboxes always out of order?

"Table for two?" a plump, middle-aged hostess asked them when they walked inside. Her nametag read "Marlene."

"Could it be a booth?" Jean asked as her eyes roved over the joint. Tammy rolled her eyes. Sometimes her sister could be entirely too picky.

"A booth it is, then! Come right this way."

They followed the woman to a booth in the front window roughly two meters from the door. Marlene, who was also the server, took their drink order, and once the two Kallenbergers had ordered their burgers, Jean cleared her throat and said, "You've always lived around here?"

Marlene smiled. "Since the day I was born! Why?"

"You ever see anything weird?"

The woman's smile faltered as her eyes narrowed. "Why?" she repeated.

Jean beamed up at her with gleaming white teeth. "Oh, my sister and I are just nosy. We're passing through on our way to Wilkes Lake and thought we'd stay here a few days. We heard Graves Grove might have a few...interesting features."

Tammy cleared her throat and glanced warmly up at Marlene to placate the woman's expression of increasing discomfort at having been put on the spot. "We want to know about the ghosts," Tammy said. "If you're not comfortable talking about it, you can forget we said anything."

"Not comfortable!" Marlene gave a nervous little laugh. "Oh, honey. You don't talk about things like this here." Her voice dropped a few notches. "Nobody wants to think anything is wrong."

"What do you mean?"

Marlene cast a worried glance over her shoulder as if to make sure the restaurant's other patrons were giving them no notice. Then she said, "My nephew, Toby Clutterbuck, went missing when he was three. He and his parents had gone on a picnic down at the park. He wandered away in a flash—you know how toddlers can be—and nobody saw him again."

"I'm sorry to hear that," Tammy said, wondering if one of the vamps had nabbed the boy. "Did the police do much to help?"

"They're always a little overrun," Marlene said somewhat enigmatically. "Anyway, I'd better go put your order in."

She hurried off into the kitchen.

"So, that was weird," Tammy said.

Jean's forehead furrowed. "Okay, a missing kid. Anything could have eaten him."

Tammy winced. "Yeah." Motion outside the window caught her eye. She turned and saw the reddish-brown dog trot by again. As it passed the window, she could have sworn the dog looked right at her.

Jean followed her gaze and stiffened. "I don't like that dog."

"Why not? He's kind of cute."

"He doesn't seem dog enough to me. Turn your detector back on."

Tammy dutifully withdrew the clunky device from her oversized purse and powered it up. She pulled up the map overlay and saw a dot with a rather concerning label retreating from their current location along the sidewalk.

Jean leaned in for a better look.

"Oh, darn," she said.

Tammy watched as the labeled dot paused and then crossed the street. She peered out the window and saw the russet dog doing the same.

Oh darn, indeed.

"Hey, Marlene?" Jean called.

The server hurried out of the kitchen holding a spatula—looked like she was the cook as well. "Yes, what is it?"

"That dog out there. Whose is it?"

"You mean Copper? He doesn't belong to anybody. Just sort of owns the place, I guess."

"How old is he?"

Marlene put her free hand on her chin. "I don't know, he's been around for as long as I can remember. Don't you worry about him being loose, though; he wouldn't hurt a fly."

THEY MET back at the motel to map out their plan.

"How are we going to catch a dog?" Jean asked as she paced back and forth with impatience. Tammy stood in front of the mirror touching up her makeup once more; she always managed to smudge it somehow. "I mean, they can run *fast*."

"Grandma Kallenberger's old dog liked peanut butter," Tammy said as she smeared fresh blue eyeshadow onto her eyelids. "We could set a trap and bait it with that."

"But this dog isn't really a dog. He's going to be smart. We'll have to outwit him somehow."

"We'll just have to make sure he doesn't know he's walking into a trap, then."

"Oh yeah? How?"

Tammy snapped her eyeshadow closed, feeling a swell of pride that she'd thought of something Jean hadn't. "Easy. Here's what we do."

THE NEXT day, Tammy strolled down the sidewalk into the heart of Graves Grove, taking note of her surroundings. She passed a park dominated by an enormous sycamore that had no business growing in this climate, eyed a charming bronze statue no doubt commemorating some long-dead important person, and passed a busy general store when she finally spotted her quarry. Copper, as Marlene had called him, was sniffing around a garbage can outside a post office, probably seeking out some discarded morsel.

Tammy pulled two dog biscuits out of the basket hooked over her arm. She'd cemented them together with peanut butter—a delectable doggy treat.

"Hey, boy!" she said, then whistled to get Copper's attention. His ears pricked up, and he approached her, tail wagging.

She held the treat out for him to take. "You look like a hungry boy," she cooed, patting him on the head while trying not to recoil from her knowledge of the pooch's true nature. "Go on, eat it."

Copper bit the glued-together biscuits out of her hand and scarfed them down, then looked up at her as if wanting more.

"Sorry, buddy, that's all I've got right now." Tammy's heart raced. She gave Copper another pat on the head, and as she watched, his eyes closed and he slumped to the sidewalk, snoring.

Tammy whipped out her phone and speed-dialed Jean's number. "Got him," she said.

"Good. Where are you?"

"Outside the post office. Quick, I don't want anyone to see this."

"I'll be there in a jiffy."

A click indicated that Jean had hung up. Tammy let out a nervous breath and glanced up and down the street once more. An older woman in worn, shabby eighties clothes pushed a creaky pram down the opposite sidewalk, muttering to someone Tammy couldn't see, and to Tammy's dismay, a teenage girl with jet black hair was coming up the sidewalk right toward her.

Tammy stepped aside to let the teenager pass, but the girl stopped beside her. Tammy noted she was wearing a t-shirt advertising some sort of punk band.

"May I help you?" Tammy asked, praying the girl wouldn't ask about the dog.

"What did you do to Copper?" the girl asked, crossing her arms. She looked young, 18 at the most.

"I gave him a biscuit," Tammy said. "Why?"

The girl gestured at the snoring dog. "Why do you think?"

"I—I didn't drug him, if that's what you think."

"Yeah, because dogs just take naps in the middle of the sidewalk."

Tammy's heart raced. She had to change the subject, and quick. "Honey, what's your name?"

"Lisa, and I'm not your honey. I ought to call the—"

Just then, the yellow and white Volkswagen bus lumbered up the street and lurched to a stop beside Tammy, Lisa, and the tranquilized Copper. Jean hopped out and opened a side door, leaving the engine running. "Okay, buddy, let's get you back to your owners," she said, leaning down to scoop up the dog.

"Nobody owns Copper," Lisa retorted. "What are you doing to him?"

Jean glared at the girl. "He's clearly sick. We're going to get him some help."

"But you just said—"

"Tammy, get in the bus!" Jean wrapped her thick arms around the dog and hauled him up into one of the seats, and Tammy scrambled into the passenger seat before the overly-inquisitive Lisa could say anything more.

Jean slammed the side door, got back behind the wheel, and gunned the bus down the street toward the motel. Tammy glanced behind her to watch Lisa's dwindling figure. "That girl is going to call the police on us."

"No, she won't. You heard what that waitress said yesterday. She said the police around here are overrun."

"Whatever that means."

They turned into the motel parking lot. Tammy got out first and unlocked the door to their room so Jean could haul the sleeping dog inside, then closed the door after Jean laid Copper on the floor between the twin beds, where Jean and Tammy had earlier dumped a protective circle of rock salt on the carpet.

The salt completely encircled the dog, who twitched in the throes of a dream while he lay there in drugged silence. The two sisters waited for half an hour in breathless anticipation before the animal stirred and cracked open an eyelid.

"Good, you're awake," Jean said, taking charge of the situation as she always did. "*Mutata te!*"

Tammy rolled her eyes. "Why does it always have to be Latin? You know English works, too."

"Shut up."

Copper groggily sat up, then shrank back in fear as he took in his surroundings. Then his lovely russet fir rippled and stretched, and the next thing they knew, a balding, somewhat deflated-looking middle-aged man sat in the center of the salt ring, his face long.

"What gave it away?" the man who had been Copper asked weakly. He wore no clothes because Copper hadn't been wearing any, and Tammy handed him a towel from the bathroom as a courtesy.

"Doesn't matter," Jean said, unaffected by the man's nudity. "What's your name?"

He coughed. "Copper."

"Your real name."

"It's Copper. John Matthew Copper."

Tammy covered her mouth to stifle a giggle, and Jean shot her a look of irritation.

"Okay, John Matthew Copper," Jean went on. "We know you're a shifter. Why're you hanging out in this shitty little town? I thought your lot stayed in cities where there's more fresh meat."

Copper's jaw clenched. "There's good people here."

"And about four dozen creeps, if we count up everything we've seen on our detector. You're one of them."

To Tammy's surprise, tears welled up in Copper's eyes. "I'm not a creep. I'm a good person."

"No shifters are good people. Good people don't need to hide who they are."

"You're wrong."

Jean leaned over and selected a knife from the array of weaponry laid out on the dresser. "I don't think so."

Copper yelped and leapt to his feet still holding the bath towel to his front, but he couldn't step out of the circle of salt to get away. "Lady, please. I've never hurt anyone. I make people in this town happy. God knows they need a little cheer around here. You should see them smiling whenever they see me. Do you know what that's like, when people are just genuinely glad to see you? It's the best feeling in the world."

Jean lowered the knife but maintained her grip upon it. "You're a *shifter*."

"Accident of nature, not my fault. Parents were good people, too. We weren't like the other ones."

"I don't have time for this," Jean huffed. "I'm late for my fishing trip, and I intend to clean this town up before we leave it."

"Let him talk awhile," Tammy said, moved by Copper's words. "He can't hurt anyone while he's trapped in that circle."

Jean stepped aside. "Okay, you talk to him, then."

Nodding, Tammy sat cross-legged on the floor in front of the man, who sat back down as well. "I'm sorry I drugged you. We're just not used to the idea that monsters can be nice."

"No worries, that biscuit sandwich was delicious." Copper smiled, and Tammy couldn't help but grin back at him.

"How can we know to trust you?" Tammy asked.

Copper spread his arms wide. "Do I look like a killer to you?"

"Sorry, but in our experience, most killers look normal at first glance."

Copper sighed. "Figures."

"Do you know why there are so many monsters around here?"

He shrugged. "Some kind of spell attracts them, I guess. It's like a feeding ground out there. I can't stop any of it from happening, so I just do what I can to distract people from the inevitable. I was an insurance salesman before I started living as a dog full-time," he added. "I hated my job. People are *not* genuinely happy to see you when you sell insurance. I finally said enough was enough, skipped out of town, and found this place. Life's been good ever since."

"You're not the only shifter in town, you know," Tammy said. "We saw others on our detector."

"Oh, they're friends of mine," Copper said. "Cara disguises herself as a raccoon and hides herself up in the woods. She used to be a schoolteacher over in Edmonton. After I found this place, I rang her up and invited her to come stay. Every few months we change back into human form and go out for dinner and a movie. I still have my bank account."

"And the others?" Tammy asked while Jean made a face.

"They were burned out on life, just like us. Missy, she's usually a cat, but sometimes she changes it up and turns herself into a rabbit, but then she's afraid the real cats will try to eat her. Edgar likes being a turtle, and that's all of us."

"So the four of you don't kill people."

"Never."

Jean cleared her throat. "You are aware that Graves Grove is overrun by ghosts, demons, a banshee, a Jikininki, several vampires, and a boatload of fairies?"

"Yes."

"Then if you care so much about making people happy, why don't you go after some of those creatures yourself so they stop killing people?"

Copper blanched. "We don't know how."

Jean picked up a thick book from where she'd set it beside the weaponry. "Okay, dog. I'm going to give you the benefit of the doubt since you look so pathetic with that towel draped over your crotch. Is there a library in town?"

Copper's cheeks turned pink. "Well, yes."

"Good." Jean thumped the book's cover with her index finger. "This book here tells people everything they need to know about slaying monsters. I'm going to go make some photocopies. Tammy, you keep an eye on Dog Boy here while I head out."

With that, Jean strode out the door and slammed it behind her.

Copper looked to Tammy. "She trusts you alone with a shifter?"

Tammy shrugged. "You're bound by the salt, and even if you did find a way out of it, I've got a whole arsenal behind me. I've got that book memorized, too, you know." She tapped on her temple and winked. "It's true you just want to make the people in this town happy?"

"It's the only thing I know how to do. I was a terrible insurance salesman."

Tammy felt a giggle well up in her chest, and before she knew it, she was laughing so hard that tears streamed from her eyes.

AS TAMMY and Jean reloaded the Volkswagen bus the next day, the punky teenager named Lisa sauntered up to them in the motel parking lot.

"I'm sorry I thought you were hurting Copper yesterday," Lisa said. "I stand corrected."

"Oh?" Tammy said, facing her.

"Yeah—I've just seen him down by the sycamore, looking cheerful as always." She smiled. "I love that dog. We all do. If something ever happened to him, I think the whole town would implode."

And maybe it would, Tammy thought.

Once the bus was fully packed and Lisa had wandered off toward home, Jean drove Tammy down to the park dominated by that unnervingly large and creepy tree. It didn't take them long to find Copper—he lay on the ground beneath the shade of the sycamore gnawing on some kind of glowy chew toy.

Copper's ears pricked up when he saw them, but he didn't rise. Leaning in for a closer look, Tammy saw that Copper had been gnawing not on a chew toy, but on the lifeless corpse of a fairy. It lay draped across his paws, missing several body parts.

Tammy scratched the dog's head. "You've been reading up, I see. That fairy stunning spell is tricky to learn."

Copper winked.

"Keep your copy of the book safe, okay? At least until you've memorized it."

The dog gave a curt nod and resumed his grisly task. Tammy tore her gaze away from him, unable to watch.

"Hey, look at that," Jean said, pointing.

Not far from them, a raccoon, a cat, and a turtle had gathered around another dead fairy lying in a broken heap on the ground. The cat batted it with one paw, and the turtle took one wary step in reverse while the raccoon just watched with beady eyes, seemingly amused at the whole affair.

"See?" Tammy said. "Not all monsters are bad."

Jean shook her head. "I've officially seen everything. I mean, look at all the creeps we've killed over the years. After Mom and Dad died, I didn't think we'd..."

Jean trailed off, and Tammy said, "Wait. Were you just about to talk about your feelings?"

Jean wrinkled her nose. "Who the hell does that? Let's get going. I'm late for my fishing trip."

MAGICK

D.M. KILGORE

GRAVES GROVE
SUMMER 1938

Magdala Agatha Mersy rummaged through the surplus of jars that threatened to topple out of her Magickal Cabinet. She snorted. *Magickal.* The only thing magical about the rickety old cabinet that housed the ingredients she needed for spellcasting was its ability to make whatever she needed disappear. She had dried sage in her collection. She *knew* it. So why couldn't she find it?

Because the cabinet was cursed. Her whole life was cursed. *She* was cursed. A walking, talking, mess of a curse. Unable to locate the sage, she shoved the jars deeper into the cabinet and slammed the door shut. The bottom hinge gave a high-pitched *ping* before snapping. The door dangled precariously from the remaining hinge. Magdala glared at it. "Magickal, my ass."

She really needed that sage. Not that the spell called for it. Sage had notable calming properties. Anxiety about recasting the failed spell had her so on edge she could almost hear her nerve endings screaming.

She wanted a calming cup of sage and honey tea before she attempted the spell again. Everything had to be perfect this time. The pressure was immense. There was no way she was going to attempt the spell again unless she could find the sage. Nope. Not this time. This time it had to work. It just had to.

She paced the length of the small, one-room shack as she pro-conned her way through the idea of casting without the sage tea. "Maybe a dose of nervous excitement would help the spell," she pondered aloud.

"Or maybe it would backfire even worse than the first time."

The screechy unwelcomed reply drew Magdala from her inner deliberations. She turned to find the dreadful creature perched on the windowsill, its beady eyes boring holes into her. Stupid, nosy raven. Always had to poke his beak in at the worst times.

"You really want to risk that?" he asked, cocking his head to one side.

Magdala spread her arms wide and spun in a circle to give him a better look at her ensemble. "How could it possibly get any worse?" she glowered at the stupid bird. *Damn.* Despite her promise to herself not to engage the glorified crow in future debates, she'd given him a grand opening. He had a way of always winning that annoyed the hell out of her.

"You could wind up eternally naked," he cackled.

Magdala shot him her best evil eye while hankering to turn him into a toad. Then she could toss him into her cauldron and chalk it up to a craving for frog legs. She waited to see if her yearning would render results. He ruffled his feathers and cackled louder in response. She knew he was protected from her puny attempts at evil, but that wasn't going to stop her from trying. She hated him too much to give up that easily. "Why don't you just go home?"

"And miss the fun? Never." He flew over to the mantel and settled in for the show.

Magdala sulked. She'd been under more than enough pressure before the arrival of the Coven Mother's Familiar. The anxiety twisting through her stomach slithered higher, like a snake determined to choke the life out of her, and settled around her throat. The foul fowl was going to report everything back to the coven. There was zero room for error now. Everything had to be absolutely perfect. She was doomed.

Wringing her hands and muttering to herself, Magdala resumed her pacing. The hem of her long black robe swept against the dirt floor, causing small dust storms to swirl around a scruffy white cat sprawled near the hearth. Coughing and sneezing, it shot her a dirty look. Magdala shrugged apologetically. Tufts of white fur fell off the poor creature's scrawny legs as it disappeared through a small crack in the wall. Magdala wished her own escape could be so easy.

"Pitiful. Just pitiful," the raven clucked. "I mean, all cats are pathetic, but that one? That is the sorriest looking feline I've ever seen. You really went all out with that spell."

"Oh, shut up!" Magdala grabbed the nearest object—a wooden spoon—and chucked it at the bird. She missed him by a mile.

"You're pitching is almost as bad as your spellcasting!"

Magdala growled in his direction. It was her only defense. She knew he spoke the truth. She paced faster.

"Careful now. You're going to cause another 'Black Sunday'!" he crowed, prancing along the edge of the mantel.

Clearly, he was having the time of his life. Magdala hoped he'd fall into the fire. If only she knew his name she could banish him. She'd tried several times to trick him into telling her, but he was as clever as he was annoying. That was the most maddening thing of all. She knew he would always be able to outsmart her…and she knew that he knew that she knew. Truly maddening.

Magdala stopped pacing, took a deep breath, and willed the miniature dust storms to cease—not that today was even a Sunday. That's just how much the pesky bird got under her skin. Those "Black Sunday" storms hadn't been her fault. She hadn't even been anywhere near the Plains in 1935. Just like she hadn't been anywhere near New Jersey in 1936 when the Hindenburg crashed. That never stopped the raven from suggesting that one of her badly-cast spells had caused the calamities of the world. Nor had it stopped him from placing well-timed whispers into the wind…whispers that caused the townsfolk to give her side-glances and a wide berth as she passed them on the streets.

Her family's reputation for being truly wicked was well-established. Sadly, it wasn't her wickedness they feared, it was her unpredictability. Magdala sighed. When it came to being truly wicked, she was a complete and utter failure. If only spellcasting was as easy as double-double toil and trouble and eye of newt and wing of bat. The powerless had no idea how hard a witch had to work at being wicked.

Herbs had to be planted, tended, and harvested with extreme care. Every ingredient had to be pure and perfect. Potions had to be blended meticulously. The stars, moon, and planets had to be just so. The words of the spell had to be delivered in a perfectly timed meter and enunciated with exact precision. If any one element was the slightest bit off, the entire spell would fail.

Magdala should know. In over a hundred years, she'd never once cast a successful spell. She wasn't truly wicked at all, she was just truly terrible…at spellcasting. Maybe it was her slight lisp. Or maybe it was her inability to correctly calculate anything that involved the use of numbers. Maybe it was because her astigmatism made it impossible to accurately follow the movements of the moon. Or maybe it was because her left leg was half an inch shorter than her right, causing her cauldron dance to always be just a little less elegant than it should be. Maybe it was because she was a tad bit dyslexic. Or maybe she was just destined to be the worst witch…and not in the "oh, isn't she wicked" way she so longed for. She really had no idea what combination of personal flaws attributed to the long list of failed spells. She only knew when it came to being a wicked witch… she was a joke.

The spell she cast for a sprawling Mock Tudor home with a plentiful herb garden had generated the dilapidated shack she currently called home. Nothing would grow in the stony soil. Flowers and herbs were always withered or dead well before it was time to harvest them. The spell she had cast for a Familiar—she'd wanted a silky black cat she could name Shadow—had delivered a pathetic, half-bald, white cat she hadn't even bothered to name. The love potion she'd slipped into the town's most eligible bachelor's favorite bottle of whiskey had sent him straight into the arms of every available woman in town...*except* Magdala. And the spell for turning her rags into riches? Well...

She glanced down at her tattered black robe. A stereotypical pointed hat, ugly shoes with tacky buckles, and striped stockings completed her ensemble. Shuddering, she rolled her eyes and shook her head. Of all the failed spells she'd cast, this one was the worst. Naturally, no one knew the truth. Magdala was all about fashion. She wasn't a very wicked witch, but she was a wicked-good dressmaker. And she had great taste.

Desperately wanting the beautiful dresses pictured within the pages of her hidden stash of women's fashion magazines and catalogs, she'd devised a spell. A wonderful spell that would allow her to be an eternal fashion-icon. She'd so desperately wanted a fancy new sewing machine and an endless supply of fabrics and notions for creating a fashionable new wardrobe...but the spell, as usual, had backfired. Instead of a new Singer machine and an endless supply of materials, she'd conjured up a rusty old toaster and condemned herself to wearing the clichéd witch's garb twenty-four seven, three sixty-five.

Magdala hated the drab costume she'd cursed herself into as much as she hated her drab life and even more than she hated the raven that delighted in tormenting her about it. She couldn't stand it any longer. Sage tea or no sage tea, anxiety or not, she had to rid herself of the ridiculous outfit.

Decision made, she cast out a telepathic message to her unnamed Familiar. The cat didn't respond. She cast out another message with a bit more force. Slowly, the cat made its way back in through the same crack in the wall it had used to depart. Shedding large clumps of fur across the dirt floor as it approached, it looked up at its master for further instructions. Magdala mentally conveyed the plan to the pitiable feline. It attempted a rebuttal, which came out as series of yowling "me-you-alls" than actual "meows." She shot the feline a mental warning and less than gently insisted the plan would work. Head drooping, the cat meandered off to do as it was told. The pathetic thing wobbled across the floor towards the raven.

Nothing about the cat was right. It didn't even know how to meow or even walk properly. There was no way the plan would work...but the cat didn't need to know that. She just needed the raven to fly away long enough for her to recast the spell. She needed to focus, and she couldn't do that with the bird eyeballing her.

The cat, who apparently suffered from ADHD as well as male-pattern-baldness, forgot steps one through three of the plan and skipped directly to leap at the raven. It missed, of course, landing just close enough to the fireplace for its tail to get singed. As the smell of burning cat hair wafted through the air, and the raven fell over in a fit of cawing and cackling, Magdala wondered if she could spell herself back in time...preferably to 1690's Salem.

Magdala watched the cat disappear through the crack in the wall again, leaving only a trail of fur and smoke in its wake. On the mantel, the raven continued to roll around in a fit of bird-laughter. Magdala gave up. Time was wasting. And when casting spells, timing was everything.

She grabbed the box of ingredients and items she'd worked all week to perfect and collect. This time it would work. She was sure of it. She'd taken extra measures to make sure this spell would be different. Her Uncloaking Spell—that was the clever name she'd given it—would soon allow her to be rid of the banal witch's garb, and she'd finally have unlimited access to the latest and greatest fashions. Magdala was going to be a one-woman fashion show with just the snap of her fingers. The thought was wickedly delicious.

Ignoring the raven, she went outside to check the position of the sun. She licked a finger and held it in the air to test the wind direction. Finally, she stooped and pulled up a handful of dirt and grass—well mostly weeds, if she was being honest—and lifted them to her nose. Things couldn't possibly be any better. Everything was in order. The timing was perfect. The ingredients were fresh. And she knew exactly where she'd gone wrong last time. She'd forgotten the sacrifice.

With a huge smile plastered across her face, Magdala went back into her ramshackle hut. She looked the raven directly in its beady black eyes as she grabbed her most beloved copy of *Marie-Claire* from the stack of magazines beside her makeshift bed. She hated to give it up, but there had to be a sacrifice. The raven wasted no time pointing out the ridiculousness of using a magazine as a catalyst for the spell. Magdala pointed out the pretty feathered hats on page 12. The raven shut up. She didn't care what he said, she knew it was the missing ingredient. How could she expect a spell to give her what she wanted if she didn't at least provide an example of what she desired?

Magdala lit the yellow candles she'd purchased from the General Store for this very occasion. She'd never mastered the art of candle-making and had decided long ago that store-bought candles were just as good as homemade ones. Lighting the jasmine incense, she crossed the room and smudged the door and window. For good measure, she decided to smudge the walls, the mantel (much to the raven's displeasure), the hearth, and any other flat surface she could easily reach. Her living space prepared, she placed the ingredients on the table, and checked the cauldron. It had been heating on the fire for exactly three hours. Perfect. One by one, with careful precision, she added each specially-selected herb, oil, dried flower, and finally a spider's spinneret to create a bubbling concoction. Next she added a shiny new zipper, a dozen random buttons, a handful of sequins, a strip of fancy French lace, and even a square of Italian leather. Only the magazine remained.

With painstaking care, she removed each page that featured beautiful clothing and accessories. She hummed a catchy tune as she folded each page, wrapping it in one of several assorted fabrics, she visualized herself wearing the new beautiful clothing. She tied off each packet with a colorful ribbon, and then, one by one, added them to the boiling brew. A puff of sweet-smelling steam wafted up and out into the tiny room.

Now it was time to speak the words. She gave the raven the briefest look before she started chanting, "Goddess, goddess, hear my plea, let me be clothed in endless finery. Give me jewels, bronze, silver, gold. A sight for all eyes to behold. Matching shoes, scarves, and hats. The latest fashions, give me that. When I snap my fingers, let it be, as I ask, so mote it be."

Magdala spun herself in frantic circles repeating the chant three times while turning clockwise, then three more while turning counter clockwise. Caught up in the frenzy, she wasn't exactly sure that was the proper procedure, but it felt right. Certain she felt the power flowing through her veins, she lifted her arms high above her head and snapped her fingers. The raven, who had been silent throughout the spell, suddenly let out a loud cackle. Magdala opened one eye, then the other, and looked down at herself. She was naked.

"I told you so, I told you so!" the raven cawed, hopping up and down.

Magdala stared at the raven, at the cauldron, at her naked body, back at the raven. She didn't get it. Everything had been perfect...the sun...the ingredients...the words.

The raven danced in circles on the mantel yelling, "Naked! Naked! Naked!"

"Shut up! Shut up! Shut up!" Without thinking, Magdala reached down to remove a shoe to throw at him. Right. She was barefoot as well as naked. The raven was overjoyed. He fell over in another fit of cackling caws. Ignoring him, Magdala stomped over to the closet and slowly pulled back the curtain. Empty. Not a stitch of new clothing. Not a stitch of old clothing either. Grabbing the ragged quilt from her bed, she wrapped herself in it, and then searched the room for anything she could use to beat the raven within an inch of his life. Due to the protection spell she knew she couldn't kill him, but maybe she could maim him.

The distant rumbling of voices and laughter drew her attention to the window. She could vaguely make out the Town Square where a crowd was gathering around the bronze likeness of the town's founder, Samuel Madsen Graves. What was going on? It wasn't his birthday, or Founder's Day, or any other day that should have caused such an assembly. An uneasy feeling began to pool in Magdala's stomach. The raven flew over to see what she was looking at.

"Can you see what's going on?" Magdala asked.

Craning his neck to get a better look, he ruffled his feathers, stretched his wings, and took off without answering her. Oh well. At least she was rid of him.

Magdala sighed. Where had she gone wrong this time? And more importantly, what was she supposed to do about her clothes—or more specifically, her lack thereof? Even the perpetual black robe was preferable to running around town naked. She supposed she could gather up enough oils and herbs to barter herself enough material to make one housedress. She couldn't wear the quilt into town, though. The idea crossed her mind—briefly—to just spell herself a simple dress. No. No more spells today. Maybe not ever.

Magdala did what she always did when her spells backfired. She looked for the Silver Lining. She could sew. A pillowcase could be made into a temporary dress easily enough. She'd seen flour-sack dresses before, so why not a pillow-sack dress? She'd be able to go into town without looking completely ridiculous. Maybe with the whole town staring at Samuel Graves, she wouldn't even be noticed. As she set about gathering needles and thread, she wondered again why the whole town was staring at that silly statue.

She'd just put the finishing touches on her new "sack-dress" when the raven returned.

"Just wait until you see what you've done this time," he cawed, bobbing his head.

A sinking feeling settled over her as she pulled the pillowcase over her body.

"Oh. That's attractive," the raven hooted. "This spell might be your best yet."

"Go fly into a hurricane," Magdala muttered as she headed out the door.

The closer she got to town, the clearer she could see the crowd and the statue, and the more certain she was that whatever was going on, it had her name all over it. She squared her shoulders and prepared herself to face the music.

Literally.

The enthusiastic strains of swing music emanated from some invisible source, drowning out the gasps and comments of the townsfolk—for the most part. Lovely. Frank Sinatra and the Four Sharps' "Exactly Like You." The same tune she'd been humming while working her spell.

From the back of the crowd, Magdala studied the statue and compared it to the mental picture she'd memorized of a pretty outfit in *Marie-Claire*'s June issue. Princess fitting. Shaped collar. Buttoned front. Flared hem. Short set in sleeves with turned back cuffs. Patch pockets. The hem fell just above the knees. Good thing Samuel had nice legs.

She wasn't sure how the spell had gone wrong, but she'd managed to render herself naked while the bronze likeness of the town founder magically changed into the exact dress she had visualized when she snapped her fingers. She looked around. The townsfolk would be ogling *her*, not the statue, if the spell had gone accordingly. The dress, though cast from bronze like Samuel himself, was perfect. She might be a horrible witch, but she had excellent taste. It would look stunning on her. Especially in a lovely shade of ruby red.

"This is by far the best disaster you've ever created."

Magdala turned and glared up at a nearby oak tree. The raven flapped his wings happily. She bit her tongue. The townsfolk thought she was crazy enough without knowing she could understand the flying menace's grating caws and screeches. Seeming to understand her reasons for remaining silent, the bird took it upon himself to cause a bigger scene. He flew out of the tree and landed right on Samuel Grave's bronze head.

Someone in the crowd yelled, "Shoo!" and snapped their fingers—or maybe they clapped their hands—Magdala wasn't sure because everyone gasped loudly at almost the same moment. Samuel Graves no longer wore a dress. Now he wore a casual bronze summer suit. Magdala recognized it from page 9. She gazed longingly at the statue. Was it going to change clothes every time someone snapped their fingers or clapped their hands?

She snapped her fingers. Nothing. A few people turned to look her way, but Samuel continued to wear the suit. She had to know how it worked. She waited until everyone turned back around. She clapped her hands. Nothing, other than a few strange looks from the townies. How did the spell work, then? How or when would the clothing change again? Magdala waited. That's when she realized the song had also changed. Was that it? The song changed, the clothes changed? What song was this, anyway? She strained to recognize it.

Turning to the nearest bystander, she asked, "Do you know what song this is?"

"What?" The woman eyed her warily.

"The song. Do you know what it's called?"

"What song?" The woman's rosy complexion paled. She backed away slowly and disappeared deeper into the crowd.

Magdala turned to the gentleman on her left. "Excuse me, sir. The music? You hear it, right? Do you know what song it is?"

"Isn't there enough crazy going on here today without you adding to it?" He glared at her, and then he too turned and disappeared deeper into the crowd.

Magdala asked three more people before allowing herself to believe she was the only one who could hear the music. She wasn't sure if that was a good thing or a bad thing. The only thing she was sure of at this point was that she needed to take her basket of herbs and oils over to the General Store and get herself enough material to make at least one proper dress. The crowd gasped just as she turned away. She looked back as the familiar tune of "A Tisket, A Tasket" filled the air. Samuel Graves now wore a lovely bronze sundress, a big, bronze, floppy-brimmed hat, and bronze summer sandals, and he had a bronze picnic basket draped over one arm. Magdala rolled her eyes as the crowd oohed and ahhed.

Apparently, Samuel Graves was going to be the eternal fashion icon of Graves Grove.

MAMIE RUE'S REVENGE

DEANNA FUGETT

It won't happen again. I swear it. This is the last time.

The blinding fluorescent lights threaten to reveal the depths of my depravity. As if connected to my thoughts, the long, shining tubes above flicker. Now's my chance. Just one more...

I glance around. No one's even in the same aisle as me. Good. Last thing I need is for some blabbermouth nark to ruin my day. This is the last time, after all.

Whisking a bottle of pricey hair mousse from the shelves, I tuck it inside my jacket pocket alongside numerous other trinkets hidden within. Getting one final swiping session out of my blood couldn't possibly hurt, could it? He'll never find out.

My thieving days are over after this. It will stop now. It has to. Moses will leave me if it doesn't. I vowed to him just a couple nights ago. My days as a klepto are done with.

Over. Finito.

Now on to new and better things. What those better things are... not so sure.

Turning the corner at the end of the aisle, I bump into none other than the solid frame of Avalean Harper. Oh, great. Miss goody two-shoes, editor-in-chief, who thinks her farts smell like roses. That's all I need right now.

"Hello, Maggie." She flips a bouncy curl to the back of her hair. "Haven't seen you around lately."

Yeah. That's 'cause I'm trying to avoid ya.

"Guess we've just missed each other." Humph. Leave me be, giant lady.

I rock back and forth on my feet, trying to imply that I wanna get past her, but her Amazonian-like shoulders block my way.

She leans down for a closer view of me. "You look mighty chipper today. Rosy cheeks and all."

I stab her a glare and arch my eyebrow. 'Cause I'm in the middle of a theft, lady. It always makes my cheeks red when my adrenaline is pumping. But you don't need to know that. "Having a good day, is all."

"It would appear that way." She widens her stance, planting her tree-hugger boots to the floor, further keeping me from getting past. "But not everyone in Graves Grove is having such a good day."

What does this woman want? Beads of sweat form on my brow. Not good. "Listen, I'd love to stay and hear all the town gossip, but I'm sure you'll be writing about it in the *Graves Grove Gabbler* any day now."

She teeters on her large feet and steps aside for me. "You still haven't gotten a subscription yet, have you?"

I glare at her. "Ain't got money for those fancy internet screen-thingies your newspaper comes out on these days."

She palms her hips. "Really, Maggie? It's 2027. I would think you'd be with the times by now."

I briskly pass her by.

"We still have the *Gabbler* in print form for all you…less fortunate folks," she calls out after me.

I pretend to not hear her and carry on to the checkout. Have to buy at least one thing or it'll look suspicious. Throwing a packaged nail file at the clerk, I shove $1.50 in her hand and promptly leave the store without my receipt. Save the stupid trees and all that jazz.

Hitting the streets, I chuckle. I did it. My last heist. The gnawing of guilt that should accompany a wrong deed died inside of me a long, long time ago. But I will be a new person, for Moses. Only hope he'll come home this time.

Shuffling down the road, I'm careful not to bump my new loot out of my inner pockets. I clutch my jacket around me so nothing will fall to the smoking black tar below. Sweat trickles down my back. No one ever questions why I always wear my jacket, even in the summertime. Maybe they just know to keep their mouths shut.

Glancing up, I notice the Grovey Chops salon across the street. My footsteps fall in a faster pace as I try to avoid the badgering eyes of Agnes and all the other women in this town that frequent that place. Never did understand all the ridiculous pampering those ninnies did for themselves. Boring old gossips. That's what they are.

At the center of the town square I run into a familiar sight. The bronze statue gleams in the summer sun. Old Samuel is wearing his raincoat and fisherman hat today. I swear just yesterday it was the stylish coat and trousers. Oh well. That used to terrify me as a child. It's just old hat now. Same old, same old. Day in, day out. Funny how the only thing in town that ever changes is that stupid statue.

Nearing the town's edge, the roar of the river meets my ears as I glance at the old sycamore tree. It's meters and meters away, but shivers run through me as I struggle to keep my eyes from it. I promised all those years ago I wouldn't ever touch it again. Wouldn't even look at it. Not after Peggy went missing. But that's in the past. I'm not about to indulge the town rumor mill with all their deluded superstitions about that spot. Blast these goose-prickles on my arms.

I continue on down the path, only to gaze up to the old dilapidated manor with boarded-up windows and doors. They wanna tear that place down. That burns my biscuits when I would gladly live there. I don't care 'bout no ghost of Mamie Rue Le Doux. She don't scare me none. Living in that joint would be so much better than my dinky trailer. If only Mamie hadn't died a few years back, maybe she'd be lookin' for a roommate. 'Course livin' with a crazy person doesn't sound too good either.

The Graves Mobile Home Park sign in the distance graces the tops of the trees. Never thought I'd spend the rest of my days in that rundown place. Pa had to go on and die without leaving me no inheritance.

I scuffle my feet in the dirt leading to my trailer.

The creaking stairs that lead to my dented metal door make me more nervous by the day. Don't know how many times I've called Mr. Harrington to come and fix these steps. Guess I'll just have to sue the pants off of 'im once I fall and crush my legs in. Then I can move somewhere nice. Somewhere pretty. Maybe I will just buy up that ol' manor.

A smile tugs at my lips as I enter the dimly-lit trailer. I head back to my bedroom, shoving piles of clothing and bulky plastic bags aside to get there. Opening my jacket, I bend over my bed and shake the loot onto the Canadian flag spread across it. Stolen goods pour from my inner pockets on top of my most prized possession.

That flag was the best steal I've ever managed. Moses hates it and wishes I would trash it. But every time I gaze at it, it makes my blood curl through my veins with energy and warmth. I'll never forget the feeling of triumph the first night I wrapped myself up in its glory, letting my victory literally cover me as I sleep.

Gazing at my treasures, I savor this feeling one last time. Breathing in my pretties. Energy courses through me as I fondle each new trinket with my cracked and wrinkled hands. Too many years of hard work. I smile. Either that, or not enough stolen lotion.

Maybe I'll take a stroll over to Moses's place. His porch is so friendly and sunny. Great place to just be until my Moses comes back. Lord knows when he'll be home. That man's been on the road more often than what's good for 'im. I miss him, I do.

Almost as if on cue, the diesel engine of a big-rig vibrates my chest as it roars into the drive beside my flimsy-walled trailer.

Moses! He's back.

My beating heart bangs in my chest.

My treasures. He can't find them!

Frantically, I pull the flag around them, wrapping up each corner. One, two, three, four. Snug as a bug, my treasures be.

I hold the flag full of goodies to my chest as my eyes fly around the room.

Where to hide them, where to hide them?

Panic creeps up my spine as footsteps rattle the porch outside.

The key clinks in the door.

No!

Under the bed? Too obvious.

I lunge for the closet. He won't suspect the most easily accessible place to hide things, will he? I start shoving the loaded flag up onto the top shelf. One corner sets itself free and out falls a shiny bottle of perfume.

It was part of the sample section. So that's not really stealing, right?

I thrust the rest of the slowly escaping items upwards. With a push of my hand, the entire thing spills around the sides and onto my chest and toes.

Ouch, dang it!

Dropping the flag, I scramble to pick up the pretties scattered all over the ugly, corded carpeting. My back muscles scream as I bend and twist to retrieve every...last...one...oh, no.

Moses's black trucker boots.

I cast my gaze up his rail-thin legs covered in denim, all the way up past his chest, to the worst-looking frown I've seen in years.

"You did it again, didn't you, Maggie?" His skinny black hands are firmly planted on his bony hips. "You just couldn't help yourself, could you?"

Ugh. That stern voice he only uses when he's extremely ticked is back. My shoulders tense as I push the loot behind me and away from his sight. Shame has escaped me long ago, but disappointing him wasn't what I had planned in the cards today.

What if he leaves me? Fear creeps up inside of me.

He can't leave me! I ain't got nobody else.

"Why'd ya do it? I told you I'd leave you next time, Maggie. How could you do this to me?" His eyes well up, resembling the rich wine he likes to sip on cool evening nights. "You're not even trying to change."

"I am." He's gotta believe me. "I *am* trying."

"You promised me, Mags. Not two days ago."

"I know, I know. This was my last loot. I swear it."

"You expect me to believe that?"

"Yeah, I do. Because you love me. Because you know I would do anything for you."

He shakes his head, his tight, graying black curls not budging from the movement. He stays silent for a moment. "I just don't know with you anymore."

My heart aches as he turns and heads out of the room. My knees seem to sink into the floor with the weight of a thousand tons. This can't be it. This can't! Forcing my legs to stand, I crash into the living room just as he's exiting the front door.

"You can't leave me!"

"Oh, but I can." He starts to close the metal door behind him, then stops. He opens it further and stares at me with sad eyes. "Just answer me this one question. Why, Maggie? Why do you do it?"

I quickly search my mind for an answer.

Do I need this stuff? Hell, no.

I might be poor, but I got plenty of crap.

My eyes do a quick scan of the room. More than half this stuff was swiped from somebody or someplace else. Honestly, I ain't got no room for any more junk.

I'm starting to think I need to call one of those Hoarder shows for an intervention. But then everybody in this town would see on TV all the stuff I've taken from them over the years. My sin on display for the whole freaking world to see. No thanks.

Moses begins to inch the door shut.

The Canadian flag lying in a rumpled-up pile in my room flashes before my mind. That same warmth begins to spread. Energy. Excitement. Triumph. That's it!

"It's the thrill."

"The thrill?" he repeats in a monotone voice.

"Yeah, it's like a bunch of energy runs through me, exciting me. Making me feel young again." He returns a blank stare. I turn to slink away, my heart falling into the pit of my stomach. "You wouldn't understand." Silence fills the room.

"Well now, I get that." His voice slices through the heaviness in the air.

My breathing halts. What did that man just say? "You do?" My voice cracks.

"The excitement. The longing for more youthful days." His eyes perk up and he enters the trailer once more. He grins at me and opens his arms, waiting for my embrace.

I skitter over to him and run my chubby arms around his sides, squeezing as if my life depends on it. "So, you understand?"

He stiffens and holds up a finger. "To a point." I back off and stare up into his face. "I still don't approve of you stealing. But if we can find a way to bring back that excitement. That youthful feeling…something to replace your thieving tendencies. Then maybe…"

My heart soars. He's going to give me another chance. "Anything. I'll try anything. You know I don't want to live like this anymore."

He claps his hands together. "I've got it. More wine!"

My heart sinks a little. "That's your thing, Moses. Not mine."

His shoulders slump. "You're right, you're right." He scratches the grey stubble on his face. "Something exciting...hmmm..." If he could appear any deeper lost in thought, I'd be afraid he'd lose himself completely. "I got it!" he cries as he claps his hands again. "Mamie Rue Le Doux."

Is he serious? "You know I don't believe in ghost stories, Mo."

"But a real ghost. What's more excitement than that?" He does a little happy jig. "That'll be enough excitement to last a lifetime. You'll never steal again!"

Oh, man. He's gone off the deep end. "But there's one minor problem." I need to talk some sense into him. "She's not real."

"I saw her. You know I did, Mags."

Backing away from him, I cross my arms. "You saw a shadow, Mo."

"Of a woman pushing a pram! You know they don't even make those anymore!"

"It was just a shadow."

"I know what I saw. She's there, Mags." He shuffles his feet. "She never left."

I shake my head. Looney old fool. Believing in child's tales. Will this get him off my back for a while? At least it'll stop him from leaving me. "Fine. I'll go. But don't be getting disappointed when we don't see no ghosts."

WE WAIT until the moon lights up the night sky to lumber over to the manor. Moses's shoulders hunch as it comes into view. He gazes down at me.

"Did you hear about the little Pearson girl? The one who lives in your neighborhood?"

I roll my eyes at him. "Which one? There's seven of those brats."

"The youngest."

My heart falls to my stomach. "Yeah, they had to take her off life support last fall."

Moses's boots stop their clomping. "She died because she ate the food in Mamie Rue's basket."

A chill runs up my spine, and I mentally brush it away. "Ghost food?"

A slight grin creeps onto Moses's face. "Thought you didn't believe in no ghosts."

Clenching my fists and pursing my lips, I march past him. "I don't." I spin on my heel, and he almost crashes into me. "But everyone knows how Mamie always carried that stupid picnic basket around in her pram."

Moses's eyes light up. "They say she was doing a switch. Little girl had something Mamie wanted."

"Like what?"

"A baby doll." Moses takes in a sharp breath as he notices the looming form of the manor. We near it, and the tension rippling off of him increases with each step. "Mamie offered the starving girl her picnic basket in exchange for it." He looks mournful now as his eyes soften. "Poor little girl didn't know you can't eat ghost food."

Slapping my hip, I break the stillness of the night air. "You believe the craziest things." I shake my head. Man's got a screw loose if he believes such rubbish. Enough of that.

I gaze up at the impending form before us. The shadows on the manor appear ominous, like a dark entity waiting to swallow us whole. But that's 'cause Moses got me all riled up. If he had never mentioned the old Mamie ghost, this would be no different than walking around the trailer park at night.

We reach the wrought-iron fence, and I wrap my pudgy fingers around the rhombus-shaped spindles, sending tingles of cold rushing through my fingertips to my forearms.

Moses gets to the gate before me and swears as he struggles to open it.

"Nobody bothers to take care of these grounds." He tugs on the gate, which is snugly enveloped by a bushel of weeds. He kicks at the weeds and smooths them flat with his boot, yanking to finally release the gate from its entanglement. We sweep through, and it flings closed with a thud.

I stare upward at the Le Doux manor in front of us. The Le Douxs had owned this property for years. After Mamie Rue died, no one's lived here since. There's been plenty of speculation as to why, but only a trip back in time would give away the truth to that. And I ain't seen no time machine lyin' about.

Toppling trees arch their once-beautiful limbs above us as we head for the manor entrance. Crows mill about the uppermost branches as they sway in the breeze. They scatter and caw as a heavy wind rustles their branches, sending chilly whooshes of air up my shirt and pant legs. The air smells dry and old. Leaves prickle my ankles as they skitter by.

I cling to the back of Moses's arm as we inch up the porch of the unsightly manor. Being this close makes me realize how unkempt it really is.

And I had wanted to live here.

Guess I need to get my vision checked. I rub my eyes and stare at the broken-in narrow window panes that grace each side of the doorway. All the other windows on the front are boarded up 'cept for these two. Guess when no one is small enough to fit through 'em, it don't matter.

Moses reaches his arm right in, attempting to get to the doorknob on the other side. "Gosh dang it!" He rips his arm back out from the splintered glass and grips the bloody extremity to his chest.

"Moses! What do you think you're doing?" My chastisement is met with a sour look. I turn my face from him. "Shouldn't have tried such a dumb move."

He makes an irritated noise in the back of his throat and coddles his arm. I reach out to touch his elbow. "Lemme see the damage."

He extends his arm to me, cherry red oozing over his dark skin. I grab a tissue from my pocket and wipe away the blood as Moses flinches.

"Don't be such a baby." I sigh and put my hands on my hips. Not even a centimeter-long cut he got. Bet it still stings like the dickens. "All right. Time to call it a night."

"It's not that bad." Moses brings his arm back to his chest. "We're not going to stop just because of a silly little cut."

A thunk resonates from inside the manor. *Inside.*

My heart sinks into my stomach. "What in the heck was that?" My eyes go wide for a moment.

Moses points at my face. "See? We can't quit now. Not when things is just getting exciting."

He smiles at me, and I can't seem to force myself to smile back. "I ain't going in there."

Moses grins even wider. "Then now we hafta go in. No ifs, ands, or buts about it. This is the perfect thrill. Remember, Mags? This is what we're after."

I'm not after trying to get killed by a homeless squatter, that's not what *I'm* after. I keep silent. The look on his face tells me he's not gonna back down anytime soon. Fine. I'll do it. But only because this is so much fun for him. I'd much rather be back in the trailer, curled up on the couch watching Hoarders right about now.

Moses reaches for the doorknob. He twists, and whaddayaknow? It pushes right open. He squints and crinkles his brow. "Guess I shoulda tried that first." He lets out a couple of forced chuckles turned into coughs and sputters. The heavy door stops midway, and Moses has to push through to get it wide enough to pass.

Darkness smothers us. "Why didn't we bring any flashlights?" A shudder runs through me as the dank air fills my nostrils. Smells like a dump.

Moses steps in further, and I follow. A dim stream of moonlight fills the hall, revealing a rather impressive front parlor to the left. There are stairs to the second floor in front of us. It has a wide, winding stairway that is cut off halfway, as if the entire thing had given way and fallen in on itself. There'll be no going upstairs looks like.

A shadow moves against the wall caped by the moonlight. I flinch and cling to Moses, pointing as it creeps slowly against the wall. "Wha… wh…what is that?"

Moses laughs. "Here, boy!" A pitter-patter of feet near us as a dark shape encroaches closer. My hands are licked by a slobber-mouthed dog.

"How did Copper get in here?" I pat the short-coated town mutt on his head.

"Maybe there's a hole in the walls somewhere we aren't aware of?" Moses brushes my hand with his as we both give the mutt some much-appreciated scratching. He enjoys it for a few moments longer, sneezes, and shakes his head. The padding of his paws fades into the next room.

Moses chuckles. "And you told me you weren't afraid of no ghost."

I can faintly make out the shaking of his head in the darkness. I fold my arms across my chest. "I ain't. And this ain't no better than stealing."

"Just you wait. Mamie's here. I know it." He grasps my hand with his callused, work-worn one. "We just need to find her." He inches to the left of the room, toward the parlor.

A shiver runs up my spine as the temperature plummets. A sour, dusty odor fills my nose as a wave of air rushes past my legs. My heart stills, and Moses dead stops. The tension in his body is as severe as mine, and it rotates around us like a tornado. A whisper calls out in the darkness, and I swear I'm going to break Moses's fingers.

"Looks like she's found us first." Moses's voice is so high-pitched, it makes the annoying grate-on-your-nerves voice of my neighbor girl sound angelic in comparison.

Another wisp of nail-biting wind swirls past, and the whispers intensify. The hair on my arms and neck stand at attention, and I bite the inside of my mouth until the iron taste of blood slides over my tongue. Why did I agree to this stupid idea? This isn't a thrill, this is downright horrific.

A shadow passes briefly through the moonlight. A woman.

"That's no dog." My words come out icy cold. Chilly puffs of breath escape my mouth. "Let's get outta here!" I dig my nails into Moses's arms and turn to drag him out the door, but he's stuck still as a stone.

"Shoulda just let you keep stealing." His voice is weak but rings through the silence of the room. The eeriness of the whispers crawls up my neck and tingles my ears until they hurt. The pounding in my chest grows painful. I turn back to the non-budging Moses.

Standing there in the moonlit corner is a woman with a pram. She's translucent with hints of washed-out color. Her A-lined dress flows as though a breeze blows through the room. I suspect the wind a few moments ago was her waltzing about. Her hair under her faded moss-green hat wiggles weightlessly as her dress below. Her dress dangles and sways to and fro as she hovers inches above the ground. Her eyes are hollow and make my stomach turn into an empty pit of anguish.

The semi-translucent pram is moth-eaten and worn. She gently pushes it back and forth as though soothing an infant inside. The once-round wheels squeak and thud like the distant noise of an old locomotive on a rust-encrusted, bumpy track. The sound fills the room.

Squeak. Thud. Squeak. Thud.

She stares intently into the pram with her vacant eyes. I tug on Moses one last time, but he is a solid, unmovable rock. Why won't he run outta here with me? I catch a glimpse of his face as the moonlight flickers our way. He is mesmerized. My eyes turn back to the apparition in the corner.

One creaky centimeter at a time, she twists her neck until her face stares my way. Her translucent skin reveals a sixty-something year old woman, who in her youth most likely had been attractive. Her dark, empty eyes manage to stare me down. My blood runs cold as shivers encompass my entire body.

"So, you're a thief?" Her voice is filled with hollow echoes. My shoulders slink further down my body. "Someone stole something awfully precious to me once."

My eyes widen as my mouth goes from cotton dry to desert-like.

"I don't like thieves."

My shaking intensifies, and the temperature plummets once more. "I'm not a thief. Not anymore. I swore it off. I promise."

"Stealing makes me angry." She inches closer and falls out of the moonlight. "Have you ever had a child stolen from you before?"

I shake my head vigorously.

"Do you know the pain? The anguish that can cause a mother?" Her presence surrounds me in the darkness. The coolness of her skirts rush around me in circles.

I shake my head. "I aint' got no kids, ma'am."

"But you like stealing, don't you?" She circles to my back.

"No." I whimper. "No, it's over. I won't steal anymore."

"You're right you won't steal anymore. I won't let you." She whispers in my ear and circles around to face me again. The stench of a crypt is heavy in the air. I can barely make her out, but I can feel every centimeter of her.

"You've been a bad, bad girl. Stealing my baby. How could you hurt me so?"

"I never stole your baby! I swear it!"

"She didn't steal your baby, ma'am." Moses tries to pull my hand, and a force pushes him back so he tumbles to the ground.

I'm alone with the ghost of Mamie Rue.

She continues to circle me slowly. The whispers are back, and every one of my cells screams to be released from this torture. Another icy current of air swoops me up from behind, pushes and drags me toward the moonlit corner where the pram stands.

Soon I am facing the black, soulless eyes of the creature. Mamie Rue places her frail ghost-hand on me. Her skin is like thousands of tiny needles being pushed into my arm.

"You stole my happiness. Now I will steal yours."

Her face contorts as her eyebrows arch high into her forehead and her mouth gapes into a hollow black hole of smiling, anger-infused fury. She twists her other hand high and jabs toward my chest as shoots of black, sparkling beams press into my body. My chest heaves upwards, and the hold she has on me is unyielding. Coldness fills my insides, hollowing me out, as my soul is being yanked out of me. Ripping, tugging, it leaves my body.

The black beam encompasses my soul with an icy grip as my body collapses to the floor. I am still me, but in my body no more. Simply part of the air around me, still entangled within the beams that refuse to let go.

I'm being pushed now.

A force stronger than my will is forcing me into the pram. Closer and closer I get.

A porcelain dolly lies in the pram, covered by a little blankie. The nearer I get, the more I can make out the cracks that line her once pretty and rosy face. Her hair is dark ringlets surrounding two cherub cheeks. Soon, I am so close I can feel the dolly. The pushing continues until blackness engulfs me.

I open my eyes. I am on my back. Black, moth-eaten siding surrounds me. Pretty, discolored lace lines the edges.

The fright of Mamie Rue's face appearing over mine clutches my throat. I attempt to cry out.

Nothing. No words.

Where has my voice gone?

I have a body again. I can feel it.

"Oh, aren't you the sweetest baby ever?" Mamie Rue's echoing voice slices my soul like a butcher knife carving a slab of meat.

Baby?

I try to move my arms and legs. Nothing.

I look down my nose and see chubby baby doll arms.

"Now you will be my sweet baby doll. And no one will ever steal you again."

DOUBLE-EDGED SWORD

MATTHEW HOWE

The old bitch knew something. Oh, she was coming off all sweet and concerned, but Mike wasn't fooled. Mike wasn't the kind of guy who got fooled easily, and this rube simply didn't have the chops to pull it off. Her hand kept flitting up to cover her mouth as she spoke. That was the obvious tell, but it was more than that—the tenor of her voice, the way her eyes kept darting up to the right, the weird pauses before answering his questions.

She was lying. Lying her fat ass off.

"I really don't know any more about it than that," Avelean Harper said. "And may I say again, I am so, so sorry for your loss."

Mike heard what she was really saying: *I couldn't give a damn that your kid is gone. Just get the hell out of my office.*

"How is your wife handling it?" Harper asked.

"Not good. She's still at the clinic." Graves Grove had no hospital, just a small clinic staffed by an aging Dr. Davis and two equally ancient nurses. "They have her sedated, under observation."

"So sad," Harper said, and he knew the interview was over.

He stood up, offered a hand. "Thank you so much for your time, Ms. Harper." He didn't have to play the role of grieving father. The pain and loss were so strong he felt like he was drowning.

Mike allowed Avalean to take his arm and lead him gently to the door. It took all his self-control, which was considerable, to stop himself from smashing her face in. Tying her to a chair. Having a go at her with a lit cigarette. Not that he had a cigarette; smoking had always seemed to be monumentally dumb.

"Again," she said as they reached the door. "I'm so sorry. If I hear anything, I'll be in touch."

He paused, turned toward her. He hadn't said anything about the tree the whole time he'd been speaking with her. He'd stuck to routine stuff. How many times has this happened before? Were any of those children ever found? How competent were the police? It had all been bullshit. A set-up for this.

He turned and looked her right in the eyes. "The tree ate her," he whispered. "I saw the tree eat her."

Her eyes widened a touch. Bam. He had her.

She knows, Mike thought. *The bitch knows.*

AS HE walked back to the Inn, he tried to ignore the glances from the townsfolk. They were full of sorrow that only made his worse, but something else. Fear. The last time he'd seen people this scared had been in Haiti. Miragoane, a port town in the south run by a warlord named Akatsuki Payen. Payen was a real charmer, known for hacking to death anyone who got in his way. Mike had no business with Akatsuki, and, beyond a courtesy call and courtesy bribe, had stayed out of his way. He'd dealt with his target and gotten out.

But he'd seen it in the faces of the citizens, the strain, the tension, the wondering: *am I next?*

He saw the same thing in Graves Grove. People were scared.

He stopped by the Constable's office from where the search for his missing daughter was being coordinated. Mike already knew what the cop, an Officer Kandalmass, was going to find. Nothing. Because he already knew what had happened to little Karey. The crews dragging the river and searching the forest were for show. Their efforts had a rehearsed, phony feeling to them, like they'd been through this before. Many times before.

For three days, the station had been a buzz of activity, volunteers manning phones, others coordinating search parties. All that was left of the effort was a cardboard tray of half-drunk coffees from the Grove Diner and a few stale doughnuts no one had cleaned up yet.

He could hear Kandalmass in his office, on the phone. Before going in, he paused by the bulletin board. It hung on the southern wall of the station, an ordinary five by three cork board, the kind you'd see in every school classroom back when Mike was a kid. It had been transformed into a gateway to hell by the pictures. Pictures of missing children. Hundreds of them, going back who knew how long, the quality of the photos, the clothing and hair styles changing, the pain and desperation in the handwritten pleas for help constant. And the latest, his little Karey, pinned in the upper right corner.

It was a picture they'd taken at her second birthday. Looking at it, he felt like someone was crushing his heart between two rocks. But he kept looking, let the pain flow. Pain was a great motivator. He recognized that he'd become two people since his little girl had vanished. The man inside screaming his sorrow, and the other. The one who came out when it was time to go to work. The one who set traps for small town newspaper editors that they fell into without even realizing it.

And now the second trap.

Kandalmass hung up the phone as he stepped into the doorframe and knocked.

"Mr. Newman," Kandalmass said. "I just got off the phone with the dive team. I'm so sorry, nothing to report."

Mike nodded. He let a heaving sob rip through him. "Thanks. Thanks for trying. I just wanted to let you know, we're going back to Vancouver. Deb's mom is there. It'll be better."

The cop tried to cover. But he sucked at this as much as that Harper woman. He couldn't hide the relief that flooded his eyes, that tugged the corners of his mouth up oh just that tiniest bit. "You have my card," Kandalmass said.

Mike nodded. "Yeah. I'll check in every couple of days. Thank you again for all you've done."

Kandalmass got up and came around for a handshake, but Mike moved past the proffered hand and seized the cop in a tight hug. "Thank you," he whispered again.

He stopped himself from breaking the cop's neck.

DRIVING OUT of town, they stopped at a light on Main Street. Down the hill he could see the river and the top of the tree. The tree that had taken his daughter.

Deb was in the passenger seat. An orderly had helped her out of the wheelchair and into the car. She was staring straight ahead, face blank.

Movement caught his eye and his head snapped to it. Situational awareness. He'd learned it in the Marines. What you didn't see was going to kill you. Though his military training, time in the spook service, then his freelance career, Mike's situational awareness had grown paper-cut sharp.

The movement was a blur of reddish brown, low. The dog, he realized before his eyes even found focus.

Copper. Someone had told him the mutt's name was Copper. Russet colored and old. Mike had never seen a dog that old. Yet it still seemed to get around just fine.

And the eyes. The mutt's eyes were wide and deep. There was something behind those eyes. Something smart. The dog was watching him. He got the sense the mutt was sad he was leaving.

The light turned. Mike drove on. Out of Graves Grove.

As he threaded his car up the winding mountain road that led out of town, as the last of the houses on the outskirts of town faded behind them, Deb coughed. Her dull eyes brightened, and she pulled the seat-belt off herself. Deb had always hated them.

"So?" he asked.

"I told them I was allergic to whatever the hell was in the IV they wanted to give me, so they hit me with pills. I palmed them, then played dummy."

"Learn anything?"

"The Doc. Doctor Davis. He didn't say a lot. It was his attitude. He was..." She looked for the word. "He was trying to hide it, but couldn't. He was psyched about something. Excited. Like a kid at Christmas." She realized what she'd said and now she did sob, a real sob. She let it work through her, then he saw her give a small shudder as she pulled herself together. "The cop came by at one point, Kandalmass, to check on me. I heard them whispering about the full moon," she said. "And another word. *Talakoth.*"

He nodded. He'd look it up later.

"Tell me again, what you saw." Deb was stronger than him, he realized for the hundredth time since he'd married her. As tough as he was, he'd still spent half of the last three days bawling his eyes out. No way could he have spent it pretending to be quietly sedated while he eavesdropped on a doctor both of them had decided was acting suspiciously.

"I was on the blanket. Karey was playing by the tree, in the roots." The sycamore by the river where they'd decided to have their picnic had the biggest roots Mike had ever seen. A city of roots. The kind of thing he would have loved as a kid.

"Something grabbed her," he said. Grabbed was the wrong word. He'd seen it at the periphery of his vision, he'd seen something explode. Not with fire and smoke, but with darkness. His eyes had flicked that direction and for a nanosecond he'd seen it. A fine net of tendrils had sprouted from the roots of the tree. They had enveloped his daughter, only a hank of her blonde hair hanging free, then had snapped back into the roots taking his daughter with them. Just a flash. Most people wouldn't even have seen it. Most people wouldn't have been able to process.

But not Mike.

"That tree," Mike said. "That tree took our Karey."

Deb was quiet. He knew what she was thinking. It was crazy, insane. But Mike had absolute faith in his own senses honed from years of putting himself into the most dangerous crapshoots imaginable. What he'd seen that tree do changed everything, it changed the nature of the world around him, but he'd seen it. Period.

"The editor of the newspaper, that Harper bitch, the cop, and now the doctor. They all know," he said.

"Yeah. They know what took her," Deb said. She was crying now, quietly. "But do they know why?"

"Exactly," Mike said.

THEY FOUND a hotel in Risingville, checked in. There was a used car dealer a few blocks down, and they bought a 2027 Toyota Manx. It was beat up, but the battery seemed good and it ran fine.

A sporting goods store yielded hunting camo, a pair of decent binoculars, and a few other items.

When it got dark, he left Deb at the hotel and drove back into Graves Grove.

He kept to the outskirts of town, avoiding the busier streets, until he found Harper's house. Harper, the cop, the doctor who'd treated Deb, they were all in on it, but he figured Harper was the brains.

A number of cars were parked in the street running perpendicular to Harper's house. Perfect. He parked among them, jumped into the small backseat and reached up to adjust the mirror. The reflected view through the rear window showed Harper's house in all its simple modesty.

Her garage door opened at j
late-model car out and into the nig

Mike climbed back into the fr
and, lights off, went after her.

She drove through town, not mo
up in front of an old Tudor styled ma
had been abandoned for years. He hung
binoculars.

Harper got out of her car, took a quick look … and practically jogged up the path to the front door.

Mike watched for another ten minutes. He was about to get out of the car and move closer on foot when Harper came back out of the house clutching something. He dialed the binocs to a higher power. Saw she held a cloth sack. Through the open window, he could hear a distant rattle from it as she walked. She was moving fast, with the short, choppy steps of someone who was glad to be getting out of a place they didn't like.

Interesting.

She got in her car. Mike followed her back to her house. She parked in the garage and closed the door. Whatever she was up to, it seemed like she was done for the evening. Just to be sure, he watched for another hour. His instinct was right. Unless she'd made him and snuck out the back—unlikely; Harper's chores were done for the night.

So what had her little mission been all about? What was in that sack she'd been carrying? A few ways he could find out—break into her house and have a look, break into her house, tie her to a chair, and heat a fork on the stove.

Or go back to the mansion. The answer was there. Every sense screamed it.

He drove back.

The house was silent. Two large brick pillars framed the driveway. There was a faded plaque on one of them he could still read by the bright moonlight: *Graves Manor: Mayor's Residence.*

ant had lived there. During his three nightmar- ad absorbed enough of the town's history to know that probably Samuel Graves, the town's founder. This had been use.

He went up the driveway. The house loomed over him. He wasn't a guy who scared easily, he'd proven that a hundred times and more. But something about this place set his teeth on edge.

Something important was inside.

The house was even more wrecked on the inside than the outside. The thick coat of dust turned out to be his best friend as Harper's fresh footprints couldn't have been more obvious if they'd been made in fifteen centimeters of new fallen snow.

He followed them to a bookcase where they abruptly ended. There were other marks in the dust, wide arcs like something had swung open.

Some kind of secret door bullshit. He started to look around for some sort of hidden switch when a voice spoke from behind him.

Mike spun fast, his gun appearing in his hand. He was as pissed with himself as he was scared. No one snuck up on him. Ever.

But when he turned it wasn't a person with a gun behind him, it was a woman pushing a baby carriage. An old fashioned pram on wheels. Nothing like the mag-lev carriage he and Deb had bought for Karey.

Only the woman wasn't a woman. He could see right through her. A ghost. An honest to God ghost.

Mike reholstered his pistol. Even .42 hollow points weren't going to do shit against a ghost.

He took a better look at the woman. She'd been old when she died, her face etched with sadness. In the carriage sat a doll. A little ghost doll. Which was weird. Weirdest of all were the doll's eyes, human eyes full of terror and pain.

Mike and the woman stared at each other for what must have been twenty seconds. Then she spoke again. "Moby Dick," she said. And then, as silently as she'd come, she vanished.

Moby Dick? What the hell was she talking about?

Then he got it. Turned back to the shelf. There, among the moldering books, was a copy of Melville's classic. He grabbed it, pulled. It came right out and fell to the floor with a puff of dust.

Looking behind it, he saw nothing but bookcase. He peered closer. There was a knothole in the smooth surface of the wood. He stuck a pinky inside, absurdly afraid that something was going to bite it off.

He felt nothing.

Mike looked around, found a long, thin splinter of wood, and jammed that into the knothole. It went back a good ten centimeters before it met resistance. He pressed harder. Something clicked.

The bookcase swung out on hinges that screamed with rust.

It opened on a stairway going down.

"Thanks, lady," Mike whispered. He switched on his flashlight and went down.

The stairs were stone, damp with moisture and moss, but he could see someone had been down them recently. Harper.

They went down maybe ten meters before ending in an arched stone corridor. He hurried down it to the door at the end. The door was wood banded with iron. It had been secured once, but the lock, a huge, steel padlock of a style he'd never seen and probably hadn't been used for decades, had been left hanging. Harper had been in a hurry.

He tossed the lock aside and opened the door. It swung open with more screaming rust.

The room beyond was maybe six by six meters. Stone walls. Stone floor. Ceiling of heavy wooden beams and more stone.

In the middle of the space, a stone altar of some kind. Resting on that, a coffin.

An open coffin.

An open, empty coffin.

He'd already guessed it, but the beam of his Strikefire revealed an inscription on the base of the coffin: *Samuel Madsen Graves.*

That sack Harper had been carrying. He had a pretty good idea what was in it had previously been in this coffin. The mortal remains of this Graves guy.

Odd thing was, Graves was said to have been buried beneath that monstrous tree. Looked like his followers had dug him up at some point and snuck him here for safekeeping, and now they were hauling him somewhere else for God only knew what purpose.

He turned his flashlight to the walls and gasped. The back wall wasn't made of stone blocks, but one huge, smooth piece of rock. Someone had carved a representation of that sycamore tree down by the river. The tree that had taken his Karey.

On the massive trunk one word had been carved: *Talakoth.*

The tree had been carved without foliage. Each branch arched up stylistically and ended in a number of points as smaller limbs branched off. At the end of each point, a name had been written.

He recognized some of the names instantly. The same names that adorned all those *Have You Seen Me?* posters on the Constable's bulletin board. Every branch, he saw, had a name written at its tip. He scanned them. *Jason Smyth*, *Alice Sawyer*, *Bobby Flanders,* and there, on the furthest, highest branch to the right: *Karen Johnson*. His little Karey.

Every branch tip had a name. Karey's name had been added last.

Mike stepped close, reached up, and touched his fingers to the stone. For a second, just a flash, she was with him, her spirit and warmth filling him, the joy he'd felt when he'd first seen her tiny, squished face burning bright in his heart. And then gone, leaving nothing but cold and empty behind. He knew then something he'd been trying to dodge from the moment she'd been taken. The hole that had been ripped in his soul when she'd been taken was never going to heal. No matter what he did, that pain was always going to be with him.

He fell against the wall. He didn't know how long he stayed there, just crying, but movement interrupted him. He sprung straight, the gun coming up again.

It was the ghost again. She'd come down the stairs. As he watched, she walked to the carved tree and touched her fingers to a name of her own. *Archie LeDoux*. And he got it. Like him, she'd lost a child.

He walked to her. "Talk," he said.

The ghost spun on him. "About what?"

"What you know about that tree. What you've overheard, legends, rumors, everything."

"Why?" the ghost asked.

He pointed to the name of her son. "That's why."

The ghost stepped back, moved toward the stairs, then stopped. She turned back to him. "The tree didn't take my son."

"But something did."

The ghost waved an arm at the carving. "*Something* took all of them. Fairies, murderers… It's all for the same purpose. The tree just…helps."

"And what is that 'purpose'?"

She hesitated.

"Please," Mike said.

The ghost sighed. Then she talked. And talked. And talked.

THE SKY was lightening to the east when he finally left the house. A big moon, one day away from full, was setting in the west.

His heart ached. He was more exhausted than he'd been in his entire life. But the pain inside him, that kept him going. Because he knew a salve for hurting.

Sharing it.

As he drove out of town, he called Deb. Explained a few things.

Told her what he needed.

AT THE hotel, he got a few hours of sleep. As dusk hit, he went back. He stopped by Graves Manor, then headed into town, parked a few hundred meters north of the sycamore, and followed the river south.

He crawled into the woods as the sky to the east began to lighten. Not with dusk.

With moonrise.

Through the screen of trees, Mike saw it come up. Fat and red. Blood red. He thought again about what he'd seen in that basement. The carving of the tree, the names at the end of each branch and that name *Talakoth* on the trunk. He'd looked it up back at the hotel and all he'd been able to find was a reference to some ancient being from beyond the veil of human existence. But having seen his daughter eaten by a tree, having seen a ghost, he had no trouble believing Talakoth was real.

The moon was nearly at zenith when he heard them. They came down from Main Street in Harper's car. They parked on the street near the tree and got out. Three of them, Harper in the lead, carrying that sack. Behind her, Kandalmass and an elderly man he could only assume was Dr. Davis.

They reached the base of the sycamore and stood a moment. Then Harper opened the neck of the bag and gently dumped the contents out.

Bones. Human bones. Mike was pretty sure if you counted them you'd get to 206. A complete skeleton.

"Are we ready?" Harper asked.

"Yes," the other two responded.

The three of them reached out, placed their hands palm up over the pile of bones.

In their other hands, knives appeared. They drew the blades across their exposed palms and let the blood that flowed rain down on the pile of bones.

There was a strange sound, a low, subsonic growl more felt than heard. As Mike watched, the tree seemed to shimmer, then shake and then it sprouted those tiny tendrils he'd seen surround and take his daughter.

They swarmed the pile of bones, covering it in a black, shimmering mass. A mass that slowly began to take on a familiar shape.

A human shape.

At last the tendrils parted and revealed a man. He lay on the ground, naked, panting, staring up at his followers. "Then..." he whispered.

"It is accomplished," Harper said.

The man looked around, dawning wonder in his eyes. "Then I have returned?" He sat himself up, leaning on the bole of the tree. Kandalmass and Davis helped the man to his feet while Harper helped him into a bathrobe.

Strength had returned to the man's eyes. "My faithful servants, your reward will be eternity. As I now am, one day you shall rise, immortal." He reached into the branches of the tree and picked three seeds. He handed one to each of them.

The three fell to their knees, silent, weeping. "Now rise, my friends," the man, Samuel Graves, Mike now realized, said. The town's founder. Reborn. Just as the ghost had told him he would be. "Rise and taste the great victory we have won over the forces of nature. After tonight, each of you will go forth, gather followers as I did, found your own communities, and plant the seeds which will one day grant you immortality."

There was more talking. Bullshit, mostly. Promises of eternal devotion to whatever the hell Talakoth was, promises of eternal devotion to each other.

Then they all piled into Harper's car like a bunch of kids going on a night out.

Mike ran back to his car and picked their trail up halfway up the hill. They were going back to the mansion. Of course. He let them get inside, fire up a few battery powered lanterns, and settle in. He heard glasses clinking, bright conversation.

While they partied, Mike circled the building and quietly chained each door shut.

Then he walked around the front and pulled a tarp off a crate he'd hidden under a wisteria bush.

Mason jars. Filled with gasoline. A rag sticking out a hole he'd punched in each cap.

He lit the rags and heaved them through the mansion's windows.

The place was a firetrap, with all that splintered wood and broken furniture. It went up fast. He heard them inside, running for the door, banging on it when they found it chained shut, screaming as the smoke and flame started to grow. He heard Samuel Graves shouting orders.

And another sound above the roar of flame and the screams—sirens.

Mike faded into the woods, watching.

The screaming had stopped by the time the trucks got there. It took them three hours to get the fire out. Listening to the firemen and cops as they packed their gear, Mike got the sense they didn't know anyone had been in there. They'd come back after the embers had cooled and search. Then they mounted up and roared back into the night.

But Mike stayed. He knew it wasn't over.

An hour after the cops and firemen left, he heard movement from inside. Slow, shuffling movement. The building had more or less collapsed, and out of the soaked ashes, he saw something crawling. Something that had once been human and was now blackened, red and skeletal. It was crawling, moaning, in agony. And why not? He'd burned Graves and his followers to a crisp.

And yet, even as he watched, he saw charred flesh slowly turn red as it filled out with new fluid, saw burned, reddened flesh slowly turn pale as new skin formed.

Graves managed to get to his feet and take a few tottering steps.

Mike met him on what used to be his porch. They just stood there a long moment, staring at each other, as the skull that was Graves' face slowly filled out and his hair sprouted fresh. "Who are you?" Graves asked. His voice was a dry croak.

"That last little girl whose life and soul you stole, that was my daughter."

"She gave her life for a greater good," Graves whispered.

"Spare me, Graves," he said. "Mamie Le Doux told me everything. I know the legend. Karey died so you could rise again. They paid for your immortality."

Graves smiled. His face had finished healing. His eyes shone with strength and vigor. He smiled. A sick, greedy smile. The smile of a man about to declare *checkmate*. "Correct. The benevolence of Talakoth has fallen upon me, and I am remade immortal. Your mission is futile, as you have just seen. Perhaps you thought fire would destroy me?"

"Maybe," Mike said.

"It won't. Nor will a silver bullet, or a wooden stake through the heart. Try as you might, you cannot kill me."

Now it was Mike's turn to smile. "Who said anything about killing you?"

Doubt flickered in Graves' eyes. That's when Deb stepped out of the shadows where she'd been watching. She swung the crowbar. He never loved her more than when he watched her break both of Grave's knees with it. The man screamed, high and shrill, and fell, moaning to the smoldering ash and dirt.

Mike knelt, a knee on Graves' chest, driving the man into the ground.

"See, Graves," he said. "Immortality's a double-edged sword. Yeah, I can't kill you. But because I can't kill you, it means I get to hurt you. And hurt you. And hurt you. And keep hurting you." He grabbed Graves' left hand. He broke fingers as he spoke, punctuating each thought with a muted snap and a scream. "Because you're coming with us, Graves. You're staying with us as long as we live in a cozy little room I have down in my basement. It was going to be Karey's playroom, now it's going to be our playroom. We're going to hurt you until you wish you could die, and then we're going to hurt you some more. And if it works out, we're going to have more kids and we're going to teach them what you are and what you did, and they're going to keep it going. You got reborn, pal. But into a world of pure shit."

As understanding dawned in Graves' eyes and he began to protest, Mike gagged him, handcuffed him, dragged him to the van Deb had rented, and threw him in the back. Then they drove away, fast, taking the curves hard, not caring about the thudding and muffled cries of pain they heard from the back.

Somewhere, probably in his imagination, he heard Karey.

Heard her laughing.

Clapping and laughing.

QUERY

KELSEY KEATING

Raven DeMarco
1210 Parkdale Ave
Graves Grove, BC V0C 3A0, Canada

Melissa Mumble
Russet Literary Agency
2320 South Huntington St
Ottawa, ON K1P 1J1, Canada

Dear Ms. Mumble,

Did you ever climb trees as a child? Toby Clutterbuck did. During a picnic with his parents one afternoon, the toddler waddled over to the sycamore tree in Graves Grove and was never seen again.

The Sycamore of Graves Grove, my first ever children's book, is complete at 40,000 words. I think it will fit along with your other titles, *Spot the Cat's First Day of*

School and *Bumper Bill Goes to the Dentist*, as school and doctors both are scary for children.

The children of Graves Grove often play on the sycamore tree, but anyone who has been close enough to see their friends go missing knows better than to get near its roots. Minnie Dribble, the main character of my story, has seen the sycamore eat three of her friends, leaving drops of blood behind, and she's determined to chop it down. She dives deep into the mystery of the tree and learns of its origin, planted by the town founder and watered with his own blood.

Minnie knows the tree has to go. Her adversary, Mrs. Avalean Harper, will stop at nothing to keep the tree standing, even if it means stopping Minnie.

The Sycamore of Graves Grove is based off of a true story of my own life.

I am fifteen years old, and I live in Graves Grove, British Columbia, Canada. I have seen the tree eat people. This is a true story. I've included the first ten pages and a synopsis for you to read.

Thank you for your time and consideration,

Rebecca DeMarco

Rebecca DeMarco

AUTHOR BIOGRAPHIES

MARK ANDERSEN

Mark Andersen makes stuff up. He's the author of a contemporary fantasy series, Merlin's Thread. For eleven years, he wrote science articles for Oilfield Review; for nine of those years he was the journal's executive editor. Sadly, he couldn't make things up during that part of his writing career. He has a PhD in physics from the Johns Hopkins University and worked in the oil industry for thirty-four years as a research scientist, domain expert, and writer.

Visit Andersen at www.markandersentales.com.

J.S. BAILEY

As a child, J.S. Bailey escaped to fantastic worlds through the magic of books and began to write as soon as she could pick up a pen. Today her stories focus on unassuming characters who are thrown into terrifying situations which may or may not involve cursed mirrors, evil paintings, and family vacations from hell. Bailey lives in Cincinnati, Ohio with her husband and cats.

Learn more about her books at www.jsbaileywrites.com.

E.D.E. BELL

_. Bell writes unique fantasy fiction that blends traditional and modern elements. A passionate vegan and enthusiastic denier of gender rules, she feels strongly about issues related to equality and compassion and loves to inspire thought through her writing. She eats a questionable amount of garlic and loves cats and trees.

Learn more at www.atthisarts.com/authors/edebell.

S.R. BETLER

Born and raised in New York, S.R. Betler now lives in Kentucky, where she passes her days collecting stray animals, torturing her characters, and inventing new worlds while attempting to keep her husband and offspring from destroying this one.

CATHRINE BONHAM

Cathrine Bonham is the real life name of an unused pen name. When she isn't writing stories of her own, she is busy reading stories by others. Her greatest achievement is whichever book you are reading now.

You can visit her blog at www.dolphin18cb.wordpress.com.

DAKOTA CALDWELL

Caldwell grew up on a Kansas farm, working with livestock and dreaming of outer space. He is now a college student who writes more than he goes to class (when he thinks he can get away with it). *Project Nomad* is his first published work, though he has dozens more books planned.

MACKENZIE FLOHR

Flohr is the author of the popular young adult fantasy series *The Rite of Wands*. A storyteller at heart, she loves to inspire the imagination. Mackenzie makes her home in Michigan, where she is currently penning her next adventure.

Learn more at www.mackenzieflohr.com.

DEANNA FUGETT

While Deanna Fugett isn't writing or connecting with others via social media, she can be found dancing around the kitchen with her four kids. She secretly enjoys writing more than reading. Her first novel, *Ending Fear*, was released in 2017.

Learn more about Fugett at www.deannafugett.com.

RAYMOND HENRI

Raymond has enjoyed writing from an early age. After exploring a variety of other formats, he just recently started writing novels. His character driven stories reflect the diversity of the places he has lived and the jobs he has had, focusing on animals and film.

MATTHEW HOWE

Matthew Howe has worked in the film industry in just about every position imaginable. He's shot documentary series for networks such as Discovery Channel and The History Channel. Those gigs led to opportunities to actually write the shows. In addition, he has written and sold dozens of feature screenplays. His first novel, *Waypoint*, was published in 2016.

AVILY JEROME

Avily Jerome is a writer and the editor of Havok Magazine, an imprint of Splickety Publishing Group. Her short stories have been published in multiple magazines, both print and digital. She is a wife and the mom of five kids. She loves living in the desert in Phoenix, AZ, and when she's not writing, she loves reading, spending time with friends, and doing crafts.

KELSEY KEATING

Keating moonlights in the realm of writers, weaving tales of adventure, fantasy, and romance. A student of media, Kelsey considers acting a hobby, critiquing movies a calling, and riding unicorns through rainbows a daily expectation. Driven by her love of Fantasy, Kelsey's novels reflect the wonderment imagination can dream up.

Learn more about Keating's work at www.swanitude.com.

D.M. KILGORE

D.M. Kilgore is a Freelance Writer, Novelist, and Literary Hitwoman. She loves dipping her toes into the sparkling stream of whatever genre she happens to be dancing by when inspiration strikes. She's currently prancing through poetic puddles, making a splash in the blood-tinged waters of suspense filled thrillers, and twirling her toes in the glittery streams of young adult paranormal fantasy. She insists she's found her niche, if not her groove.

If you can hear the music, dance along at her official website: www.dmkilgore.com.

CAITLYN KONZE

Caitlyn Konze may seem like your typical librarian, but through her secret identity as a writer she hopes to write stories that make her readers ponder the divine, invest in Kleenex, or sleep with the light on. Though a number of Caitlyn's short stories and poems have been published, her passion is speculative fiction novels.

ELISE MANION

Elise, her husband of two and a half decades, and Franklin the weenie dog are recent empty-nesters living in northern Nevada. Elise has written two novels in her King Brothers trilogy and short stories for the anthologies *A Winter's Romance* and *On the Edge of Tomorrow*.

Learn more at www.elisemanion.com.